Fireflies
AND
ZeroEs

LIZ LARSON

BELLE ISLE BOOKS
www.belleislebooks.com

ISBN: 978-1-958754-29-0
Library of Congress Control Number: 2023901309

Designed by Sami Langston
Project managed by Jenny DeBell

Printed in the United States of America

Published by
Belle Isle Books (an imprint of Brandylane Publishers, Inc.)
5 S. 1st Street
Richmond, Virginia 23219

BELLE ISLE BOOKS
www.belleislebooks.com

belleislebooks.com | brandylanepublishers.com

For Charlottesville, with love;
"not for the virtues,
but despite the faults."

TABLE OF CONTENTS

The news was everywhere, inescapable: on every site, every social media outlet, every channel. Worse than that, it was right outside.

Jason was still in bed as he started to scroll through the headlines on his phone, a visitor in his childhood bedroom in an otherwise empty house. A knot of disbelieving dread began to form in his stomach as the words slipped over him, leaving only the images of scowling, screaming faces, illuminated by a sea of flaming torches.

As shadows resolved themselves into the Jefferson statue and the Rotunda, the world he had always known suddenly looked alien in torch-lit miniature. Headline after headline. The news was all the same.

We were there yesterday.

Something in him wanted to cry out, scream at the CNNs and MSNBCs and all the rest. What right did they have—strangers who two days earlier couldn't have picked out Charlottesville on a map—to grant themselves the authority to tear his home apart, to condemn the entire life of a town as a single moment of violence?

It's not like this, he thought. *It was never like this.*

Jason's phone rang. Seeing the caller ID, he answered quickly, his voice still raspy with sleep as he muttered, "Hello?"

The young woman's voice on the other end was icy. "Jase, get me the hell out of here."

"Hold on," he said, beginning to rise. "I'm on my way."

Five minutes later he was in the car, quickly closing the six-mile gap between himself and the picture on every front page in the country. He took the long way to Tara's hotel, avoiding the University and keeping downtown at a safe distance. There was a heavy stillness in the air, an uneasy feeling that called to mind an approaching thunderstorm. He could feel that things were only getting worse. He didn't want to see, didn't want to know.

Tara was like a caged wildcat, pacing the hotel room as she let him in, cursing and looking like she might send a fist through the television that was blaring minute-by-minute updates. She, too, had been transformed, and it rattled Jason further to see his friend and bandmate swallowed up by the surge of anger that had overtaken his home. "This fucking town," she kept saying. "Fucking racist assholes. Fuck!"

Jason watched helplessly, wishing he knew what to say, but his own roiling emotions took over and put him on the defensive. The rally was a violation, an assault that left him at a loss for words, and with a sinking feeling that when his anger did find its voice, tears would follow. "It's not Charlottesville," he insisted. "*They* did this. They came from out of town to make a scene. It's not *us*."

Of course she was unsatisfied. "Why here, then? In this fucking racist town that hasn't once owned up to the fact that it was built by slaves, or shed any light on the literal Goddamn skeletons in its closets." Without waiting for a reply, she announced, "We're leaving. Let's go home. Now."

But I am home. He couldn't bring himself to say it aloud, but as he watched Tara pace—swearing all the while—all Jason could think about was home.

He remembered the tug of his mother's hand leading him across the University of Virginia Grounds on a mild fall day, recalled sometimes running to keep up, sometimes fidgeting in place as he waited for her to pass down to him the name of yet another ancient tree. The tropical-sounding names had stuck with him better than he cared to admit: magnolia and crepe myrtle and ginkgo.

He remembered the first time he gazed up at the statue now at the center of so much controversy. "Who is that?" he had asked, and nodded knowingly as only a small child can when the answer floated down, once again, from his mother.

"Robert E. Lee," she had said simply, and without explanation. "His horse's name is Traveller."

"Traveller," he'd repeated, eyeing the massive metal beast. To his four-year-old self, the name of a horse in a statue was much more important than the name of its rider, or whether he had ridden in the Civil War, the War Between the States, or the War of Northern Aggression—each of which Jason would come to hear it called over the course of his public-school education.

He remembered the afternoon walk from his elementary school to his mother's biology lectures, where he would draw her students' attention as he pored over the sports section of the *Daily Progress* with an air of importance. He remembered navigating gameday crowds by his father's side, and once even being hoisted onto his shoulders to witness the exuberant chaos when the football team finally handed Florida State its long overdue welcome-to-the-ACC defeat.

He remembered cool mountain streams and hot, sunny fields; yes ma'am and no sir to strangers with voices like molasses—women in the grocery store who knew his family tree three generations back and sent well-wishes to them all, and men in rickety old pickup trucks who could tell you the weather for the next month better than any TV meteorologist. He remembered balmy Halloween nights for trick-or-treating and gray, fifty-degree Christmases when dreams of snow gave way to the reality of racing onto a soccer field among friends.

He remembered it all, and Tara knew none of it.

"This fucking town," she repeated. She stopped pacing and eyed Jason with a look of disdain. "How can you even try to defend this place?"

"I'm not defending slavery or anything," Jason insisted. "The past is. . . ." He trailed off, felt a pang of missing their other bandmate—the friend whose absence had drawn them to Charlottesville—who *had* been there for all those years when this town was their whole world.

If only Max were there, he'd craft the perfect line about past and present and the challenge of reckoning with history. But all that echoed in Jason's head was the Faulkner quote even he knew by heart: *The past is never dead. It's not even past.*

Chapter 1

Stepping out of his own car and hearing the crunch of gravel underfoot, it took Jason a moment to get his head straight. Everything felt off, somehow, even as the muffled sounds of pounding drumbeats and screeching guitars filled the night air. It was the right event—a celebration of the band's return from a year on hiatus—but the venue was impossibly wrong. Even Jason, who'd leapt at the idea of opening their reunion tour with a hometown show, could see that. They had no business trying to cram an extravagant New York City-style party into these equally extravagant yet totally incongruous Virginian surroundings.

Tara, stepping out of the passenger's side as a valet rushed, too late, to open her door, wore a scowling expression that echoed Jason's thoughts. "Remind me why we're at a fucking plantation manor?"

Jason stood frozen in place, fiddling with the collar of his leather jacket as he waited for the frantic valet to accept his keys. "It's not a plantation . . . I don't think."

"It's Virginia. Of course it's a plantation."

"Yeah, well, not my idea," Jason muttered.

"Is he even coming?" Tara demanded, her dark hair and all-black ensemble almost disappearing into the shadows as she and Jason fell into step toward the columned entrance to the house. She didn't need to name their absent bandmate for Jason to understand, and to know why the question was directed his way. Max had a reputation for being difficult to pin down, and Jason, his best friend since childhood, was more likely than anyone to guess where he might be—and if he had any intention of coming out of hiding.

"He said he was."

"Not what I asked. Is he coming?"

Jason sighed, watching his breath billow out in a frosty cloud illuminated by old-fashioned lanterns as they neared the house. "Max says he's coming."

Tara's only reply was the click of her high-heeled boots on the brick steps that landed them only inches away from the party—*their* party—from the night they'd waited over a year for.

"You know what?" she said finally. "I don't even care. As long as he's at the concert, Max can do what he wants." She reached for both doorknobs, preparing to fling the double doors open in a dramatic entrance, and added, with a small nod in Jason's direction, "We're back."

And as the doors swung wide, Jason knew that they were. It washed over him all at once: the heat, the sweat, the scent of booze, the roar of their latest hit through an overdriven sound system, the screams of the crowd, all eyes fixed on him and Tara.

It only took a second to lose her in the crowd, and to find himself right back where he belonged. "Jason!" "Jason, over here!" "Oh my God, Jason!" "Jase, hey Jase!"

Any reservations about the venue, the stuffiness he half expected to find inside the centuries-old building, drained away in an instant. The furniture had been removed, the walls were draped in thick black fabric, and speakers had been wired up in every possible corner of the house. Most importantly, the crowd was there, and—New York or Virginia—five hundred close friends and adoring fans guaranteed a good time.

"Who has a drink for me?" Jason demanded with a grin, surveying the crowd. Everyone was talking, shouting, yelling at once, clamoring for attention yet hanging on his every word. Cocktails were produced, which he rejected one by one before downing a shot of whiskey—or what remained of one after its trip across the room.

Buoyed by the buzz of one, two, then quickly three shots, Jason wove his way through the crowd, making the rounds from one clique to another, scribbling autographs, pulling fans in for hugs and back-slaps, and refusing photo op after photo op. "Now?" he'd ask, adopting a façade of mock incredulity. "No, no, no, not without my guitar." It was a policy stolen from Max, an affirmation that they were a band first and celebrities second. With the band, Jason could be a hero, but even at their own party, he was just himself.

He tried to bask in the moment, to drink in every second of it. It was fun, refreshing even, to experience it all again as if for the first time. But Jason couldn't help noticing the one striking difference between this party and the *real* first time. Max, despite his promises, had yet to make an appearance.

Jason paused by the bar and pretended to contemplate his options before reaching for his cell phone—just to check the time, he told himself, trying to silence the voice in the back of his mind that wondered whether Tara was right about Max not coming. He was on the verge of shooting off a quick "ETA?" text when a girl he thought he recognized appeared by his side, maintaining a careful hold on a quartet of shot glasses. "Jason! Oh my gosh!" she greeted him eagerly, extending the drinks in his direction.

Mustering a grin, Jason pocketed his phone and made a show of taking all four glasses from her before accepting one and downing it, grimacing slightly at the sharp, artificial fruit flavor. "How's it going?" he half shouted over the music.

"Great!" was the enthusiastic reply.

"Where do I know you from?" He was less sure she looked familiar now, and it was at least the third time that night he'd used the same line, but fans never seemed to mind being the ones to supply the details of the last time they'd met.

"Oh!" the girl let out a little laugh, giddy with the importance of being recognized. "Me and my friends met you after you played up in D.C. one time. You remember me?"

"Yeah, yeah, of course," he played along.

"That's so crazy!" She was smiling, almost seemed to be flirting by the way she was eyeing him, and he could sense a question forming on her lips.

"What's up?" he asked, returning her smile.

"Have you seen Max anywhere?"

Not the question he'd had in mind.

Or rather, it was exactly the question on his mind, and Jason was immediately annoyed that this girl—who had all the makings of a very compelling distraction—had failed to live up to her potential.

"Haven't seen him," Jason said, helping himself to a second shot from her collection and using it as an excuse not to engage further.

"Oh." The girl looked disappointed. She gave a little shrug, then downed the remaining shots herself, and with a quick, "See you around!" disappeared back into the crowd.

Jason sighed, not even interested enough to watch her go. His presence was no longer a novelty—to himself or anyone else. They were all waiting for Max and Max alone. But likely Jason was the only one dreading the lonely hours after the party if Max really did decide to bail.

He tried to shake those thoughts aside and return to the moment, but the rush of his and Tara's arrival was long gone, and he fell to contemplating the party, as if watching from a distance. Now that he saw the space all decked out, he understood Max's insistence on holding the event in Charlottesville; the square footage alone would have been impossible to find in the city, and with the lights low and speakers blaring, it was easy to forget where they were. He just wished he could forget everything else.

He felt a tug on his arm and looked up to see that Tara had reappeared, her expression serious as she nodded for Jason to follow her. He did, struggling with the greater height all around just to keep her in view, before realizing where she was headed. He elbowed his way over to one of the interior walls where he could use the dark curtains as a guide, feeling his way along until his hand pushed through to air as the wall dropped away. He fumbled for the break in the heavy fabric and, finding it, ducked through into the relative quiet of their private coatroom.

"Hey," Jason said. His voice was too loud for the small space; he could hear that, even with the noise of the party ringing in his ears.

"Hey," Tara replied quietly. From her tone, it sounded like he was the one who'd summoned her, the one keeping her waiting for whatever came next. She sank back against a stack of instrument cases and withdrew her cell phone from the pocket of her slim black jeans. "He's not coming."

Jason fumbled for his phone, and a moment later the same text message illuminated his screen. He didn't say anything at first, just peered distrustfully into the eerie bluish glow. "Okay," he said finally. "That figures." He read and re-read the text as if in a drunken haze, despite suddenly feeling about three drinks more sober than a moment earlier.

Jason pocketed his phone as Tara began to tap away at hers. "He's acting like a child," she muttered, half to herself, still typing what Jason suspected was an irate response.

"C'mon, that's not fair."

"Not *fair*?" Tara's eyes shot up to meet his, her stare incredulous. "We were supposed to surprise everyone with a show tonight and now he's bailing."

Jason sighed. He knew she was right, but where Tara felt anger, he was left with disappointment, and he couldn't bring himself to side against Max, even now. "Tara, let's not—"

"Not what?"

"Just . . . this." He gestured vaguely. "Who's this helping?"

Tara folded her arms across her chest. "Well, I *thought* I was helping Max by dropping what I was doing to come back on tour after an entire fucking year of radio silence."

Jason sank back against the coats that lined the opposite wall, no more than a few feet away from Tara but suddenly a world apart. "He's just . . . he's still working through some stuff." He paused. "I mean, touring again . . . it's a big deal. For all of us."

"Oh, no, don't play this 'all of us' game. This is Max," she insisted, her voice rising. "Just him. Just him yanking us around, just him flaking out, just him ditching us. Again."

"Tara!"

The bite in Jason's tone shocked her into momentary silence. "Well," she mumbled, sounding more composed, "I just think if we're getting back together, we should be back together for real."

Jason sighed again, running a hand through his sweat-dampened shock of dirty-blond hair. The year on hiatus had made it easy to forget, but the past several weeks together brought everything flooding back. All of the good, all of the bad. The years of fighting and scrapping for any low-paying gig they could book, the rush of being discovered, of making it big, of learning life was just as hard at the top—and doing it all alongside his two best friends in the world. What had happened to them?

He darted a probing glance in Tara's direction and suddenly he could read it all in the frustration on her face. Max had happened to them. Once in the positive—rushing into each of their lives with his crazy dream of rock stardom, and once in the negative—fleeing from the fame he had engineered and shutting himself off from the world for months at a time.

And now Tara was retreating too, back into the distracting glow of the virtual world, but more significantly, into the defensive shell of *rightness* that sheltered her, that made it safe for her to dole out blame and condemnation.

It wasn't fair to expect Tara to see things in the same light, Jason reminded himself with some bitterness. She didn't know; she hadn't been there from the start. Not the real start, anyway, the formative years that created the boy, the young man now nearing thirty but firmly rooted in teenagerhood that the world celebrated on stage.

Tara knew well the genius songwriter who, on an especially prolific tear, would arrive at rehearsal unslept but bursting with energy as he distributed scribblings of their next hit single. She was used to the stubborn nonconformity with which he insisted on playing only his bass, never performing any of the intricate guitar solos he spent weeks perfecting before passing them along to Jason. But Max—temper, sulkiness, and all—had always been destined for that world of fame, and his band's renaissance atop the charts was merely the next step in the trajectory Jason had watched develop over the course of their shared adolescence.

Jason alone remembered the shy kindergartener clinging to his mother's side as she balanced a toddler on her opposite hip and sounded out the unfamiliar English words to wish her son a good first day of school. He alone had forced Max out of his shell with a verbal deluge of his own and the sometimes-violent coercions of friendship common to all boys of that age. And he alone had watched the ensuing transformation from start to finish.

Tara didn't know the third grader, the indiscriminate lover of all things musical, whose awe at the hulking size and impossibly low tones of the double bass in a school orchestra performance had fixed the course of his life's trajectory. "And it's the same strings as a bass guitar and everything," Max had gushed. "If you can play *that*, you can play any kind of music. Everything has bass in it—everything!"

She didn't know the ten-year-old who made the daring second-story climb to Jason's bedroom window one night, silently letting himself in with an illicit copy of *Enema of the State* that neither boy had been allowed to buy. They'd huddled under the covers, contorting a pair of headphones to both listen at once. At the end of the disc, Max had declared in a serious whisper that it was the best album he'd heard yet, and that he'd be able to play every song on it by the end of the week. He kept his word, and the album its status in his esteem until the final notes of *American Idiot* echoed through that same bedroom five years later.

Tara only knew Max as he was, not as he had been, making it possible for her to believe that the moody turmoil that now seemed to follow him everywhere really could swallow him up, could nullify everything he and the band had worked for. But Jason knew the truth; the friend they knew and loved was still in there, and nothing, not even his sullen descent into the hiatus, could hold Max down forever.

A simultaneous buzz of phones drew Jason's attention back to the coatroom.

"Alex is on his way," Tara reported, then added under her breath, "I can't believe he's still making time for this crap." She was already in the process of typing out what Jason could only assume was a friendlier response to the person actually bothering to make an appearance that evening.

"I mean, it's his brother," Jason replied, hoping that would satisfy her. He was starting to feel buzzed again and resented that he had to fight it to be mentally present for whatever conversation Tara, ever sober at events like these, intended to hold.

Alex, too, had been a part of Jason's world since childhood, the younger sibling perpetually eager to be roped into whatever scheme Jason and Max had gotten into their heads. But only as the recent storm started to brew did the adult Alex find a home among them—and an unconventional one at that.

It had surprised both Jason and Tara the first time the "Max" who appeared beside them at a publicity event turned out to be an apologetic Alex, blushing uncomfortably but otherwise the spitting image of his older brother. "It'll never work," Jason had sworn, too familiar with their subtle differences to be fooled by the stand-in, but he was quickly proven wrong. It had been a relief and a disappointment all at once, but as Max's emotional storms raged, grew, and became all-consuming, Jason knew there was no better option. They could all see that Max was headed for a breakdown, and the more private the band could keep it, the better.

"Brother or not, it's some deal he's got going," Tara grumbled. "The kid's still in school, right? He's at UVa?"

"Not still—again, I think," Jason said. "He was somewhere else before. We went to a graduation thing. . . ." He trailed off, suddenly feeling strange about his use of a "we" that excluded Tara, and hastily added, "I mean, Max and I did."

"Anyway," Tara said, the edge returning to her voice, "he's busy with his own life. If I were him, I'd—"

"Tara, let's not."

Frowning, she slumped backward against the stack of instrument cases behind her. "Fine. But you know I'm right. Max needs to either figure it out or not. I'm not going to play this game much longer."

"No one's playing games," Jason said. And then, in a rush of impulsivity, he added, "But I am gonna *play*." In two steps he was across the coatroom, fumbling with the latches of the guitar case on which Tara's elbows rested. She stepped aside, giving him space to retrieve the instrument.

"Sure." Tara's comment was almost certainly accompanied by an eye roll. "The fans will love that: no melody, no lyrics, no bass solo. Just you, strumming some fucking chord changes."

Jason offhandedly extended a middle finger in her direction as he secured his strap locks. "Shit, Tara, it's not like we need Max's permission to have a good time." But even as he said it, he could feel the words weren't true, were just covering up his own frustrations, which were better lubricated with alcohol but no less pressing than hers.

He'd committed though, and he flung the heavy fabric aside. He resented Max's flakiness and the razor-sharp accuracy with which Tara called him out on it, but he was filled with a new wave of defiant pride at the shouts and exclamations that ensued as he strode across the room, made famous once again by the guitar in his hand.

Chapter 2

SUNDAY, 4:50 A.M.

The room was spinning—softly, in the comfortable haze of the night's drinks—as Jason fumbled his way to an overstuffed, high-backed sofa, and with it, the promise of a few hours' sleep. His head was beginning to throb, but exhaustion promised to win out over the distraction of pain.

Across the room, Tara and two others he didn't recognize leaned up against a makeshift bar, smaller but nearly as well-stocked as the permanent feature on the first floor. He could just make out the murmur of conversation but couldn't have pieced together more than the occasional phrase, even in a clearer state of mind.

Settling onto the couch, Jason tugged at the hood of his sweatshirt, cocooning himself more fully for his long-awaited slumber. His leather jacket had been lost to the crowd in the midst of his impromptu solo act, and he'd been forced to rummage through the cramped coatroom for a hoodie as the old house emptied and a late-night chill set in.

He kicked off his sneakers and swung his legs up across the far arm of the sofa, letting his socked feet dangle in the direction of the soft chatter. As he shifted around, his muddled attention was drawn to the glass-paneled doors on the opposite wall, which afforded him a view of the balcony, still inexplicably populated in the cold February predawn.

Jason's interest was vaguely piqued, but the heaviness of his eyelids proved impossible to overcome, and, swallowing a yawn, he settled deeper into the cushions and started to drift off.

"Jase!" It was Tara's voice, now carrying across the room.

"Hm," he murmured, half asleep.

"We're leaving. You coming?"

"Mm." Jason resisted opening his eyes. He hoped she would take the noncommittal grunt as a refusal, which she momentarily seemed to, judging by the quiet hum of conversation and shuffling of feet that followed.

A minute later, he heard the familiar click of her high-heeled boots crossing the room. "I thought Al—uh, Max, left already?"

She wasn't going to let him sleep through whatever this was. Grumbling to himself, Jason shoved back his hood and shifted up to a seated position. He rubbed at his bleary eyes and let his head rest in his hands. "I'm sorry, what?"

"Out there." She nodded to the balcony. "I mean, that's"— she glanced around cautiously, then lowered her voice as she continued—"Alex outside, isn't it?"

"God, how are you still lucid?" Jason mumbled. He dragged his head up and blinked away the haze to reexamine the scene beyond the glass doors. At first, he could only make out rough outlines of the figures on the balcony—one tall and lanky, the other shorter and stocky—then gradually registered the combative body language, shouts and gestures of a pair about to come to blows. But the angle afforded him a shadowy three-quarter view of a face that certainly looked a lot like Alex's—or Max's— same thing.

"That's Alex," Tara decided, nodding in the direction of the taller man as she folded her arms across her chest. "And he's about to deck that dude."

"Nah, he wouldn't," Jason replied. As he spoke, though, the other figure on the balcony raised a gloved fist and took an off-balance swing at Alex's jaw. A quick dodge caused the punch to miss its mark, and the counterstrike hit home—painfully, judging by how the recipient staggered backward, bumping into the glass doors before regaining his footing.

"What the hell did he say to that guy?" Tara wondered aloud, her voice filling with concern. "We should—I mean, or should we? Shouldn't one of us go out there?"

"Sure," Jason yawned, "go for it." He was starting to shake some of the weight of his earlier grogginess, but the pounding in his head remained and he was reluctant to surrender his comfortable seat. Something about the escalating conflict forced him to share Tara's uneasiness, though; it would have come as no surprise to see Max fight back against a drunken harasser, but he had never known Alex to lash out, even when provoked.

Was it Alex though? Jason could convince himself the facial features were those of either brother, but the gestures, the mannerisms, everything about the way the figure on the balcony carried himself was so true to Max he struggled to believe it was really Alex out there. Wishful thinking, he decided, trying to ignore the weight of disappointment settling in his stomach. It was Alex, undeniably. They had spoken at length earlier in the evening and had even broached the uncomfortable topic, shouting to be heard but comfortably anonymous on the fringes of the crowd.

"How is he?" Jason had half yelled, then repeated even louder when Alex gestured that he hadn't heard before leaning in closer.

Alex gave a nod of recognition but was silent at first, pausing to sip his club soda. As he did, it left Jason wondering how he'd ended up sharing the title of Man of the Hour with the two soberest people in attendance. Tara's sobriety was situational, at least—she had a strict personal policy of never drinking around fans, which she always explained in terms of a twofold identity. Tara the drummer had been molded by a stack of Led Zeppelin albums and a rebellious streak, courtesy of her white father. Tara the woman, however, was in full command of the so-called caution gene inherited from her Black mother, and the caution gene was unequivocal about staying sober among rowdy crowds.

Alex, meanwhile, was always sober, somber even, to the point that Jason had begun to wonder how much his presence at events was doing to quiet the rumor mill. A present yet borderline depressed Max wasn't much better than one who was absent entirely.

"He's . . ." Alex had started to say, then reconsidered. "You know how he is."

"Yeah, I know, I know." Jason had heard the edge in his voice but hoped Alex would attribute it to the volume with which he'd had to shout above the music. He *did* know how Max was, having had a front-row seat for the downward spiral that had begun two years earlier, following the release of the band's third album.

To that point, the reviews had been unconditionally glowing. Their debut five years prior had been broadcast to the world with the headline, "Meet your new pop-punk obsession: The Generation." They had suffered no sophomore slump either, and with the release of the band's second album, Max's unique flair for bass-driven melodies began to draw the attention it deserved. "Move over cowbell," one review declared, "this NYC trio says it's time for MORE BASS."

Their third album was their best yet—the whole band felt it—but as the praise and accolades poured in, an ever-so-slight trickle of criticism began as well, and something in that new critique unsettled Max.

"Punk is life, but what about *love*?" one headline wondered, and suddenly the question was everywhere. Three albums in, why *hadn't* the world heard a love song from The Generation? Or even a breakup song, for that matter? Overnight, the internet made it a running joke, one that Max—the genius behind the band's treasure trove of lyrics on growing up, on politics, on literature—refused to find funny.

Jason had tried to shrug it off, by that point well used to the ups and downs of Max's creative process. "So, we put a love song on the next album," he'd said. "No big deal."

But something in Max's single tight-lipped nod and his immediate move to change the subject said that it *was* a big deal, and one that he didn't want to talk about. That was around the time he'd started sending Alex to events, only personally appearing for rehearsals and performances, and even then, avoiding the crowds he'd once embraced. Not long after, he'd begun to slip away from his bandmates, too.

Then came the declaration of the hiatus, a decision made by Max alone, but one there was no point in fighting. His announcement to the band, their agents, and their manager had been canned and unenlightening. "They can't tell me what to write," Max had repeated angrily. "It's *art*. It doesn't work like that. Enough of this bullshit." He seemed to be staging the hiatus as a punishment: if the fans weren't happy with what he had to offer, maybe they'd be better off with nothing at all.

The popular narrative was that Max just couldn't handle the criticism. Something in Jason refused to believe it was that simple, though. "What's this really about, man?" he'd asked, searching for answers in the deep, dark pools of Max's troubled eyes.

And only once they were alone, truly alone, the isolating walls of the hiatus complete, had Max replied, his voice barely a whisper. "I can't do it, Jase."

"Can't do what?"

"Write a love song."

Jason's fumbling reaction had been to downplay the concern. "It wouldn't be selling out," he began, a rebuttal forming in his mind. It didn't matter if Max was dead set against writing a love song; it wouldn't take the next "All the Small Things" or "Check Yes Juliet" to satisfy their fans. Just look at what Fall Out Boy had done with "Sugar We're Goin' Down," or My Chemical Romance with "I Don't Love You." Jealous, insecure, devastated . . . Max could redefine love song any way he chose, and the pop-punk faithful were sure to approve.

But Max had cut him off. "I know it's not selling out. I just . . . just can't." His voice was starting to shake with a swell of anxiety that Jason could feel from across the room. "I can't. I can't do it. I can't—can't give them what they want."

Had he not seen the look in Max's eyes, watched the shakiness unsteady his hands, and felt as if he could hear the panicked thrumming of his friend's heartbeat, Jason might have shared Tara's often-voiced question of whether *can't* was really *won't*. But he had been there. He had seen that whatever demon was eating away at Max was fighting hard. The inability—or refusal— to write a love song was a symptom, only the tip of the iceberg.

But now, one full, tumultuous year, and one arduously crafted love song for Charlottesville later, they were back. And things were getting better, back to normal even. Or so Jason had told himself as he stood watching the crowd, waiting for Alex's confirmation that despite his latest absence, Max really was back.

"He said you stopped by," Jason began, trying to nudge Alex into continuing their conversation.

"He says he talks to you."

"I mean, yeah, he's started to again . . . it takes a while though, you know?"

Alex nodded, and he, too, seemed to be surveying the crowd. Quiet was his usual mode, and his lack of response didn't rattle Jason. In a way, it was like untangling Max. You just had to know how—and how long—to wait.

"He was smart to call you when he did," Alex said, leaning in once again.

"Yeah?"

"He gets so . . . in his own head. You bring him back to reality."

Jason laughed, but the sound was swallowed up by the wall of noise that surrounded them. "Kicking and screaming, most of the time."

A smile flickered across Alex's usually serious face. "He needs that."

"Yeah," Jason said, more to himself than to Alex. He wanted—needed—to know more, but he could sense Alex's reluctance to talk, the fiddling of his fingers on the hem of his jacket betraying his discomfort at being put on the spot. "Anyway," Jason had added with a shrug, and Alex responded with another nod, a silent agreement that the conversation had run its course.

It had been difficult for them, moving past their preassigned roles set back in childhood, when Jason and Max were inseparable partners in crime and Alex the ever-present little brother, practically a sibling to them both. And making him a substitute Max did nothing to alleviate this tension. Jason was continually at a loss for how to approach Alex, the not-quite-comrade, not-quite-bandmate—the perpetual *not-quite*.

Even an assertive younger sibling could have been engulfed by Max's shadow, and the quiet, bookish Alex was all too easy to absorb. The very spaces Max inhabited were capable of swallowing Alex whole. Tonight, as usual, he'd spent most of his time in the coatroom once his performance—a grand entrance marked by painstakingly rehearsed nonchalance—was complete.

Which was why it came as such a surprise to see him now, on the patio, looking every bit the part of a prize fighter in the glowing outdoor lights, spitting insults and reloading for another blow.

"I'm going out there," Tara declared, reinforcing her earlier conviction, but still making no move toward the doors. Jason didn't reply. He found himself engrossed, enjoying the drama of the conflict without regard for its consequences. It was good to see Alex sticking up for himself, he decided, even if it came in such an unexpected manner.

Then, all at once, everything changed.

Jason felt himself move in slow motion, heard Tara's scream only mutedly—

He stumbled, slipping, diving ahead, felt the wall of chill air hit his lungs like a slab of ice as he flung the doors open into the night. He tried to yell out, to break the frosty silence.

He scrambled to the edge of the balcony and steadied himself against the lone column left standing, the last remnant of what moments before had been a sturdy row of brickwork. His stomach churned as he looked down.

A heap of bodies. In the dark he could just make out two forms tangled and sprawled on the patio below. As he watched in disbelief, one staggered to its feet and stumbled, limping, off into the pitch blackness beyond the dim glow of the house. That left one body: a tall, lean figure he recognized all too well.

Jason's heart was racing, and he could feel himself shaking, clinging to that column for dear life as both chill and fright threatened to upset his balance. Tara appeared beside him—or maybe he just became aware of her presence as she placed a trembling hand on his arm.

"That's Alex," she said quietly, helplessly, sounding small and far away.

Jason swallowed hard, summoned up everything within him, and forced a shout to carry through the night air. "ALEX!" But it was pointless. The dark, the haziness, the shock; none of it was enough to obscure the fact that the body below could not hear him, might not ever hear him.

Jason felt Tara shivering beside him, and instinctively, without breaking his stare at the body, he drew her close under his right arm, still hugging the column with his left. "We have to get down there," Tara stammered, teeth chattering, as she nestled into his side.

His first impulse was to leap. Get down as quickly as he could. But Jason shook it off, tearing his gaze away from the unimaginable scene below, only slowly releasing the column as he ushered them both back inside. "Yeah, you, uh, call . . . call someone. I'll go down."

"The—the police?"

"Right, the police."

"Jase?"

"Yeah?" His focus snapped to Tara's face, and, in his state of shock, he was surprised to see her eyes filled with tears. Although they were back inside the warmth of indoors, she continued to shake.

"I—I don't know the address."

"What?"

"The address—here—wherever this place is. They're going to ask."

"Oh. Right." Jason racked his brain, came up empty. "Wait, your friends, you were about to leave together. Where are they? Someone must know."

"They left." Tara's voice was small again, though the shivers were subsiding. "You were all zoned out, we were watching"— she shuddered, couldn't bring herself to say his name—"and I told them to go ahead."

"Okay," Jason declared, inhaling deeply. He could feel the rush of clarity that so often accompanies a moment of crisis. "Your—your phone. The GPS. It'll know. You call, and—and meet them out front. I'll go . . . out there." He gave her shoulders a quick squeeze before taking off, first at a jog and then an all-out sprint, racing for the back corner of the house, toward a set of stairs he remembered being just off the main room.

Jason burst through a doorway to the spiral staircase, a dim, narrow service corridor, and tore down the steps. His mad scramble sent him tripping over the first few stairs before regaining his balance—only to come skidding to an abrupt, shocked halt.

A misstep—no, a stumble into a very real obstacle—had nearly upended Jason, and what he could make out in the half light of the stairs threatened to do the same.

"Max?" The name escaped his lips breathlessly, involuntarily, in a burst of shock.

He had tripped over the crumpled form of—well, it had to be Max, if Alex were outside—but from here, with only a side view of the ashen face, it could have been either brother. But . . . how? Jason shook his head in a futile attempt to clear the lingering haze before stooping to examine the body that had, from the look of things, been unceremoniously tossed down the stairs. He felt warmth, was instantly relieved, and was reaching to feel for a pulse when the figure began to stir.

"Hey," Jason gasped, "hey, are you okay?" His mind was racing to match his heartbeat. What was happening?

The figure shakily raised his head, and managed a weak murmur Jason couldn't quite make out. But as the dark eyes flickered open, two things became clear: it was Alex, and he was badly hurt.

What the *fuck*?

"Al—Alex!" Jason stammered. He knelt close beside Alex's head in the narrow staircase. "I thought you were—we saw—on the balcony. . . ." His stomach dropped again. *Max.*

Even crouched low as he was, Jason had to place a hand on the wall to steady himself. Alex murmured again, still inaudible.

"I'll be right back," Jason said aloud, more to announce his intention to himself than to Alex. "I have to go." Blurred, shadowy images kept flashing back and forth in his mind—the face on the balcony, Alex in the stairwell—

How had he not known Max's face? Even from a distance, even foggy headed, even . . . everything. He should have known his best friend's face. A new series of mental images took over as he saw himself flying ahead of his own progress through the house, rushing to Max's side, pulling him close, listening for a dying word, wishing desperately for a different ending. It couldn't all end like this, it just couldn't.

My fault my fault my fault, beat the rhythm of his footsteps as he cleared Alex's crumpled form and raced down the stairs. *No more surprises*, he found himself silently pleading as he ran with quick, deliberate steps along the final stretch of hallway separating him from the open spaces of the first floor and the wide double doors that opened onto the back patio.

The polished hardwood flooring was slick beneath his socks, and it required a moment of conscious effort to keep himself upright as the echo of Tara's phone call caught his attention. She was still all right. Good.

"I don't know, just hurry, okay?" Tara was practically shouting, her voice high and panicked as she paced the lobby at a gait more closely resembling a run than a walk. "Okay, yes, thank you." She punched at the face of her phone to end the call and looked up just as Jason swung around the corner, wild-eyed and mouth slightly agape. "What?" she exclaimed. "Oh my God, Jase, what?"

"I—I don't fucking know," he stammered. "I think it's Max out there."

"*What?*"

He was halfway across the room, making his way toward the

back patio and the horrible scene that awaited there, but Tara's repeated question drew him to a halt. "I found Alex," he blurted stupidly. "He's in those back stairs, and if it's not him out there—"

Tara was already running. She swept past him, bursting through the doors out into the icy not-yet-morning. Jason tried to keep pace, but found himself falling behind. He rushed out into the cold just as she was kneeling beside the flattened form.

Jason halted his motion, awaiting the verdict as Tara rose, shaking, her features drawn with concern. She spoke slowly, deliberately, Jason hanging on her every word. "Who . . . in the *hell* . . . is this?"

"What do you mean?" Crossing his arms for warmth, Jason strode out to meet her, his heart still pounding.

"I don't know who this is, but it's not Alex, and it's not Max, either."

Jason approached slowly, and shuddered as he leaned down to inspect the body he'd been so sure was Max's. Up close, they could see blood beginning to pool on the bricks and a glassy stare he knew would be burned into his memory. But all the same, he was overcome by a flood of relief. "His eyes," he said, looking up to Tara for confirmation. Max's were a much darker brown. Alex's too.

Tara nodded, silent and shivering once again.

Chapter 3

SUNDAY, 7:30 A.M.

The glare of the stark white hospital lighting and ambient frenzy of activity were dizzying. The past hour . . . hours . . . however long . . . had been a blur, and Jason felt as disoriented as if he'd been dumped on an alien planet. He probably looked that way too, pacing frenetically with his damp, socked feet shoved halfway into his still-tied Converse, and his shoulders wrapped in the rough blanket he'd been handed by a shaken-looking young officer as they waited to answer questions outside the mansion.

"Pick up, pick up, pick up," he muttered, listening to yet another repetition of the five rings before Max's cell phone shunted his call to voicemail. Again.

"Dammit!" Jason spat, flinging the phone into the ground. It bounced and skittered across the corridor before coming to rest face-up, its brightly lit screen still shining up at him. He regretted the slip instantly, letting his worry escape as anger. He could feel the tears rising, and his hands shook as he clutched at his makeshift robe and bent to retrieve the device.

The knot in his stomach was oppressive, and he thought he might be sick. It didn't make sense. He didn't know what *it* was, even. It felt like an attack. But the idea that someone could have come after them—or after Max—seemed absurd. Unreal. Not the type of thing that actually happened.

Jason felt a hand on his shoulder and jumped.

"Jase, it's just me."

He heard Tara before he could rise and face her. She had been crying, and was clutching a wad of tissues.

"And?"

"Alex is going to be fine." Her voice was flat and matter of fact as she delivered the news. "They said his leg is broken, but he's okay." And with that, her composure fell away and she was sobbing again, overcome with the same tumultuous combination of emotions Jason was struggling to hold in check.

"Hey," he said, pulling her into a hug. "Hey, it's okay." The words spilled out absently and he felt the reassurance fall flat as it left his lips. It *wasn't* okay, and they both knew it. He silently cursed himself for not being able to feel what should have been a tremendous relief, but made no difference to the panic eating away at them both.

No one had been able to reach Max, and Jason was sure he should have heard back from the police officers dispatched to check his house by now. It wasn't like he'd sent them chasing down a New York address. Max was in Charlottesville—he had been since practically the start of the hiatus. It couldn't have taken them more than twenty minutes to drive out there. . . .

But still no word. For at least the hundredth time that morning, Jason swore he felt the buzz of a text message and darted a frantic glance at the screen, only to find a blank, dark surface staring back at him.

His mind was racing with worries that, even in his current state, Jason knew were bordering on ridiculous. Did he give the police the right address? Would they know where to look, to check everywhere Max might have holed up for that particular night? He should have gone with them to . . . well, he wasn't sure *what*, but the feeling of uselessness inspired by all this waiting and not knowing was becoming unbearable.

Tara was still sobbing into his shoulder, but Jason hardly noticed. His attention was finally captured, however, by a commanding voice behind them: "Excuse me, sir."

Jason spun around, bumping Tara aside in the process, and found himself staring up into the stern and slightly haggard face of a broad-shouldered man. The man was dressed in a clean but wrinkled suit, though he lacked a tie, and it took Jason a moment to process that he was neither a doctor nor a nurse.

"Yessir?"

The man shifted his weight around, and as he crossed his

arms across his chest, Jason caught a glimpse of a gold badge on his right hip. Another cop.

The officer introduced himself in a low rumble of a Southern drawl—a detective, his name immediately slipping from Jason's memory—and tersely asked if they would come to the police station for an interview. From his tone, it wasn't a question.

"Now?" Tara's voice wavered, but her tears had subsided.

"Please."

"But Alex—"

"Ma'am, your friend is stable, and we have an officer stationed by his room."

Her eyes darted from the detective to Jason and back. "Can't we stay?" she asked, her voice quick and high with anxiety. "We haven't even gotten to talk to him yet."

"Ma'am."

The detective's stony demeanor made clear his unwillingness to compromise, and as he ushered them down the hallway, he seemed to be grumbling to himself, impatient with his chore of shepherding around what amounted to little more than a pair of helpless and distracted children.

Jason and Tara had just settled themselves in the backseat of the detective's car when a true buzz of his phone sent Jason's heart leaping into his throat. "Mine, too," was Tara's frenzied whisper as she started to dig through pockets for her own phone.

"Just Izzy," Jason reported with a sigh as the message opened on his screen. No word from Max, just a rare text to their personal cell phones from the band's manager. The band tried to keep their personal and professional lives—and therefore cell phones—separate, but Jason guiltily realized he'd left his work phone at home. Considering the circumstances, the urgency of communication was warranted.

"Hearing rumors about police @ ur party?" Izzy's text asked. As Jason stared at the screen, a follow-up message arrived. "Call ASAP."

Now Tara was typing away on her phone, and the next message to appear in the thread was hers. "Yes cops. Don't know anything. About to talk to them."

After a moment's wait, Izzy's reply came through. "I'll keep it quiet. Call when u can."

Tara looked up to catch Jason's eye across the backseat. "I couldn't just tell her," she whispered.

Jason nodded. His gaze fell to the floor as he searched for a reassurance to offer, some hope they were wrong and Max would call any minute, but all he could find in amongst the dust and stains of the mat at his feet were more worries and dread.

They rode in silence the rest of the way to the station, save for the occasional crackling of the police radio. The detective led the way inside before passing Jason and Tara off to a uniformed officer who ushered them into a brightly lit room that felt more like they were back in a hospital waiting area than about to be interrogated. "He'll be right with you," the officer promised, and as the door closed and silence set in, Jason found himself fidgeting in his seat and racking his brain for anything he might have missed saying in the first round of questioning outside the mansion.

Although, to be fair, he couldn't be sure of anything he had or hadn't said in the chaotic moments after the first police car pulled up to the house and he went running out to meet the officers, trying to tell the whole story—of the balcony, of the stranger disappearing, of Alex in the stairwell—all in one breath.

The officer stepping out of the passenger's side must have been younger than Jason, and could have passed for eighteen in his wide-eyed, nervously attentive state. He'd begun scribbling down notes as Jason spoke, and would have let him ramble on interminably had the other officer not cut them off.

"Take a deep breath, sir," she had said, with the tired patience of a mother trying to calm the victim of a painful knee-skinning. "Do you mind showing us inside?"

Jason half expected her next question to be about where his shoes and coat were on such a cold night. "Yeah, uh, yes ma'am, of course," he stammered, and led them up the brick walkway, hopping lightly from foot to foot as he felt the iciness of the ground soak through his socks.

Tara joined them in the lobby, having been drawn from Alex's side by the approach of sirens. She, too, blurted out a jumbled mess of information, but managed to convey the immediate need for medical attention.

Then more sirens had swarmed the property, and just as everything seemed to be happening at once, Jason and Tara found themselves relegated to waiting out of the way. Eventually, the young officer who had first attempted to make sense of Jason's account escorted them outside and began to ask a more focused string of questions—a list provided by his higher-ranking partner, Jason suspected. It had still been dark, the late-winter sun an hour away from casting its first feeble rays over the frosty valley, and Jason's violent shivering as the questions continued to fly led the officer to hand him the blanket that even now, in the warm and bright interrogation room, remained bunched around his shoulders.

The continued presence of the blanket registered with Jason, jogging him back to the present. He shrugged it off and made a halfhearted attempt at folding it while they waited for the detective to return.

As he considered the blanket on the table before him, a pang of loneliness hit, and a memory of Max came rushing back to Jason. He could practically see him waiting there under the glow of a streetlamp, blanket-wrapped and carefree. They had just finished the final recording session of their first studio album and, at Max's insistence, made an exclusive party of it at their apartment, notably lacking in guests but complete with drinks and celebration. It had been a cold night then, too, and a still-unfamiliar city that welcomed three a.m. with a pair of caped heroes laughing as they raced its streets on an urgent quest for a late-night snack.

Of course, they were no heroes, and the capes were well-loved fleece blankets thrown on for warmth among the swirling snowflakes. Jason's bore a garish pattern of cartoon owls, and Max's an oversize logo of the university they had seen Alex off to at the start of the fall. Tara had departed earlier in the evening, to a home that was actually *home* in a part of the city whose name forever eluded her bandmates, leaving the two transplanted Southerners to continue their discovery of the magic of city nights together.

Magic was the only way to describe that feeling, carefree and weightless as he'd chased after Max, shouting and laughing all the while. They'd raced past one, two, probably half a dozen bodegas all told, before Max's path began to circle back toward home and they spilled into the flickering blue-white light of a newly familiar haunt, loaded up on bags of popcorn and potato chips, and flew back out into the night.

Their flight had carried them back to the steps of their apartment building, where Max skidded to a halt, sending Jason tumbling into him and the snacks scattering around their feet.

"What?" Jason had asked, somewhere between a whisper and a yell as adrenaline and breathlessness competed for his voice.

"Look up."

He did. The snow was falling faster, in fat, wet flakes that had started to accumulate on the tops of their heads. Directly above, in the orangey glow of an old-style streetlight, the drifting and spiraling flurries were mesmerizing.

"Wow." Jason's voice had faded to a true whisper, and even the sounds of the city streets seemed muted by the increasing snowfall.

"You dropped the chips," Max said, flashing a sideways grin in Jason's direction. But neither made a move to reach for the scattered goods.

They had stood there in silence for . . . how long, Jason didn't know; it could have been a moment, or it could have been forever. Finally he broke the silence. "How do you always do that?"

"Hm?" Max pretended not to have heard and made a show of leaning in closer until Jason's head nearly rested against his shoulder. In the moment, Jason had forgotten his own question, but Max hadn't. "Do what?"

"Notice things . . . like that." Jason gestured vaguely to the sky full of snowflakes. *Beautiful things*, he meant, but didn't quite have the words to say.

"I don't know," Max trailed off, then straightened up and stretched, widening the space between himself and his friend. It was a moment of uncharacteristic hesitance to accept an implied compliment. "I'm always looking. Sometimes I get lucky."

They had been lucky then, one of the few times Jason knew it both in the moment and in retrospect. The future had been wide-open that night, a far cry from the uncertain present.

The interrogation room door swung open, snapping Jason back to reality, and in strode the detective who had greeted them at the hospital. Instantly, Tara was on her feet, leaning across the table that divided the small room. "What's all this about? Did you find Max?"

"Take a seat, ma'am."

She bristled at the severity of the detective's tone, but obeyed his directive as he settled himself in the chair across from them.

The detective flipped open a folder and began to page through its official-looking contents. Between his large frame and the low grumbling that accompanied every moment of exertion, he seemed to occupy an immense amount of space. He continued to fuss in near silence for several endless moments, during which neither Jason nor Tara dared breathe.

"Let's see here," the detective finally muttered, looking over a sheet from his folder. "Do either of you know this man?" As he spoke, he passed a photograph across the table. It was the body on the patio, the sight of which sent an unexpected shudder down Jason's spine.

"No sir," Jason said as Tara solemnly shook her head beside him. Just seeing that lifeless face again, he felt the gravity of the situation sinking in.

Grumbling slightly to himself, the detective reclaimed his photo. "Did either of you get a clear look at the individual who fled on foot?"

Tara shook her head again. "No. It was dark."

"He was shorter than the . . . other," Jason offered, trying to force himself to remember an identifying detail, something, anything. But he hadn't seen much, and recalled even less. "He was wearing a dark jacket," he managed to add, "and limping pretty badly, um, after they fell."

The questioning proceeded along the same lines for several tense minutes, and Jason figured they had been about as useless as a pair of witnesses could be. Finally, the detective flipped to a second, nearly empty folder he'd kept hidden beneath the first. "Moving on. You also reported a friend of yours missing this morning. If you know anything about where he might be, now would be a good time to speak up."

A wave of nervous energy flooded the room. Tara sat bolt upright. "He—he texted us last night, but we haven't seen Max in almost a week. Monday, I think," she stammered, the color draining from her face.

"This text message," the detective replied, jotting a note on one of his documents, "what did it say?"

"Nothing." Tara's voice was shaky. "Just that he wasn't coming to the party."

The detective turned to Jason. "You received this message as well?"

"Yessir." Jason drew his phone out of his pocket, pulled up Max's most recent message, and held it out across the table for the detective to read.

As the detective squinted at the small screen, Tara interjected, "So he's *missing*—you didn't find him?"

The detective remained stony-faced. "No, ma'am." He looked back to Jason. "And other than this text message, you haven't been in contact with your friend since Monday either?"

Jason hesitated, searching for the best way to frame his response. He hadn't expected to be forced to admit that he hadn't faced the same wall of silence Tara had spent the past week resenting. "Uh, yeah, we did talk actually," he said, keeping his gaze lowered to the tabletop to avoid the judgmental stare he could already feel from Tara's direction.

"When?" The question came from two places simultaneously.

"It was, uh, it was Friday," Jason muttered, eyes still downcast. "He called me, asked me to come over. But that doesn't have anything to do with where he is now. You checked—he wasn't at home?" He could feel his voice moving too quickly, the words rushing out as if he could somehow speed up time, skip over the questions, and go straight to the answers. *Just tell us*, he mentally pleaded. *Tell us what you know. Tell us where he is.*

"No, sir." The detective paused, flipped to a blank page and scribbled a brief note. "How did he seem on Friday?"

"Fine, good, I don't know. Not like he was about to disappear," Jason said, still rushing, and beginning to sink down in his chair by degrees as the intensity of Tara's accusing glare increased. "He hasn't exactly been *happy* lately, but he seemed fine."

"Oh?" Tara interjected, her voice betraying an immense effort of restraint. "You had some sort of secret meeting and he just seemed 'fine'?"

Jason rubbed at his temples, trying to dispel the headache that was creeping up on him. He could tell that her worry had, at least for the moment, been overtaken by the irritation with Max that had reared its head the previous night. "Tara, please don't."

"To be clear," the detective said slowly, "this is or is not unusual behavior for"—he checked his notes—"Max?"

"I mean, that's hard to say—"

"Lately, *everything* Max does is unusual behavior," Tara interrupted. Jason could feel his own exasperation building, and not just with Tara. He should have told her earlier, confessed the times he and Max had shared when no one else was welcome in that tumultuous world. But how callous would he have sounded, announcing the times he'd spent with a friend she, too, missed terribly? And worse, what would she have thought of Max? Jason's self-imposed silence had made sense at the time, but now he wished he could crawl under the table to avoid the furious weight of her glare.

"May I remind you," the detective's rough voice cut through the room, "that anything you can tell me will only improve our chance of finding your friend."

Only a chance of finding him. The meaning sent Jason's stomach churning. "Okay," he said, drawing in a deep breath. It was a futile attempt at steadying his nerves and shutting out the confrontation he could feel brewing with Tara, but he managed to refocus his attention on the detective's question. "Max seemed okay on Friday, really. He's always got a lot going on—in his head, I mean—but lately it's been better. He's *fine.*"

The detective nodded and continued taking notes. "When you say, 'a lot going on' . . .'" he paused and motioned for Jason to continue.

"I—I don't know," Jason muttered. "It's just Max. He's always been like this."

"Has he seemed anxious or restless? Any signs he might be eager to depart of his own free will?"

"Like, run away?" Jason exclaimed.

Tara mumbled something inaudible, provoking a shocked glare from Jason. The detective seemed content to let their disagreement play out, still silently writing.

"No," Jason said, eyeing Tara distrustfully. "He didn't run away. She's just frustrated with him about something else. It's not important."

"Not important? He disappeared for almost a year—I think that's pretty important if we're trying to figure out where he is!"

Tara's outburst seemed to pique the detective's interest. "Your friend has gone missing before?" he asked. "Was this ever reported to the police?"

"Not that type of missing," Jason made a fumbling attempt at clarifying. "He just . . . needs his space sometimes." He paused for a moment, then continued, regaining steam as he spoke.

"And never like this! It's—it's insane! We have no idea what's going on here, between that fight at the party, and Alex in the stairwell, and now Max, too! It was supposed to be him on that balcony and something happened and he wasn't there, and now his brother's hurt and he's just *gone!*"

"Sir—"

"I don't get it!" Jason burst out. He could feel the panic rising up within him, and this time made no attempt to rein it in. "Alex gets attacked, Max goes missing, someone who we all thought was Max ends up dead, and you're asking me if he *ran away?*"

The detective let out a heavy sigh of discontent. "Coincident or not—" he began slowly.

"Are you even *listening* to me?" Jason rose out of his seat as he spoke, his voice approaching shouting volume. "What if he's in trouble? What if we all are? What if we're next, and you're too busy pretending Max ran away to do anything about it?"

Tara's admonition came with a slight gasp of a suppressed sob. "Jason, stop it."

The detective nodded in her direction. "You would be wise to listen to your friend here. This is an active police investigation, and I assure you, we are considering all possibilities."

The heavy silence that settled over the room conveyed that was all he had to say or hear about the matter, and Jason sank back into his seat. He felt the sting of defeat, of being put in his place. And until he'd said it aloud, he hadn't realized just how sure he felt that someone had come after Max. There was no other explanation; he wouldn't disappear like this.

As Jason stewed, the detective began flipping through the pages from the first evidence folder, eventually seizing upon one document, which he referenced briefly before returning his attention to his pair of witnesses. Jason met his stare with an icy glare of his own, but Tara had withdrawn, huddled back in her chair with her arms folded tightly, eyes downcast.

"Now," the detective began, but he was cut off by a purposeful knock at the door, followed by the intrusion of the officer who had first taken charge outside the mansion.

"Detective." Something about the way she said it made it clear that the greeting was also an instruction, and the massive man grumbled his way to his feet, stuffing his folders under his arm. There was no promise to return, only a command to wait where they were, and the silence that followed the closing of the heavy door felt eerily final.

Jason shot a glance over toward Tara, hoping to gauge her mood, but also hesitant to provoke her further. She now sat with her elbows on the table, head cradled in her hands. It was possible she was crying again. Jason slumped back in his chair, sighing as he fell to mindlessly inspecting the speckled pattern of the tabletop.

Much to his surprise, Tara's wavering voice broke the silence. "Jase, what are you doing?"

"Hm?"

"You're just—you're scaring me a little." Her voice sounded small and far away, not the admonishment for his defense of Max that he'd expected.

Jason exhaled slowly, trying to collect his thoughts before attempting a reply. He was starting to scare himself, too, letting his mind race and jump to conclusions. Max and Alex had both been attacked, that much he felt sure of. The rest . . . not so much. He'd thrown out the jab about their safety to garner the attention of the detective, but he couldn't help but worry that he was onto something. Maybe they *were* in danger. "Well, yeah, I'm scared too," he muttered.

"Why are you even bringing all that up? It just makes it worse."

Jason leapt back on the defensive. "Why am *I* bringing things up? You're the one making it sound like Max just decided to run away."

"Well, what if he did?"

The sudden opening of the door precluded Jason's next reply, and in strode the officer who had questioned them at the mansion—whom he was beginning to suspect was a detective herself. She settled into the seat across from Jason and Tara. "Hello again," she said, forcing a brief, restrained smile before repeating the introduction she must have offered at their earlier meeting. He was right: detective. Briskly, she continued, "We're almost done here. I just wanted to touch base with you about our next steps."

Jason managed a slight nod. *At least we admit there are next steps*, he mused bitterly.

The detective flipped open a folder of her own and extracted a page of notes. She began to read, her voice a flat monotone as she recited the listed steps. "We will continue following our missing person protocol with regard to your friend. We will seek a statement from the young man injured in the accident in the stairwell—"

"Accident?" Jason interrupted.

The detective's eyes narrowed. "That's generally how we classify it when an individual with a BAC of point-one-seven stumbles down a poorly lit stairwell in the early hours of the morning."

The mood in the room shifted tangibly as Jason and Tara's eyes met in a moment of mutual confusion. "Hold on, that's impossible," Jason said. "Alex doesn't drink." His heart was racing again. Had he been wrong this whole time? It had been dark; he could hardly make out the face, but he had been so sure it was Alex in those stairs, so sure he would have *known* if it were Max. . . .

"Sir, I can only tell you what the bloodwork we received reflects." The detective's voice jarred Jason back to attention. She continued with her list, providing vague assurances of increased police presence for the concert and vigilance against threats, but none of it was sinking in. All Jason could think about was rushing out of the station and back to the hospital. If it were only true, if it were Max in that room. . . .

Tara had clearly reached the same conclusion. "We know Alex," she said, once the detective had finished her list. "He doesn't drink."

"Last night he did," the detective replied with an air of finality. She collected her folder before rising to her feet.

"He didn't," Tara insisted. "I was with him at the bar. He ordered a club soda, same as always."

The detective shook her head. "I don't know what to tell you—"

"There's some kind of mistake." Jason heard the bite in his voice as he cut the detective off and hurriedly added, "Ma'am."

"No mistake, sir."

"I don't mean with the bloodwork. That might not be Alex. He and Max—"

"Both have fingerprints in our system." The detective's voice was firm. She sighed as she looked Jason and Tara over, her expression softening. "I actually know Alex. He volunteered with a local EMT crew a few years back. He's a good kid, and I'm sorry to say, accidents do happen."

Jason and Tara shared a look of disappointment, of guilty acknowledgement at having let such a wild glimmer of hope take root. Jason could read his own feelings mirrored in her expression. They both knew it was Alex; they'd known it all along. But it had been too tempting to let themselves feel—even for a moment—like Max might not really be missing, like there was still some easy way out of this mess.

The emotional shift could be felt from across the room, and the detective's expression was sympathetic as she offered a weak smile. "I know this is a stressful time for you both. Why don't I get an officer to take you home, and we'll stay in touch?"

Chapter 4

"*What* is going on?" The question was out of Alex's mouth before Jason and Tara were through the doorway of his hospital room. Jason regretted how long they had taken in retrieving his car from the mansion, but if anything, the time seemed to have done Alex some good. He was sitting up in bed, looking alert and like himself despite the hospital gown, and had been reading a waiting-room magazine that he quickly set aside. His right leg was elevated, encased in a cast that ended just below his knee, but a slight pallor and the tiredness in his eyes were the only other signs that anything was amiss in his world.

Alex. It was definitely him.

God, he looked like Max.

"How are you feeling?" Tara asked gently, keeping a hand on the heavy door until she heard the click that guaranteed at least a sense of more complete privacy.

"Fine. What happened?"

"How much—or, um, what do you know?" Tara asked. She'd frozen in place, no doubt anticipating the news she was about to have to share.

Alex shook his head. "Not much. Someone jumped me in the stairs, and now the police are asking about Max. What's going on? Is he okay?"

"Oh." The word spilled out involuntarily and looked to bring a renewed flood of tears welling up in Tara's eyes.

"*What?*"

The urgency of Alex's plea sent a new dagger through Jason's heart. *It's his brother*, he thought miserably, unable to imagine how hard the news would hit him if he were in Alex's place. "We don't know where Max is," he said. "The, uh, the police are looking for him."

"Police . . . looking for him." Alex's voice came out as a scared whisper.

"Yeah." Jason sighed, and after a pause, he continued, and without realizing it, began pacing the room. "There was a fight out on the balcony, probably after you were already hurt . . . someone's dead, and Max is. . . ." He threw his hands up in a display of hopeless uncertainty.

Alex drew in a deep breath. "I'm sorry, *what*?" His dark eyes were wide with disbelief as they darted from Jason to Tara and back to Jason.

Jason's mind was in overdrive, scrolling through the events of the previous night, trying to make sense of any of it. "I'm going to find him," he said aloud. He surprised even himself with the statement, but as soon as the words were out of his mouth, he knew they were true.

"What . . . what do you mean?" Alex asked, still looking back and forth for answers.

"Max. I'm going to find him," Jason repeated. Suddenly he became aware of his pacing and stopped, locking eyes with Alex. "I have to."

The whole room seemed to shake as Tara slammed a fist against the heavy door. "Jase, what the *fuck*? You're not going to find him!" The outburst seemed to shock Tara as much as the others, for she quickly swallowed a whimper of a sob, clenched fist still pressed against the door. At least her bitterness had found a more immediate target; Jason couldn't say why, but it was a relief to hear her criticism aimed at him rather than Max.

"You don't know that," he mumbled, beginning to pace again as his thoughts raced out of control. It was an attack, it had to be. But that was all he knew, and it left him a long way from any hope of finding his friend. "I just need to figure out . . ." he trailed off, lost in thought.

"Figure out *what*?" Tara's voice wavered, but her anger had subsided.

"What the cops don't know, or didn't want to say, or . . . or, I don't know." He threw his hands up again. "I don't know, okay?

I don't know what happened, I don't know where Max is. I don't know, but I have to find him."

The silence that followed hung heavily in the room, and threatened to linger, as Tara shook her head slowly and buried her face in her hands.

Alex was the next to speak, his eyes fixed firmly on Jason as he did. "I'm lost here. What is going on?"

"I don't know, man," Jason mumbled, hurriedly wiping away tears that had sprung to the corners of his eyes. He took a deep breath and tried to collect himself. "I don't know," he repeated, "but I want to find out."

"Sure, of course." Alex's expression was clouded with worry as he continued to watch Jason. "What did the police say?"

Jason gave a small shrug. "Nothing. They're acting like he ran away."

Alex's eyes narrowed in concentration. "That doesn't sound right," he replied. "I saw him this week. We both did. He wasn't acting like"—he hesitated—"like before."

"No," Jason agreed, "not at all." His thoughts flashed back to the previous summer, the days before Max had finally, fully shut himself off from the world. Jason had sensed it coming then, despite telling himself otherwise, and the silent, brooding Max he'd seen in June was worlds removed from the friend with whom he'd just spent Friday night. Friday had felt almost like old times—the *good* old times—passing an acoustic guitar and a bottle of wine back and forth by the glow of a roaring fire. In June, Max hadn't even let on about his new house in the foothills west of town, much less extended an invitation that stretched late into the night.

Jason felt himself slipping into memory and glanced in Tara's direction, hoping her reaction would ground him, but he struggled to read her expression. "You would know, I guess," she muttered. She sounded dejected as she continued. "Look, it's fine. You and Max are so much closer. If he seemed fine . . . I mean, what would I know?"

For some reason she seemed to be staring directly at Jason as she spoke. He didn't know what to make of that, but fortunately Alex picked up the train of conversation. "We've just known him longer," he offered. Tara managed a weak nod.

Jason could feel that Tara needed him, needed yet another

reassurance he wasn't sure he could find, but his mind was pre-occupied and the questions eating away at him drove his focus back to Alex. "Sorry, Alex, what else did the cops say to you?"

"Um . . ." Alex hesitated. He, too, looked to be checking on Tara, but a moment later turned back to Jason. "They asked what I remembered about last night. I thought they meant what happened to me, but then one of them asked about Max. When I said we hadn't talked since Friday afternoon, they sort of let it drop. If I'd known he was missing . . ." he trailed off, shaking his head.

"And what *did* happen to you?" Jason asked.

"I'm not even sure," Alex said, considering. "I was upstairs at the party and I started feeling dizzy and wanted to step outside. Then halfway down the stairs this guy just barreled into me. It's kind of hazy, and honestly, I'm not sure the cops believed me."

A flicker of hope sprang to Jason's mind. "I believe you," he said. "Who was this guy in the stairs?"

"Don't know. I only saw him for a second."

"But he definitely . . . did something? You didn't just fall?"

Alex shook his head. "No, he pushed me, tripped me. I don't know what exactly."

"You're sure?" Jason pressed. "The cops said you were drunk, so maybe—"

"No," Alex interrupted. "Jase, you know I don't drink."

Jason's mind was racing. He could feel pieces of the puzzle coming together, found himself lost in thought as he rushed to make sense of it all.

"I have a theory," he blurted out, drawing probing looks from both Tara and Alex. "What if you were drugged?" Jason's statement was met with blank stares, so clumsily, he continued. "I mean, you ended up with alcohol in your system, and if someone jumped you in the stairs, it might've been on purpose."

Alex nodded slowly, his expression of curiosity becoming skeptical.

"I don't think anyone wanted to drug *you*," Jason went on. The ideas were coming to him as fast as he could get them out. "They must have thought you were Max. They wanted to get rid of you—or something. It could have something to do with the rest of this mess—Max being missing, maybe even that fight on the balcony. I mean, the guy who died looked exactly like you.

We thought he was Max, too, at first." He looked eagerly from Alex to Tara, awaiting their reactions, but the silence that settled into the room felt empty and confused.

Alex was the next to speak. "I'm a little lost."

"Same," Tara butted in. "Jase, what are you talking about?"

"It's connected," Jason insisted. "The police say Alex's 'fall'"—he drew out air quotes—"was just an accident, and that Max being missing and the fight on the balcony were unrelated. But Alex wasn't drinking and he didn't just fall, so there has to be more going on with the rest of it, too."

Alex frowned, the look of skepticism not wavering from his face. "There . . . might be something there," he offered.

"You think so?" Tara asked, clearly unconvinced herself.

"Well . . ." Alex trailed off. "Jase, you're onto *something*, but it sounds . . . improbable. You think someone wanted to hurt me, Max, and someone we don't even know?" He counted off the supposed victims on his fingers as he spoke and held up the three glaring loose ends for the room to see.

"Not exactly," Jason admitted, feeling doubt creep in as he backpedaled. "For all anyone knew, you and the guy on the balcony both *were* Max."

"And who would want to go after Max?" Tara's voice, suddenly accusatory, cut through the room.

"I—I don't know!" Jason stammered. Desperation was setting in, and even he had to admit his so-called theory was speculation at best. But it was all he had to go on, the first even partial explanation of what could have happened to Max.

Once again, Alex pulled him back from his thoughts, his tone calm and measured as he spoke. "If they thought I was Max, how does he end up missing?"

Jason drew in a deep breath, willing an answer to come to him. He could feel Alex, in his own nonconfrontational way, baiting him to admit the ridiculousness of his theory. Some conviction within him refused to yield, however. "I know there's an explanation," he insisted.

"I'm sure there is," Alex agreed patiently, "but you're jumping to a lot of conclusions."

"Well?" Jason threw his hands up. "I have to do something. It's *Max*. If anything happened to him, I—I don't even know what I'd do."

He looked to Tara, whose gaze slowly dropped to the floor. Alex's eyes were similarly downcast. Evidently, he wasn't alone in his feelings about their missing friend and brother.

"I don't know either," Tara mumbled.

Alex shook his head again. "Jase, we all want to find him. I just don't know if this is going anywhere."

Everything within Jason resisted admitting Alex could be right. Maybe he wasn't getting anywhere, but as long as Max was missing, finding him was all Jason could think about. "Well, what are we supposed to do, then?" he asked. "I can't just do nothing."

Tara let out a small sound of realization. "Fuck," she muttered, "we were supposed to call Izzy back, like, hours ago."

"Shit." Jason nodded. He could hear the disappointment in his own voice, and resented how pragmatic Tara and Alex were capable of being while he felt himself spooling off, chasing unrealistic hopes, desperate for a sense of purpose—anything to choke down the rising panic. But they did owe Izzy that call.

Alex was nodding, too. "The doctors said I'm good to go, so—"

Jason cut him off with a sigh before Alex could offer a practical suggestion of his own. "Whatever. Let's get out of here then," he muttered. "I'll go pull the car around." With that, he slunk out of the room, not even waiting for a reply.

Chapter 5

"C'mon, c'mon, how long can it take?" Jason mumbled to himself, drumming his fingers impatiently on the steering wheel. He had been idling in front of the hospital for what felt like an eternity, hoping each dramatic swoosh of the sliding glass doors would bring Alex and Tara into view, but so far, nothing.

At least the car was finally starting to warm; when in town, he still drove the same trusty old Subaru he had learned to drive in as a teenager. In the years since the heated seats had failed, warming up had become a tedious process on a day as cold as this one.

Jason found himself muttering absently, willing his friends to hurry, mulling over the scattered pieces of evidence from the morning, and even—to his surprise—talking to Max. "I'm going to find you," he whispered, still tapping at the wheel in a quick and nervous rhythm. "It'll be okay; it's all going to be okay."

Finally, a slow-moving pair making their way through the hospital's automatic doors grabbed Jason's attention. He hurriedly clicked the door-unlock button several times, though Alex and Tara were only beginning their approach.

Alex was stiff and wobbly in his movement, making short, unbalanced hops as he stabbed at the ground with a pair of crutches. Something about the motion and the frustration on his usually serene face made him seem younger and hopelessly gangly—in short, a picture of awkwardness. He had never less resembled his brother.

Predictably, Jason's thoughts drifted back to a nearly identical view of Max, years earlier, but from the same vantage point.

"Pick me up?" Max's text message had read. "Hospital. All ok. Just need a ride. . . ." The ellipsis was one of his tells, a written tic Jason knew meant there was much more to the story. Even if Max hadn't mentioned the hospital, the way the message ended would have sent Jason racing to his car.

That day, Jason didn't have to wait long, and it was warm enough that he had cut the ignition and let his arm hang out the open window as he scanned for signs of Max's approach. At last, the doors swung wide and admitted a figure moving so effortlessly, seemingly floating, that it took a moment for him to register that Max was supported by a pair of crutches, holding a heavily braced ankle aloft with each fluid step. When he spotted Jason's car, a grin lit up Max's face—pale, even in the soft autumn sun that follows a long Virginia summer—and he called out, "That was fast! I should move you to the top of my emergency call list!"

"What the hell happened to you?" Jason had shouted back. If he'd been thinking, he would have leapt out of the car and offered to help, but Max's approach was so rapid and natural the thought never crossed his mind.

"He had but one great weakness, that valiant slayer of Hector," declared Max, assuming a dramatic air and tossing his head back to broadcast his voice to the clear skies, all without missing a step. "Noble Achilles," he continued, "who could only be felled by a well-placed arrow to the heel." With his wavy, dark locks spilling back from his upturned face, for a passing moment he himself could have stepped from the pages of that ancient myth.

"You blew out your Achilles?" Jason had understood instantly, as able as anyone to read between the lines of Max's literary tangents. If there were ever a pun or a reference to be made, it had already left Max's lips before Jason could even think of hearkening back to a long-forgotten reading list. It was one of Max's gifts; when struck by a dramatic urge, he could be Ben Jonson one moment, Allen Ginsberg the next, and spend a fleeting, teasing second as Oscar Wilde before circling back to reality.

"Long story," Max laughed. He was always graceful, but somehow more so as he glided along in legato syncopation. His movement betrayed self-assurance and absolute faith in his body, injured or not. Jason understood immediately; the hands supporting Max's weight were his truest instrument as a musician. They cradled his bass, brought melodies to life, and recorded the flashes of brilliance that would become chart-topping songs. Of course he would trust them so completely.

Jason was almost sorry to see the journey end, to have Max slip into the passenger seat and shove the crutches behind them, but he could already feel a tinge of enjoyment at being *needed*. "Where to?" he asked.

"Oh God, I'm not ready to face Victoria and all that worry she'll start throwing around," Max had replied, busily taking command of the radio. "Your place. I'll crash with you for a while, fill her in later." He meant his mother, a woman he'd taken to calling by her first name as early as middle school. But somehow, coming from Max, it was no sign of disrespect, merely an acknowledgement that they might as well drop the familial pretenses, because they were never going to share the sort of mutual understanding that the titles of 'mom' and 'son' would imply.

And so, radio blaring out the open windows, they meandered their way to US-250 and took the familiar route west to Jason's childhood home, which at that point was just as often home to them both.

Now, as Jason repeated that same question to Alex and Tara, he was only slightly jarred by the symmetry of Alex's suggestion that they head to his house to regroup.

"Let's get food on the way," Jason agreed, surprised by a sudden grumbling in his stomach. He knew he must have been hungry earlier in that long and awful day, but simply hadn't noticed in the midst of the chaos.

They rode in tense silence until the buzz of a cell phone set all three scrambling. Jason's hand leapt automatically to the space beneath the handbrake, the home-within-his-car of every cell phone he'd ever owned. "It's me," he reported, fumbling blindly with shaking fingers to answer the call. His heart was pounding, messing with his concentration for both the phone and the road, and when he'd still failed to connect on the third ring, he swerved for the nearest driveway and slammed the car to a halt. The blare of another driver's horn rang out, its tone rising and falling as the offended vehicle sped past.

Jason answered the call without registering the number on the screen. "Hello?" *Please be Max please be Max please be Max.*

The thought raced through his mind on repeat as he braced for a voice on the other end.

It was a woman's voice. "Good afternoon. This is Detective. . . ."

Jason met the expectant eyes of Tara, then Alex. "Not him," he mouthed, before returning his attention to the call.

"Sir, we need you to come back to the station. There's been a new development in your friend's case."

"Is he okay?" was all Jason could think to blurt out. The detective gave a terse, canned reply and repeated her request. "Yeah, yes ma'am, we'll be right there," Jason replied wearily before letting the phone drop to his lap. A new wave of emotions washed over him, defeat, panic, and exhaustion vying for command of his overwrought nerves. He slumped over, letting his forehead rest on the steering wheel. "The cops want to talk to us again. Something about Max."

"Okay," Tara said, her tone measured and calm. "Let's go."

It was as if they were taking turns holding it together for one another, Tara and Alex working overtime as Jason slipped further and further into desperation. He wanted to scream. He'd had nightmares like this, the day that wouldn't end, the journey from place to place without a moment's rest, but the reality was so much worse. And still so far from over.

A ransom note. That was all the police would reveal at first.

The shock was palpable, settling over the room with a weightiness that seemed impossible. A million thoughts raced through Jason's mind: he was right, there was more going on, but facing that grim reality drained away any satisfaction he might have felt.

"I'll pay it."

"Jase. . . ." Alex's voice was small and far away. "You don't have to do that."

"No." He shook his head, "I do. What do they want?"

The two detectives across the now-familiar table exchanged a brief look of concern before returning their attention to Jason and his question. "We have translators working on the details of the demand, but sir, you must understand—"

"Translators?"

The second shock was nearly as powerful as the first. The

female detective nodded. "The details of the note are not why we called you back in. We want to know if you have any idea of who would want to harm your friend."

"I don't *know*," Jason spat, his worry spilling over as anger once again. "What the hell language is it even in?"

The detective looked to her partner before responding. "Russian."

"That's—that's insane," Jason stammered. "What do they want with him?"

"We were hoping you might know."

The room fell silent, save for the shuffling of papers and shifting in chairs of a group marked by a collective lack of answers. Even the detectives seemed drawn into the discontent.

Jason was reeling from the shock, once again at the epicenter of the emotional tremor. "I—I don't know." He glanced over at Alex. "I mean, his family's Russian, but Max is a U.S. citizen. He hasn't been over there in years . . . decades probably."

The female detective nodded. "What about domestically? Any enemies?"

A sound somewhere between a laugh and a sob escaped Tara's lips. "Oh, a few." Jason gritted his teeth, trying not to resent the fact that she'd thrown a nearly identical question in his face an hour earlier and now seemed to have an answer ready and waiting for the police. Her statement prompted questioning looks from both detectives and she continued, "Max is . . . far from subtle about his politics."

"Go on." The male detective motioned for her to continue.

"Look, none of this should even *be* political, but he—really we," she corrected herself, "have been pretty vocal on a number of issues: marriage equality, immigration reform. There's plenty of people out there who hate what Max stands for—"

"But it's never gotten him *kidnapped* before," Jason interrupted.

"Well, he wasn't usually *here* before," Tara mumbled. Jason shot her an interrogating look. "I'm just saying," she continued aloud, "up until a year ago, he was basically always in New York. It's a different world down here."

"It's our *home!*" Jason declared, incredulous.

This time, the detectives seemed not to have patience for the argument threatening to break out. "All right, politics noted," the female detective said. "Any personal matters we should know about?"

Jason and Tara briefly made eye contact, sharing a tense moment before they each shook their head. "He's pretty private," Jason replied. "If anyone's after him, they want the persona, not the actual person." He continued to watch Tara with a hint of suspicion, but for once she seemed satisfied with his assessment of Max.

The detectives shared a silent exchange once again. "Thank you," the female detective said blandly, "that's all very helpful. We will know more once we hear back from the translators. Unless there is anything else we should know, you are free to go." After a pause, she added, "We'll keep you in the loop."

"Thanks," Tara mumbled, frustration obvious in her tone as she and Jason stood to depart. She extended her hand to help Alex up, but he stayed rooted in place. "Alex, let's go."

"Just a second," he replied, turning to the detectives. "Do you have it here?"

"Have what?" the female detective asked.

"The note."

Another exchange of looks.

"Can I see it, I mean?" After a pause that almost certainly meant *no*, Alex continued, "I speak Russian. I might be able to translate."

The male detective stiffened. "And where'd you learn that?"

"At home." Alex's tone was still patient, but only just. "From my parents. Like Jason said, we're Russian by birth."

Only then did it dawn on Jason that the police, for all their displays of seriousness, were acting out of desperation as well. As the detectives handed over a photocopy of the note, he realized they were all in the same boat. In over their heads and anxious to make progress, even if that meant entrusting their key piece of evidence to their kidnapping victim's little brother. He peeked over Alex's shoulder at the blurry, grayed-out snippets of text and wondered how anyone, even a translator, would make sense of that mess.

They all waited with bated breath for Alex's verdict, which he presented after a few tense minutes. "Sorry, I'm rustier than I thought," he said, sliding the page back across the table.

"Well then," the male detective said. "I think we're done

here." He rested a hand on top of the ransom note as the three made their way out of the room as if to keep it from leaping up and following them, holding tight to his slim advantage in making sense of a case that was threatening to propel their department—and community—right back into the national headlines.

Chapter 6

A strange quiet settled over the car as they pulled out of the police station parking lot. Jason felt the day's nervous energy draining away, leaving behind a vaguely hungover feeling he couldn't solely attribute to the previous night. He could sense Tara felt the same way, but Alex was tougher to read and seemed to be puzzling over something he wasn't yet ready to share.

Suddenly Alex's voice broke the silence. "There's something that bothers me about that ransom note."

"Yeah?" Jason replied offhandedly. "There's a lot that bothers me about it."

"That's not what I mean," Alex continued, not letting himself be derailed by Jason's dismissive response. "I'm talking about the way it was written." He paused. "I shouldn't get ahead of myself. Hold on."

Jason and Tara exchanged a questioning look as Alex busied himself with his cell phone. A moment later, he was talking into the phone, and it took Jason a few seconds to process what he was saying—or rather, to realize that he couldn't.

Tara caught Jason's eye with another look of confusion. "What's he saying?" she mouthed.

"I don't know."

She wrinkled her brow in a performance of deep thought before adding to their nearly silent conversation. "Is that Russian?"

It took a moment for Jason's mind to register the language, but then he nodded, sure that Tara was correct. At first Alex had spoken slowly, as if sounding out the foreign words for himself, but now the sentences ran together, quick and fluid. He even sounded more comfortable expressing himself than he often did in his native English.

No—not his native English, Jason remembered with some surprise as they pulled into the drive-through. At the prompt of the crackling speaker, he and Tara gave their orders, but it felt almost wrong to interrupt the musical flow of Alex's conversation.

Jason caught Alex's eye in the rearview mirror and gave what he hoped was an apologetic look. "What d'you want?" he mouthed.

"*Da, da, da*," Alex muttered into the phone before holding it aside to answer. "Ah, *ananasoviy molochniy ko*—" he cut himself off, his face quickly reddening. "Sorry. Pineapple milkshake and fries. Thanks."

Jason and Tara shared a brief smile as the drive-through attendant repeated their order back to them. Whatever Alex was working on, it must be good to have him so distracted.

It was funny how easy it was to forget that neither Max nor Alex had spoken English at the start. Aside from an insatiable curiosity for new words and meanings, nothing about young Max would have led anyone to suspect he had ever spoken anything else. Within the first few weeks of his and Jason's kindergarten friendship, he was babbling away as confidently as anyone in the class. The fact that he'd spent his earlier years immersed in another language only dawned on Jason months later, when he finally secured his first invitation to a playdate at Max's home.

"Does your mom have a lot of rules or something?" Jason remembered asking as the two boys sat cross-legged on the floor of his bedroom, each diligently working on one side of a growing Lego structure that would soon engulf the better part of the available floor space.

"Nah," Max had replied with a shrug. He paused, reconsidered the placement of a green brick on his side of their fortress. "I dunno."

"How come you always come over to my house then?"

Max shrugged again, still focused on the Legos. Or, as Jason guessed even then, on avoiding the question.

"Come on, how come?" Jason had pressed.

"Your house is just more . . . normal," Max said, sounding almost embarrassed. He looked up at Jason uneasily—an evasive, boyish look he had never fully outgrown. In every adult repetition of that wide-eyed seriousness, Jason could still see the six-year-old, ashamed of the explanations he would have to give his friend about the names his parents had for him and his brother, the English words plastered all over their small apartment, the after-school snacks that looked nothing like the sugary treats that abounded in Jason's home.

"Well, the first thing is my mom doesn't know that much English," Max began apologetically when Jason continued to press. Then he had hesitated, just long enough for Jason to butt in.

"How do you talk to her?" It was an honest question from a boy who had never considered *anyone*, much less anyone he knew, speaking anything other than the scattered dialects that colored the speech of his Virginia hometown. With some amazement, he realized his new friend had been hiding not just his house, but an entire language within it. In retrospect, Jason was impressed not only by the secret but the skill with which it had been kept from him.

"We're *supposed* to speak English at home," Max had explained, "but she cheats all the time. Just me and my dad follow that rule."

Jason had nodded seriously and listened as Max began to describe what he considered the embarrassment of his home and family, waiting until the last warning had been presented to ask, "So can I come over tomorrow?"

He did go home with Max the following afternoon, and marveled at the small, cozy space that smelled of unfamiliar foods and perfumes, and which—as promised—was labeled from top to bottom with little yellow notes that reminded its occupants of every word they might need, from "telephone" to "clock" to "towel." He listened in amazement as Max was transformed into Maxim and Alex into Sasha, and the rhythms of speech rolled seamlessly into and out of the only language he knew, until Max declared in exasperation, "You have to speak *English*. Jason doesn't know what you're saying."

They'd retreated to the small bedroom Max and Alex shared, Max stewing with frustration and Jason awestruck by the novelty of the secret world into which he'd been admitted. "Your house *is* weird," he said, almost enviously. After a moment's consideration, he added, "This is cool. I never knew anyone not from here before."

"I'm from here," Max replied with a surprising stubbornness in his voice.

"Nuh-huh, you were born over there, and you know a whole different language."

Max had shaken his head emphatically. "Born isn't the same as from," he corrected. "I lived here a whole year before I even met you. That's long enough to be *from* somewhere."

Jason couldn't argue with that logic, and even then, wasn't in the habit of disagreeing with Max if he could help it. There was something instantly persuasive about the way he said things, the seriousness in his dark eyes that accompanied every declaration.

But the distinction of being *from* Charlottesville that mattered so much to Max never seemed to carry the same weight with Alex. Even years later, when their mother's English had improved to the point that Jason could hardly hear an accent in her speech, Alex would still sneak comments to her in Russian, holding tight to that thread of identity that had slipped so easily from Max's hands as he plunged headlong into making the English language his own.

Jason hadn't heard Russian spoken in years, even from Alex, but there was something instantly familiar about it, and he felt a pang of nostalgia as the words filled the car. The tone, the rise-and-fall of each phrase, it was all just right, and it reminded him of those early childhood visits to Max's, times he had almost forgotten existed in the long and colorful history of their friendship.

"I think I have something," Alex announced, and it took Jason a moment to realize that he'd ended the phone call and switched back to English.

"Explain?" Tara asked, her voice muffled by an oversized bite of the quesadilla she'd wolfed down nearly whole.

"The note!" Alex was excited in any language. "I think I figured it out." He nodded his thanks as he accepted the milkshake and French fries that Tara passed back to him, then dropped a fry into his mouth.

"Figured what out?" Jason asked, still trying to shake the fog of memory and barely processing either the words or the emotion with which they were delivered. It was yet another layer of confusion on top of an already stupefying day.

"Okay," Alex began, speaking with an air of authority, "that note was a mess—words out of order, conjugations mixed up. I thought maybe I was confused—I mean, it's been a rough day—but the more I thought about it, the more it seemed like it couldn't just be me."

Jason nodded, encouraging him to continue.

"I didn't want to be wrong, so I ran it by a friend, and he said the same thing. No one writes that badly."

"So . . . what?" Tara asked.

"So, I don't think anyone Russian is responsible for that note. It reads like someone wrote it in English and plugged it into an online translator. They're trying to fake us out."

Tara frowned. "The police didn't think so."

Alex waved it off. "They don't know. They're just waiting for someone to translate."

"Wait, wait, wait," Jason interjected, shaking his head as if to shake away the feeling of intellectual whiplash. "So, if it's fake, was Max even kidnapped?"

Alex was silent for several seconds, and when he spoke, the energy had drained from his voice. "It *is* still a ransom note."

"Like I said, I'll pay it," Jason curtly repeated his assurance. He was losing patience and couldn't stop himself from forcing Alex to bear the brunt of that burden.

"It's not money," Alex said. "I don't think. It's so muddled I couldn't tell what they want. They say they have him, that they 'took him back' or something. They call him *razvedchik*. I think they're trying to say he's a spy, but the word is wrong; they're saying he's a . . . a scout." He paused. "They have some less-flattering terms for him, too, and they say something about demands, but that's about it."

"That *does* sound all kinds of fake," Jason agreed. "Well, okay," he decided, "at least we can tell the cops and get them off the idea of this being some sort of international incident."

Alex opened his mouth to speak, then hesitated. "Do you think we should?" he asked. His lifelong position in Max's shadow had instilled in Alex a strong aversion to stepping on toes. For the most part, it served him well, but Jason felt compelled to overrule him—another common pattern in their interactions.

"We have to," Jason said firmly. Memories of a lifetime of news stories and TV dramas filled his head, all broadcasting the same message: the longer someone is missing, the more likely you are to find them dead, if at all. He couldn't let that happen. "I'll call from the house."

"*After* we call Izzy," Tara interjected.

By then, they were in their final approach toward the driveway, and Jason pulled up to the shuttered garage without another word.

It was a strange relief to be home, to know that this place still existed in a world where everything else had been turned upside down. Jason led the way up the brick walkway to the familiar old front door, shivering slightly in the cold. His key stuck in the lock, but the subtle motions necessary to make the lock give way were second nature by this point, and, with all its usual creaky fanfare, the door swung open wide.

He'd been back in the house for the past week and a half, but there remained a slight mustiness in the air of the long-empty space. Not just empty of occupants, either. It was still trapped in that half furnished state his parents had left behind in their retirement to Florida. The move had happened at the height of the band's fame; he had negotiated the purchase of their coastal condominium, through various agents and managers, from some West Coast luxury suite. Over a year had passed before he made his first visit to his parents in their new world of beaches and tourist traps, and in the intervening three years, he hadn't been back once.

This house, though, continued to draw the occasional visit. Sometimes he and Max would make the trip together, but even unaccompanied, Jason would return home to the town it seemed had grown up right alongside them.

The stasis of the house, even as it grew lonelier with every visit, was reassuring for its contrast with the change of pace beyond its walls. The city was growing, buildings springing up to the north and west of what had long felt like a small college town. The classic brickwork of downtown was dwarfed by a sea of new suburbia, and even the grandiose estates once viewed as a good distance from the city were starting to sense the approach of new developments—invasive as the kudzu vine that blanketed trees, road signs, and anything else in its path—

creeping toward their picturesque rolling hills.

In here, though, it might still be twenty years ago, Jason reflected as he flipped on lights along his route from the front hall to the connected kitchen and living space that spanned the back of the house. The bulk of the furniture of that room remained; the way he spent his time here made it possible to forget the emptiness of the dining room and study that flanked the front hallway.

He heard the soft commotion of Alex and Tara's approach behind him, as they shuffled and clicked their way through the doorway and finally flung closed that barrier to the chilly day, which was by that time fading into another harsh, cold night.

"So, this is your house," Tara said, stepping into the living area beside Jason. Only then did it dawn on him that she had never seen this corner of his world. "You . . . couldn't afford furniture, huh?"

"Ha, ha," he muttered. "My parents took most of it when they moved. It's not like I'm here enough to need more. Just this," he nodded to their surroundings, "and my bedroom."

Tara nodded. "It's a nice house," she managed. "Very . . . suburban." Jason didn't have an answer for the slight distaste in her final statement. After a moment, Tara added, "Do you have a trashcan at least?"

She was still holding a paper bag of the remains of their meal, and he took it from her outstretched hand to place in the kitchen garbage himself. "Have a seat," he said, the formality of the offer awkward on his tongue. "Anywhere—make yourself at home."

"Thanks," Tara replied. She walked over to the table and seemed to contemplate it for a moment before selecting a seat. As if she, too, could feel the lingering presence of 1998 in the room and didn't want to misstep and fluster the resident ghosts.

Jason paused by the outlet where his work cell phone had been left to charge, and after a tap of his finger illuminated its screen, a barrage of early-morning texts from Izzy sprang to his attention. Fortunately, that was all. He knew the story would be blowing up soon enough, and impulsively powered the device off.

Alex, slowed only by the need to balance his crutches in an out-of-the-way corner, made the two-hop journey to his usual seat, the unofficial fifth of the six chairs surrounding the kitchen table. He stretched his injured leg out to the seat opposite him, and Jason was momentarily flustered by the relief he felt to see Max's spot reserved in such a manner. Tara slipped into the chair diagonally opposite Alex, but somehow it seemed fitting to Jason to see her in his own usual seat, and, sharing a knowing half smile with Alex, he settled at the head of the table.

Tara was already on her phone, and it couldn't have been more than two rings before the call connected. "Izzy, hey," she said. "Let me put you on speaker."

A moment later, their manager's voice came through the tinny speaker, her tone sharp and accusing. "About time. What the hell is going on?"

Alex flinched at the bite in her voice, but Jason and Tara knew their manager well enough not to react. Izzy was never one to be trifled with, and she made sure the world knew it; at forty she still wore the combat boots and spike-studded jewelry of a high school punk, and her vast array of devices kept her up-to-the-minute on every earthly happening. She was a powerful weapon and would jump to the band's defense in an instant—but was just as ready to come down hard when they were the ones responsible for a mess.

"Um," Tara hesitated just long enough that Jason took the opportunity to jump in. He suspected his version of the truth was more limited than Tara's, but with everything so uncertain, he was eager to keep Izzy—and by extension, the outside world—at arm's length. The less fuel they provided for speculation about Max, the better.

"Hey, it's Jase," he said. "So, uh, you heard things got a little crazy last night. There was a fight, cops showed up, all that. It'd be cool to keep it quiet, you know?"

"A little crazy?" Izzy's tone was incredulous. "I heard someone *died*."

How she'd heard, Jason had no idea, but that was the magic of Izzy and her so-called sources. Her command of information was normally a reassurance, but now it sent him scrambling for words. He figured his best option was to feign surprise. "Shit, really? I knew someone fell, but—"

"Sounds like the whole damn building was structurally unsound. Next time, you run the venue by me first, got it?"

"Yeah, uh, of course," Jason stammered. "Sorry," he muttered, sensing it was not the time to point out Max had booked the mansion without their approval.

"Mm-hm. Is Max there?"

"No. . . ." Jason regretted the uncertainty he could hear slipping into his tone. Izzy may have moved on quickly about the fight, but now he'd need a half truth, at least, to satisfy her. "We, uh, actually don't know where he is right now. But we're . . . looking into it."

"Is this something *I* should be looking into?"

The room was silent as Jason looked first to Tara, then to Alex. Tara gave a small eye roll and gestured for him to continue. "Uh, probably not. I think we're good. Just . . . keep everybody away, okay? You know how he gets about media attention, and we, uh, need him back, so. . . ."

"Oh yes." Izzy's reply was firm. "I know."

They all knew painfully well the five-word refrain that had all but become a four-letter word on Max's lips: *I. Don't. Talk. To. Media.* That phrase had taken on a life of its own, had become the embodiment of his militant stance on sharing any details of his life with the public. It was Max's answer to everything since the mixed reception of their third album: questions about new songs, a broken nose, the hiatus. Especially the hiatus.

A year had passed since he'd heard those words, but Jason could still picture their most dramatic deployment like it was yesterday.

"We have to give them *something*," the frazzled-looking agent had screamed, slamming a fist into the table they had all gathered around in the band's New York rehearsal space. "You think you can do whatever you want," he pointed to Max, "but fame comes at a price: people will ask questions, and sooner or later you're going to have to explain yourself."

The outburst was met with a pout and shrug, the specialties of a petulant child grown into exactly the self-absorbed, entitled rock star the world wanted to make him out to be. "No comment."

"No comment?" the agent hurled it back at him. "And what am I supposed to do with that?" Growing still more animated, he turned to Jason. "You see what I have to deal with here? Help me out, man. Tell your *bassist* this isn't how the world works for people like him, how about it?"

Jason hadn't wanted to cause a scene. There was no point trying to, once Max was set on staging one himself. "He said no comment," he mumbled.

"Yeah, I heard that part." The agent turned back to Max. "Let's try again. How about something useful this time? How about something that gives the American public, your devoted fans, some fucking inkling of why you're about to drop off the face of the earth for who knows how long?"

"I'll try again," Max had replied, his tone even and measured. "You're fired."

There was a single eerie moment of calm before the eruption, a shouting, screaming, shoving frenzy that had to be broken up by security. They'd all jumped into the fray, and as the no-longer-agent was finally escorted out, Tara had flung her next barb of frustration in Max's direction. "What the hell was that?"

"You know the rule," Max had repeated, glowering, for what felt like the hundredth time, "*I. Don't. Talk. To. Media.*"

As much as they had hated it at the time—and from the way Tara was fidgeting in her seat, hated recalling it even now—Jason was suddenly grateful for Max's stubborn policy of silence. It meant fewer questions for Izzy as she fought to maintain a façade that even she believed to be true.

"You're rehearsing Monday, Wednesday, and then the show on Thursday, yes?" Izzy asked, prompting another serious exchange of looks across the table. Hearing the days spelled out like that, knowing that Monday meant *tomorrow* and rehearsing meant *Max, not Alex* caught Jason off guard. Suddenly his plan to keep Izzy in the dark felt horribly naïve. And his plan of finding Max—not that it was much of a plan—took on renewed importance.

"Uh, maybe not Monday," he said quickly.

"And why not? How hard to find *is* Max?"

"Oh, no," Jason scrambled for words, "it's not him. It's, um—"

And just as he found himself lacking an end to that sentence, Tara cut him off. "I ripped a callus open," she blurted out, sounding surprisingly in command of the lie. "My hand's a bloody mess. I don't think I can play tomorrow, not with a show this week."

"Fine," Izzy replied tersely. "I'll see you on Wednesday. Don't let me hear anything about y'all before then."

"Of course not," Tara said, barely getting the words out before the metallic click of Izzy ending the call. She retrieved her phone from the center of the table and busied herself with clearing the notifications that had popped up in the meantime.

Jason waited for Tara to finish, eyeing her all the while with a newfound respect. He'd been prepared to talk over her to control the narrative, and was surprised—and impressed—by the way she'd jumped in to corroborate his version of events.

Alex was the first to speak. "Shouldn't we have told your manager what happened?"

Tara nodded, looking up from her phone. "We should have. But. . . ."

"But you backed me up," Jason said.

Tara's eyes narrowed. "Oh, don't look all surprised. I'm not the enemy here." She drew in a deep breath. "I don't know. I guess now that we've decided Max isn't being whisked away to Moscow . . . maybe we give the police a day to find him before telling Izzy and getting her all wrapped up in this, too."

"Well, I'd better call the police, then," Jason decided. He paused. "Either of you know how to tell the cops you think they're wrong?"

"That part's all you," Tara said, raising her hands in a gesture of surrender.

As Jason retreated from the table, dialing the number they'd been given by the pair of detectives, he could hear Alex and Tara continuing to debate just how much Izzy needed to know. He was struck by a feeling of pride, glad to have Tara's support, to finally not be at odds over everything to do with Max. Alex's wariness he could handle; that, at least, came from a place of genuine concern. Tara's skepticism was harder to read, and all Jason knew was how much better it felt to form a united front.

The phone rang and rang, never connecting, before finally shunting Jason's call to voicemail. A recording of the female detective's voice asked him to leave his name and number, which he did, followed by an impulsive "It's about the ransom note. Call me back."

As Jason shuffled back toward the table, Alex paused and looked up to ask, "No answer?"

"No. Should I try the station?"

All Tara and Alex could muster was a collective shrug and an exchange of uncertain looks, which sent Jason back to dialing, listening to ring after ring, and finally, this time, connecting with a human voice on the other end.

"Uh, yes, hi," Jason stammered, slipping out of the kitchen

to avoid any distractions. He repeated his name and what he hoped was a coherent string of identifying details. "I'm calling because I have some evidence related to my friend's case."

The man cut him off before he could say more. "Thank you, sir. We appreciate the support, but I assure you our detectives are in command of the situation at this time."

"No, you don't understand—"

"Again, sir, thank you for your support. Is there anything else I can do for you this afternoon?"

Jason could feel a wave of anger starting to rise up within him. "How about putting me through to your fucking detectives?"

"I'm sorry, sir—"

Jason cut him off, made another desperate attempt at blurting out his information, but the officer was an unyielding wall. His worry was boiling over, bordering on outrage, as he ended the call with a shouted obscenity and flung the phone into the floor. It bounced harmlessly along the carpet and came to a stop face-up, still displaying the station's non-emergency phone number.

"*Fuck*," Jason spat as he stooped to retrieve his phone for the second time that day. He'd seen how flustered the detectives were at the station. They weren't in command of anything, and now seemed to be refusing to even hear his observations, much less take them into consideration. Why had they let Alex read the note if they weren't going to listen to what he had to say about it? And why give him a phone number that wouldn't get him past the front desk?

Jason strode back into the kitchen, still fuming. "Well, that was a fucking waste of time."

Alex glanced up, slightly open-mouthed as if he'd been cut off mid-sentence. "The detectives will call back," he said, as usual, trying to defuse the situation.

"Alex, I have to ask," Jason said, crossing the room quickly and settling back into his seat at the head of the table. "Are you *sure* that note was translated?"

Alex nodded. "Yes. Ivan agreed," he said, clearly naming the friend he'd phoned from the car.

Jason let out a groan of exasperation and let his head sink into his hands. Once again, he felt sure he was on the right track, only to find himself shut down by those around him. "What do we do?" he asked aloud. "The police aren't going to look at anything else while they're waiting on the translators."

"They'll figure it out," Alex said. "It just takes time."

"Time?" Jason's head shot up. "How much time do we have? How much time does Max have?" He took a deep breath, tried to steady himself. "I know you think I'm crazy, but I'm going to find him. Cops or no cops."

Tara sent a disapproving look in his direction. "Jase, come on. This 'go find him' idea wasn't all that funny when Max was just missing, and now that we know he was kidnapped, it's downright stupid."

"So, what was the point of lying to Izzy then?"

"I don't know, give the cops a day to find him? Or, if the note is as fake as Alex claims, maybe Max *wasn't* even kidnapped, and he'll show up on his own."

"He didn't just leave this time!" Jason could hear his voice rising, nearly a shout as his pent-up emotions began spilling over in full.

"How can you be so sure?"

"I just *am*! I know Max. You know Max. He had a reason for going away before. Jesus, Tara, think about it! We're about to debut a love song for Charlottesville he spent the past six months in exile writing. He's not just going to leave *now*."

Tara threw up her hands. "Look, whatever. I never bought his whole love song excuse about the hiatus in the first place. This makes about as much sense as *that* ever did."

"Fine. Don't believe him. It doesn't matter why he's gone. I just need him back."

Tara looked poised to reload, to fire back with another accusation, but Alex stopped her short with a quiet, "Please, let's not do this." His dark eyes darted back and forth between Jason and Tara, each of whom appeared ready to explode. "We don't know why Max was gone before, or why he's gone now. Not really. But . . ." he trailed off, hesitating, "for what it's worth, we might know more than the police do."

"So?" Tara asked, incredulous. "They're trained, or whatever."

Alex bit his lip. "Tara, this might sound horrible, but do you really have that much faith in the police in this town? After August?"

She was silent for several moments, eyeing Alex with an impenetrable look somewhere between frustration and disbelief. Finally, her expression softened, and she said quietly, "No. But there aren't a lot of good options right now."

Alex nodded. "I agree." He turned to Jason. "I need you to know I'm only saying this because of how desperate we are, but . . . if you think you can find Max, let's do it."

"Yeah?"

"Yeah." Alex's expression was serious. "Tara? What do you say?"

Tara drew in a deep breath, then let it out slowly. "All right, yeah." The smile was already forming on Jason's face when she added, a second later, "On one condition."

"An overdue apology?" Jason asked, feeling badly for the way he'd taken his worries out on her.

Tara broke into a smile as well. "Fuck that, just put on some coffee, would you?"

Chapter 7

The bittersweet aroma of brewing coffee soon filled the house. The scent carried a rejuvenating warmth, even before the first sips were taken from the steaming mugs Jason delivered to the kitchen table.

While the coffee brewed, Jason had busied himself with retrieving a whiteboard and markers, long forgotten in the bottom of his closet but now the perfect supplies for organizing their makeshift investigation.

"All right, Jase, let's hear what you've got," Tara said, motioning for him to begin with the hand not curled around her mug.

Jason nodded, sipping his coffee. "I guess let's start writing up what we know." He reached for a marker, but Tara snatched it away before he could.

"Oh, no way, I've seen your handwriting," she said with a laugh. "I'll write."

"All right, all right," Jason conceded with a half laugh of his own. He would be the first to admit he lived up to the stereotype of left-handers with terrible handwriting and was more than happy to let Tara take charge, especially if that meant she supported his crazy plan.

It only took a few minutes for scattered lists to fill the whiteboard, all chronicled in Tara's neat, narrow print: Alex's comments on the note, observations of the figures on the balcony, a rough timeline of Max's routine—anything and everything that seemed remotely relevant. "Okay, now what?" Tara asked once they'd finished, capping the marker and settling back in her seat.

"I don't know," Jason was forced to admit. He scanned the board, hoping for something to leap out at him, but it was just as jumbled as the thoughts racing through his mind. He took a deep breath. "It feels like half of this says, 'big conspiracy,' and the other half . . . not at all. Like the note. Who the hell goes to the trouble of writing a ransom note in Russian but doesn't bother to check their grammar?"

"If it even *is* a real ransom note," Tara said. She sighed, and immediately Jason dreaded the continuation of her thought. "And then there's Alex and the guy on the balcony. I'm not trying to be a downer here, I'm really not, but I don't see how any of this"—she gestured to the board—"goes together."

"We know it's a ransom note," Jason insisted, trying to brush aside her doubt. "And it has to go together."

Tara frowned as if deep in thought. "You're really convinced the fight on the balcony has something to do with Max?"

"C'mon, Tara, of course it's connected," Jason shot back. "Max, 'Max'"—he drew air quotes—"and 'Max'"—this time he waved a hand in Alex's direction—"all get attacked at once. It feels kind of amateur, but it makes more sense than any of this."

Tara's eyes widened in a look of genuine alarm. "Since when is murder-kidnapping *amateur*, Jason? You got yourself all psyched up about solving this, but it's a pretty fucking serious mess you're trying to get us tangled up in!"

"Well, what, that ransom note sounds *professional* to you?"

She drew her breath in sharply with a roll of her eyes. "Fuck, Jase, I don't know what that note says in any language. We're just going off of the fact that Alex says the grammar sucks." She paused, then added quietly, "Sorry, Alex."

Alex didn't seem to hear her, though. He was absorbed in thought, and almost sounded as if he'd interrupted his own process when he said, "I might have something."

"Yeah?" Jason asked. He could only hope Alex had landed on a more compelling insight than they'd been able to generate—one that would overcome Tara's growing skepticism.

"This is just a thought," Alex said, "but the guy in the stairs looked a lot like . . . me. It could have been the, um, victim."

Neither Jason nor Tara had an immediate response, but after a moment's thought, Tara uncapped the marker and added another note to the whiteboard.

"Okay, that could be good. What does it *mean*, though?" Jason wondered aloud.

"I've been thinking about that," Alex replied. "It's why I only bring it up now. But is it possible that he and the other man on the balcony were working together?"

Tara shook her head. "No. That's dumb. He's not going to kill his own partner."

"Not intentionally," Alex agreed. "But suppose they kidnapped Max, and they think they have this great plan of showing up to the party with fake-Max to buy some time—"

"And had no idea Max had already bailed and sent you!" Jason interrupted in a burst of renewed excitement.

"Right. I figure they saw me, panicked, and tried to get me out of the way before everyone realized there were two Maxes roaming around. Several drinks and a miscommunication later . . . here we are."

Much to Jason's surprise, Tara was the next to speak. "I actually sort of buy that."

"You do?" Jason asked.

"You don't? If he's right, their plan went about as well as their fake Russian note."

"I mean, I'm just surprised *you* do."

Tara looked slightly offended. "Jase, I'm on your side. I just want to make sense of things before going down the rabbit hole on something that could get us all killed." She paused. "I will point out, though, this theory doesn't exactly tell us what to do next."

"No," Alex began, and Jason could see the spark of an idea in his eye. "But it might help explain what our kidnappers did next."

"How so?" Jason asked.

"That note was so bad, I'm wondering if it wasn't part of the original plan. If their fake-Max at the party had fooled everyone, we still might not know he was missing."

"Right, but that failed."

"And with the cops involved, they needed a more serious distraction."

Tara scowled. "So, their first thought is 'Let's write a ransom note in Russian'?"

Alex shook his head. "Probably not their first thought. But it's not such a bad one, if you think about it. Their hostage is Russian, and it's not a language anyone on the local police force is likely to know. It's a stretch, but we believed it, right?"

"We did." Jason nodded. It took him a moment to process all of what Alex had said, but the more he thought about it, the more impressed he was with the theory. "Dude, you might be right."

"Again, though," Tara interjected, "this is all supposing Max was even kidnapped. And what does it mean for *us*?"

Alex was silent. He seemed to have run out of answers, but Jason was determined not to let their momentum die. "It means it's time for more coffee," he declared, pushing his chair back decisively.

Alex's eyes darted up to the clock on the wall. "Also, it's six. Want to put on the news and see the damage?"

"Oh shoot, yeah, we'd better." Jason made his way across the room to retrieve the remote and, positioning himself a few feet from the television, began scrolling through channels in search of the local news. Izzy would handle any stories popping up on the internet, but Jason knew well that in a small town, the local news could be an equally big problem.

"It might not be so bad," Alex offered. He seemed poised to say more, but Jason had landed on the proper channel and he fell silent, eager not to miss a word of what the young anchor and his façade of self-important seriousness were preparing to share.

The opening monologue seemed to take hours, and they all waited in silent anticipation for the story of interest. "In local news," the anchor's well-rehearsed voice announced, "an Albemarle County man was killed early this morning and foul play is suspected. Police are still investigating." The screen cut to shots of the mansion, surrounded by crime scene tape and emergency vehicles, just as Jason and Tara had last seen it when they collected Jason's car.

"The victim has been identified . . ." the anchor continued, as the scene abruptly changed to a shot of a small house in the woods—evidently the victim's—also flanked by police cars with flashing blue lights scattering shadows around the scene. "Little is known about the victim, who was seen at his home in the hours before his death. . . . No motive is known at this time. . . ."

But already Jason's mind was elsewhere.

"I *know* that house," he said aloud, surprised at his own assertion.

"Shh," Alex silenced him, and the room remained quiet until the anchor had wrapped up his report and the screen returned to its natural state of blaring commercials.

"Nothing about Max." Tara sounded relieved.

"Good," Alex said emphatically. He turned to Jason. "Wait, what did you mean, you know that house?"

"I recognize it. I know where it is." Suddenly Jason was unfrozen, striding across the room to collect a jacket and his car keys. "Let's go."

"Okay, first of all, how fucking small *is* this town?" Tara asked. "And what do you mean 'let's go'?"

"It's south of town," Jason replied, in his haste missing the point of her sarcastic inquiry, "And if we think this guy was part of getting Max kidnapped, shouldn't we go check out his place?" He grabbed Tara's coat from the pile they'd left on the kitchen island and threw it at her. He was about to send Alex's coat flying, too, but was halted by another objection.

"Wait, Jase, we need to think this through," Alex said.

"We'll think in the car." He flung the jacket in a quick sidearm motion, and Alex snatched it out of midair.

"No, listen," Alex sounded insistent. "It's promising, I agree. If we can find this house, I can be convinced to scope it out, but setting out blindly after a glimpse of it on the news is insane."

"Yeah, I'm not even that convinced," Tara interjected. "This is nuts."

Jason groaned. "Come on, let's go. I drove past that house last summer. I can find it again." Immediately he regretted sharing the detail of when he'd encountered the house. Tara's reaction at the police station to one so-called secret meeting between him and Max would pale in comparison to the anger that would follow if she found out about the time they'd spent together months after Max's official retreat into the hiatus.

Alex drew his cell phone from a pocket and began tapping away at the small screen. "Let's find it on a map first. I want to believe you, Jase, but you sound a little bit crazy."

"I don't know the address."

"Okay . . ." Alex drew out the word, and Jason could tell his patience was being tried as much as his own. "Well—"

"This is ridiculous," Tara declared, shoving her chair back and rising somewhat stiffly. "Mind if I take a lap? I need to stretch . . . or something."

"Yeah, sure," Jason agreed absently. He was trying to think, racking his brain for a way to prove he wasn't crazy—one that didn't involve revealing how he'd first come across the house. The commercial break on the TV had ended, and the anchor was back with some dull report on high school sports. "Hold on," Jason declared, inspecting the remote. His thumb alit on the rewind button, and with a click he sent the anchor, ads, and anchor again flying backward until the blue-lit house flickered back onto the screen. He spent a few silent moments looking over every inch of the image. "Yeah," he repeated, "I *know* that house."

"But you don't know where it is?"

"Not—not exactly *where*, but how to get there at least."

"Then guide me." Alex was tapping away at his phone again, and Jason wasn't sure what to think. "I'll bring up a map and follow along."

"I told you; I don't know the address."

Alex rubbed at his temples, a move halfway between frustration and exhaustion. "You know what a long shot all of this is, right?" he asked. Jason nodded. "We're not even sure this guy has anything to do with Max. If we want to find him, we have to work smart. This feels desperate."

"Of course it's desperate! He's *missing*!" Jason felt himself growing indignant now. "I don't see why you're wasting all this time!"

Alex refused to be rattled by Jason's soaring emotions. "I know," he said. "Please, humor me. We'll use satellite images and street view, and if you can guide me to that house, I'm ready to go with you. Please."

By this point, Tara had circled back into the room and was pouring herself the last of the now-chilled coffee. She propped herself up against the counter, content to linger in the background.

Jason had half a mind to storm out of there and jump in his car right then, but something in the tone of Alex's plea held him back. He could see the struggle behind those wide, dark eyes and knew Alex was hurting just as badly as he was. It wouldn't be fair to leave him. "All right," he said, closing his eyes to better conjure up the drive from memory, "you get on 29 headed south of town. . . ."

" . . . *and just fucking go.*" The voice in his mind was suddenly Max's, floating lethargically through the soft, humid air of the late May twilight. It was one of the last times they'd spent together before those long months of silence, before unanswered calls and messages drove Jason back to New York for that miserable summer of frustrated solitude.

He could still picture the fading light of that sunset vividly, the sky glowing blue-green atop the mountains as they sped under the highway overpass and were finally free of civilization. The summer dark seemed to swallow them up, bury them in the insect-chorused jungle that encroached on the road—vines and trees and bats swooping low overhead in that thick, warm air particular to a Southern summer night.

The windows were cracked, open just far enough for that air to roar and rush about them, never offering any semblance of coolness as it tugged and pulled at the car, only reluctantly granting passage into the tranquil, steaming night.

They drove for several minutes without exchanging a word, as they often did on nights like this one, when something in Max's mind was trying to fight its way out, and the only way he knew to calm it was to *go*—somewhere, anywhere, wherever his partner in crime and the trusty old Subaru could fly him.

"Turn here," he'd suddenly instructed as a pair of flashing yellow lights warned of an impending intersection, a glaring interruption of the otherwise darkened landscape.

Now Jason tried to recreate that turn for Alex. "It's—okay, the road sort of curves to the right, and there's those flashing lights. It's a state route, in the six or seven hundreds, not one of the big ones."

"By a river?" Alex asked.

"Yeah, maybe, I think so."

In the dark he couldn't have seen a river, but agreeing made more sense than letting on how uncertain the less-important details of this memory might be.

The secondary route twisted and plunged its way through the countryside, and they were slowed considerably from their highway pace. The air beat only feebly at the windows, but conversation had still seemed impossible through its heavy darkness.

Their next turns had come seemingly at random, and Jason struggled to relay them to Alex now. They soon traded Alex's cell phone for the larger screen of a laptop; street view photos proved the most helpful as Jason's memory picked out trees and terrain and the occasional weather-worn church. As they slipped farther and farther into the countryside, the details of the route became muddled, but a renewed mental image leapt to Jason's rescue. "No, wait! We've passed it," he declared with sudden confidence. "Go back, go back."

They *had* passed it—flown past it, picking up speed along a rare straight stretch of backroad, just two or three turns shy of the moonlit field where Max had said, in a voice so soft Jason hardly believed it could be his, "Stop the car."

The Subaru had jostled and bounced its way over the grassy shoulder until it came softly to rest on the edge of a wide expanse of rolling hills, grassland destined for its first haying of the season in less than a week's time. They had never stopped like this before; the drive itself had always been the source of calm for whatever storm was tearing at Max's psyche. But the request had been so earnest, so quietly desperate, that Jason complied without hesitation, though he was slow to withdraw the key from the ignition as he waited for a reaction from Max.

"You . . . all right?" he found himself asking as the silence swelled to a heaviness that rivaled the humid night air.

Max had shaken his head, and when he turned toward Jason, there were tears welling up in his eyes. Jason met his gaze but could make nothing of the troubled look, the dark, shining pools about to spill over. The words were trying to come, that much he could see, but some internal force was damming them up, rendering Max speechless as the first silent tear traced its way down his pale face.

Something in that moment, that strange and unprecedented moment, gave Jason all the clarity he needed, and, letting the keys drop into the center console, he extended his hand to Max. Without hesitation, Max had slipped his own hand into Jason's and met him with a firm grip, soft and cool despite the calluses of a lifetime of musicianship. It lasted no more than a second or two, one hand pressed against another, but Jason could sense something meaningful in that brief connection, a deeper message trying desperately to convey itself through the squeeze of a hand.

For a long time, they just sat. Side by side in the car, close, sometimes looking to one another, sometimes gazing across the expanse of grassland or up into the star-speckled sky. Then the wall had started to come away, slowly, as if dissolving, and Max began to talk. "I'm sorry, man," he whispered. "This—this past year has been tough."

"I know."

"I didn't want the hiatus either." Max's voice still wavered, but he was gaining momentum, both the speed and volume of his words growing. "That love song comment just . . . messed me up, man. I just—God, this sounds so crazy to say—just didn't have the words anymore, the words true enough to put out into the world and say, 'Here it is, my truth: my words.' Jase, I still don't have them, and it's scaring the hell out of me."

Their eyes met once again, and Jason knew to wait, to let the thoughts work themselves out in Max's troubled head.

"I know they're all expecting me to get over it and get back to writing songs, but I—I can't. I don't want to write," Max finally declared. "Or talk. Not yet. I want—I want to catch lightning bugs and lie in the grass and feel the night air and watch the sunrise and not *have* to do any of that. You know what I mean?"

A smile had flickered across Jason's face, though he wasn't sure if Max had seen it in the half dark. He reached for the door handle, which sent a cascade of artificial light tumbling down over them as the latch released.

"What are you doing?"

This time Max had certainly seen the smile. "C'mon," Jason had said, "let's do it."

They kicked their shoes off in the car and grabbed beers from the case in the back, and for the next eight hours in that lonely roadside field, they were the only people in the world. In the dark, they were free, became kids again, snatching fireflies from midair and feeling the rustle of grass around their legs and damp red clay underfoot. After races and leaps and shouts, they had tumbled back into the car, sprawled on opposite ends of the backseat with the doors flung open wide to admit the soft coolness of the gently stirring night air.

Jason had been struck by a realization as he watched Max, his face flushed and chest heaving with the joyful exertion of their childlike outburst. He had been transformed, back to himself for the first time in months, a brief and brilliant glow that rivaled that of the fireflies drifting through the night sky. Jason didn't know how long the flash of light would last before Max retreated into the dark again, only that—like the fireflies—it was worth the wait.

And suddenly the words had come easily, conversationally, as memories and stories and laughs flowed back and forth between them. They had stayed through the night and were just feeling the first inklings of sleepiness as a rosy glow drifted into the eastern sky. Max was the first to scramble from the car, to pull himself up onto the roof and stand facing the sunrise, but a moment later Jason was by his side.

"Beautiful," Max had whispered breathlessly, his gaze drifting from the sky to Jason and back as he spoke.

"Yeah," Jason agreed, and was surprised to see Max duck away, reaffirm the fixation of his attention on some faraway point of glowing sky. He tried to remember what had pulled them away from the magic of that moment but could only recall the terrific instant of flight as they leapt to the ground, and the meandering drive back, retracing their circuitous route even as more direct byways presented themselves.

Now, the stubbornness of following that same winding path was proving to be just the coincidence they needed. "I'll be damned," Alex's unbelieving voice floated up from his station. He crouched low over the laptop to better inspect the image on the screen. "Jase, you're totally right. That's the house."

"It *is*?" The question sprang from Jason and Tara simultaneously, one ecstatic, the other incredulous. Tara strode across the kitchen and leaned close over Alex's shoulder. "Holy crap," she said quietly, affirming what Jason hoped to be true.

"That's it, then!" Jason declared. "Let's go!" Alex seemed to agree; he slammed the laptop closed and began to fumble his way into his coat without rising from his seat. Tara straightened up slowly, a skeptical look clouding her features. "What?" Jason demanded.

"Nothing," she said, in the tone of a clear lie. The silent glares that followed urged her to continue. "Okay, fine, I really didn't think you were going to find the house—whoever's house it even is. The whole thing still sounds crazy."

"Oh, *come on!*"

"Well, I'm sorry," Tara said defensively. "You're going to drive over there, pull in behind all the cops, and what—hope they don't mind you having a look around?"

"No—" Jason stammered, "not—not like that. We'll wait until after the cops are gone."

"And you think they're gone by now?"

"Jesus, Tara, how am I supposed to know?"

She folded her arms across her chest. "You're oh-so-observant all of a sudden; maybe you should have noticed it was a live shot on the news. No way they're gone."

Jason shot a reluctant glance back over to the still-paused television and felt his enthusiasm drain away. "Oh yeah," he muttered, spotting the word "LIVE" printed beside the station logo in the corner of the screen. "You're right." He let his jacket and car keys fall to the table, then sank down into a chair.

"Jase, it's okay, they won't be there forever," Alex offered.

"I know, I know," Jason grumbled. "So, we wait a couple of hours . . . it's fine." He yawned, then flopped forward onto the table, using his jacket as a pillow.

"Yeah, 'fine' is the word that comes to mind," Tara quipped. She stuck out a foot and nudged Jason's knee with her toe. "Wake up, come on, this is your stupid plan we're trying to work on here."

He *was* half asleep and could feel the heaviness of his eyelids becoming almost overwhelming. Only Alex's rustling around on the other side of the table prevented sleep from coming right then and there.

"To be honest, I'm tired too," Alex said. "Getting some sleep isn't the worst idea."

"No," Jason protested without raising his head, "we need to find him. It can't wait 'til morning."

Tara drew out her cell phone. "Midnight?"

"Hm?"

"I'll set an alarm. We get some rest, give the police time to clear out."

Jason nodded, his jacket rustling softly with every motion. "You can have the bed upstairs," he started to say, but before the completed thought could pass his lips, he was fast asleep, swallowed up by the fitful, desperate exhaustion heaped on him by the emotionally grueling day.

Chapter 8

"This is it," Jason said, easing the Subaru onto the gravel drive of the house he'd recognized on the news. "I'm going to see if I can pull around back."

"Whatever," Tara grumbled sleepily. She had offered no reassurance or conversation over the course of their half-hour drive and now slumped against the window of the passenger seat. It was just the two of them, at Alex's insistence. He didn't want to slow them down, and Jason had to admit, it was wise to keep an escape plan in mind, just in case. Just in case *what*, he couldn't imagine, but given how the day had gone, he felt no need to advocate for unnecessary risk.

The small, wood-paneled house—more of a cabin, now that he saw it up close—was fringed with yellow crime scene tape, though the police had long since dispersed. The nearest sign of life had been a glowing porchlight over a quarter mile away, but still Jason was nervous. "This is illegal, isn't it?" he wondered aloud.

Tara responded with a faint mumble that Jason took as an affirmative. Jason shivered, both from cold and nerves, as he pulled the car up along the side of the small house and cut the ignition. "Hey, wake up." He nudged Tara, waiting for a more compelling sign of alertness. "C'mon, you know the plan."

"I know, I know."

Jason turned his attention to his own preparations, talking loudly enough to himself to rouse his sluggish companion. Keys, cell phone, and flashlight all found their way to his zippered jacket pockets before he pulled on a pair of leather gloves. "You remember our signal?" he asked.

It was a genuine question, seeing as their plan had been devised in the confused, achingly unslept state that followed the blaring of Tara's alarm only an hour earlier. Jason's head had shot up from the table to a sound he could best place as a droning train whistle or emergency siren. The room was still brightly lit, compounding the jarring effect of the alarm.

"What the hell?" Jason blurted out.

"It's the fucking alarm." It took a moment for his eyes to adjust before he could trace Tara's voice to where she sat, curled up almost catlike in the enormous armchair, fumbling to reach the screaming phone that had slipped down among the cushions behind her. Finally, she quieted the device, and they sat in silence, each trying to blink away the sleep that had been so unceremoniously halted. Alex, too, unnoticed during the blare of the alarm, had shoved his way up to a seated position on the couch. He yawned widely as he ran a hand through his tousled mop of dark hair.

"Morning," he mumbled. "Everyone sleep well?"

Tara shuffled off up the stairs and by the time she reappeared, they were each halfway through their first cup of coffee and had started to shake the lingering sleepiness enough to discuss their next steps.

"Keep your phone on you," Jason had directed Alex. "We may need to reach you—and if you don't hear from me, call the cops. No questions asked."

"How long should I wait to call?"

"I don't know, half an hour once we're there? Tara, what do you think?" She had responded with a noncommittal shrug while helping herself to the coffee. "Yeah, half an hour is good," Jason continued, answering his own question.

"Are you both going into the house?" Alex had asked.

"Oh, hell no," Tara replied, reclining against the countertop as she warmed her hands on her mug. "I'm not wandering into some redneck's murder cabin."

Jason had shot her a look of frustration. "It's the victim's house."

"And an active crime scene!"

"Not *crime scene*, exactly," Jason muttered. "The cops were only there because of the victim. . . ." But the look on Tara's face forced him to reconsider. "Okay, fine, I'll go in alone. I'll, uh, give you my spare car key and you'll be ready to drive us out of there."

"That's smart," Alex had agreed with a nod. "And make sure you have a signal. One that Tara can see or hear from the car. If something goes wrong, you shouldn't be waiting on me to call 911."

Jason looked in Tara's direction, feigning concentration. "So . . . panicked screaming?"

"Seriously, Jase." Alex's tone was insistent.

This time he had paused to think. "Three quick blinks of the flashlight?"

Tara had nodded and given a quiet "Mm-hm," as she continued to alternately cool and sip her coffee.

"And you be the one to text Alex to say I'm going in. I'll probably be too jittery." Even then, Jason had felt the nerves rising, and now, in the cold dark of the car, he found his hands shaking as he drew out his Swiss army knife and reached for the door handle.

"Text Alex," he said. He meant to follow it up with something more meaningful, some sort of a goodbye or thank you, but the words caught in his throat, and he turned away and stepped out of the car in one nervous, hurried motion.

Every crunch of leaves and frost underfoot seemed to echo around him in the chill night air. Jason had to pause and collect himself before stooping beneath the crime scene tape and mounting the steps leading up to the house's narrow front porch. A loose board let out a groaning squeak and his heart leapt into his throat. "It's okay," he whispered aloud. "There's no one here."

He could only hope his reassurances were true as he reached for the doorknob. Locked. That was no surprise—and why he was glad to have the Swiss on hand. He drew out the flashlight and by the light of its feeble beam managed to work his way into the lock. He tried to feel for the click of even a single tumbler falling into place, but the unsteadiness of his hands made the task impossible. He glanced to his phone for the time and was flustered to see it had already been six minutes.

Jason continued to jiggle the lock, but to no avail. It *had* to give. It just had to, or this whole ridiculous plan would be for nothing. He was gripped by a sudden fear. The victim and his partner had been here—or at least he'd convinced himself they had. What if Max had, too? What if he were still inside?

Jason had to get in. Now. He rushed from the door to one front window, then the other, prying desperately at the frames that had been bolted down tight against the cold. Nothing would budge, and his plan was falling apart.

He could feel himself panicking, but the knowledge that he wasn't thinking straight did nothing to sway his resolve. With an air of calmness, he returned the knife to his pocket and sent the flashlight beam sweeping around the perimeter, making sure he truly was alone.

It's going to hurt; you can't scream. His hands were shaking as he drew in a deep breath to steady himself, then let his fist fly. Instantly, he doubled over in pain, clutching the freshly bruised knuckles whose impact had had no effect on the single-pane glass. "Fucking hell," he cursed through gritted teeth, already re-gretting the rash stupidity he'd allowed to take over.

There had to be a smarter way, and Jason knew an answer would come to him, but there was no time. Every second he spent here felt like another opportunity for police—or worse, the part-ner-turned-killer in whose existence he now fully believed—to come flying up the driveway and take aim at the trespassers with weapons a great deal more powerful than his small pocketknife.

He flexed his fingers, wincing as the soreness leapt to shoot-ing pain. One more punch he could manage. It would have to work.

This time a pained sound escaped his lips. His fist glanced harmlessly off the glass once again, and he leapt back, jumping up and down as he shook away the renewed sting. *Stupid, stu-pid, stupid*, he berated himself. Alex's warning about despera-tion came back to him, but all of his concentration was taken up by the hurt in his hand.

A new approach was in order. He pulled out his phone and tapped the third entry in his emergency contacts. Alex answered on the first ring. "Jase? What's wrong?"

"I'm okay," he whispered, trying to keep his voice low de-spite the urgency of the situation. "I just need to know how to break a window."

"This is not a good idea. Come home, we'll regroup."

"How do you break a window?"

"Jase, seriously."

"How."

Alex sighed. "You have your Swiss, right?"

"Never leave home without it."

Jason fell to pacing as Alex talked through how to use a pointed tool to concentrate the force of a blow, and cut him off with a quick, "Thanks man, call you in twenty," before approaching the window again.

Indeed, it only took what felt like a gentle tap for the lower pane to fall away, and he gingerly reached through the jagged opening to feel for the doorknob. A quick turn of the lock, and the door creaked open.

Jason felt a shiver run down his spine as he stepped across the threshold into the cabin. "Hello," he called out. "Anyone there?" No response. The fleeting panic that Max might be trapped inside was gone. As Jason scanned the room with the narrow flashlight beam, he could see just how small the house really was. And the police had left only hours earlier; of course they would have found him if he were here.

Jason took his time walking a preliminary lap around the small space. The kitchen and living area were combined as one, and the only other rooms were a small bedroom and bathroom along one side of the house. It was sparsely furnished, but well lived-in; the muddy work boots at the door and firewood stacked beside the woodstove gave the impression that the home's occupant had merely stepped out for a moment.

Clearly the man had lived alone and had done all of his own decorating. Jason started at the cascade of shadows that resulted as his flashlight passed over the mounted head of an eight-point buck. The theme extended to the rest of the space; antlers served as a centerpiece at the small table, and the only other wall hanging was a framed photo of two men grinning triumphantly over the bloodied body of what appeared to be a bear. Feeling a sudden squeamishness at the reminders of death all around him, Jason turned away and made a point of re-examining the cramped and uninformative bathroom.

But who were the two figures in the photo? He strode back into the main room and peered at the small image, which the glare from his flashlight rendered almost impossible to see. One of the men he could place as the owner of the cabin, and even in blurry miniature it was easy to see how he could have passed for Max. The facial structure was right, and he was tall and lean enough, but his hair was cropped short, and in its natural state was a muddy brown color just starting to grow dusted with gray.

"And who's your friend?" Jason softly wondered aloud. He closed his eyes, tried to think back to the confusion of the previous morning and recall anything he could about the other figure on the balcony. He hadn't seen the man's face, only that he was shorter and stockier than any version of Max, and . . . and that was it. Between his brewing hangover and the half light of the balcony, it had been difficult to make out any detail, and both men were dressed in dark jackets and pants, covered up against the cold.

Shaking his head, Jason stepped away from the picture and completed another lap of the house. Nothing. A stack of old electric bills confirmed the name they had heard on the news, but that was it. The only surprise, given the décor, was a lack of weapons. Maybe the police had already collected the stash of hunting rifles Jason expected to find around every corner. If so, he was glad of it. The last thing he needed was another way to get himself killed out here.

What was he missing? He'd opened every drawer and cabinet, checked under the bed, everywhere he could think to look, and there was nothing out of the ordinary. Doubt began to set in, and he felt sick with the realization that the victim might be just that—not a schemer or a criminal, just the victim of a freak accident. A coincidental lookalike in the wrong place at the wrong time.

Dejectedly, Jason took a final lap, making sure everything was in its original place. A sudden rumbling of the refrigerator made him jump, and an instant later, he rushed over to it, frantic in his renewed hope of a hiding place he might have missed. The freezer door was all but cemented closed by a layer of uncleaned stickiness—from what, he hated to think—and as he yanked it open, he was momentarily blinded by the rush of light spilling out.

As he blinked the glare away, he found himself only more confused. *Who keeps a jug of water in their freezer?* He shifted the heavy glass bottle aside to peer behind it and was surprised to feel the slosh of liquid as it moved. Definitely not water. He carefully lifted the bottle to the countertop and removed its stopper.

The harsh, bitter scent stung his nose before he even bent to inspect the bottle. It was moonshine, undeniably, and surprising that the police had missed it. But an illegal distillery wasn't why he'd come to the house; Jason jammed the stopper back into the neck of the bottle and replaced it in the freezer where it nestled among various cuts of freezer-burned meat.

He was about to close the door when another item caught his eye—or rather, a series of items, just protruding from behind the bottle of moonshine. Stacked in a neat row along the back of the freezer were a series of glass vials with colored lids: two blue, two green, one red. As he reached for the first vial, he saw that its liquid contents remained unfrozen as well.

Suddenly his mind was spinning; he cupped the small container in his hand, found it fit neatly, small enough to stay hidden if he were to, say, empty it into an unsuspecting stranger's drink in the midst of a crowded party. And it was strange to find five, what felt like an incomplete set. He was sure there was at least one missing.

Jason knew it was still speculation, but the discovery of the moonshine seemed to fit. It wouldn't take much to destabilize Alex, and they had all seen him sipping his usual club soda as he mingled with the crowd. The drink would have just tasted slightly bitter; he knew Alex was too polite to complain to a bartender or suspect him of having muddled the order.

This is good, Jason thought, but even as his convictions were reinforced, he realized persuading Tara would still take some work. He eased the freezer door closed, shutting off the glare of light, and paused to allow his eyes to adjust before surveying the kitchen once more. The stack of bills had been his only other source of information, and he returned to it, flipping through the pages once again. This time, the last document in the stack caught his attention: not a bill, but a pay stub.

As he lifted the paper, he felt a new flutter of excitement. He didn't even have to read the employer's name to know he was right. *That* address he knew, having heard Tara relay it to the police dispatcher as she paced the lobby of the mansion.

He continued to study the document, trying to commit every detail to memory. Nothing seemed out of the ordinary; the man had been a full-time employee on the grounds maintenance crew, earning less than Jason would have expected. He paused, considering. The total for the month was suspiciously small, though as he squinted at it, he wondered if he'd just become that far out of touch with reality. Then another number jumped at Jason, the date that the hours worked began. January 18—he'd had the job for less than a month.

It couldn't all be a coincidence. It fit too perfectly. By now, Jason was sure of it, and was finally beginning to feel that Tara would be too. As he replaced the papers, the photo on the wall leapt into his mind with renewed importance. They had half of the puzzle, and the other half was staring back at him from that photo, he just knew it. As he headed for the door, in a moment of sheer impulse, he grabbed it—frame and all—and stuffed it under his jacket.

"It's just me," he whispered as Tara jumped at the sound of him opening the car door. As they agreed, she had slid over to the driver's side, and the engine sputtered to life as Jason slipped in beside her. "Let's go, let's go," he urged.

"Great idea," she spat back sarcastically. "I thought maybe we'd hang out a while."

"Funny." He could only manage a terse reply. It was one thing to feel confident about driving up to a house to look around, but quite another to maintain a façade of calm after breaking in and stealing a photo—with the knowledge that police would be returning in the near future, no less.

They rode in silence for several minutes, and he felt Tara's curiosity rising, until she finally nudged him. "So?"

"Alex was right. He's our guy."

"You found something?" She blurted out the question, her voice more eager than Jason had expected.

He nodded silently, guiltily. Tara had known Jason long enough to sense when he was hiding something, and suddenly her tone was deadly serious. "Jason, what the hell happened?"

"Okay," he said with a sigh, "you have to promise not to freak out." He braced for the storm he knew would follow his revelation of the stolen photo. "I did a couple of bad things. But the good news is I have a lead on the guy's partner."

"Oh God, what's the bad news?"

Jason decided to ease into the worst of it. "I had to break a window."

"You *what*?"

"I couldn't pick the lock—I panicked!"

"Great," Tara fumed, "just great. We're going to jail. Perfect end to a perfect day."

"It's okay," he said, trying to sound more reassuring than his racing heartbeat felt. "That's why I wore gloves. No fingerprints anywhere, I swear."

"Ah yes, we're down to hoping your fingerprints don't turn up in a sweep."

"Tara—"

"No, no," she cut him off. "This is awesome. Max is missing, you're about to be arrested, and now I'm stuck here in this crap town pretending I don't have anything to do with either one of you."

He let the slight against Charlottesville go, knowing it was neither the time nor the place for that particular argument, but couldn't restrain himself from taking a shot at her remaining defenses of righteousness. "Technically you're an accessory to burglary."

"*Burglary?* Jason, I swear to God, if you stole something. . . ."

He shifted around and drew the photo out of his jacket sheepishly. "It's just a picture. We can put it back, too. I just needed a better look."

"Oh my *God*. If this weren't your car, I'd kick you out right here at the side of the road." From her tone, he suspected the threat might be genuine.

"Listen, there's two people in the picture, and one of them is the victim." Jason tried to maintain his composure and not let his frustration with Tara escalate his anxiety. "It was the only photo in the place, and it doesn't look like a family reunion shot. I'm willing to bet the other guy is his partner."

Tara was silent for a long moment, her expression difficult to read as they sped on through the darkened countryside. "You know how fucking stupid it is to steal a *picture*, right? A picture that you could have taken a photo of with your phone," she added, in case it wasn't obvious.

"Well," Jason muttered. She was right, and he didn't have a

good answer for his own poor thinking. "It was dark. And, you know, I didn't think of it."

Tara exhaled slowly. "Whatever. You have it now." After a pause, she added, "You get one hour."

"Hm?"

"One hour. Then I'm—no, *you're* taking it back." She paused, then added, "I'm not kidding. Before morning, before the cops come back."

A smile flickered across Jason's lips. "Deal." In the dim light afforded by a passing truck's headlights he could see that Tara, too, had softened. "We work pretty well together, you know," he offered.

Tara sighed. "Great. We're never doing this again."

Jason was struck by a pang of loneliness, of missing Max, and he returned her sigh. "God, I hope you're right."

Chapter 9

Jason had swung back to a state of elation by the time they pulled into his driveway. He went flying up the front steps before Tara had gathered the last of her things from the backseat and started toward the door.

"Dude, guess what?" he exclaimed as he bounded into the kitchen.

Alex's head shot up from whatever he had been reading. "You forgot to let me know you were all right?" he replied, his voice tinged with annoyance and concern.

"Oh."

"Yeah. Good thing you left your GPS on and I could see you were on your way back."

Jason's stomach dropped. "Oh shit." He fumbled for his phone and was horrified to see Alex was right. "That's . . . really bad."

Alex's confused look quickly resolved itself into understanding. "The window," he said. "Oh crap."

"Yeah." Jason slumped into a chair across the table from Alex, deflated. The energy of a moment earlier was gone.

"But what were you going to say?"

"Oh!" The excitement rushed back to Jason. "You were totally right. Get this: the guy started working at the mansion, grounds crew or something, less than a month ago. Plus, he had a freezer full of moonshine portioned out into these little glass vials, just like you'd want if you were going to slip some into someone's drink. And," he paused to place the photo between them, "check it out, I think that's the guy and his partner."

By then Tara had appeared, and she quietly crossed the room to join them at the table. "He told you he stole that, right?"

"No," Alex replied tersely, sending a pointed look in Jason's direction.

"Relax, we're taking it back."

"ASAP," Tara added. Apparently unsatisfied with their urgency, she gestured for them to hurry. "Well, hurry up, look at the picture or whatever."

Alex reached for the frame, but Jason slapped his hand away. "No fingerprints," he instructed. "Here." He gingerly pulled the glove from his now-swollen left hand and passed it to Alex, who slipped it on before lifting the photo and beginning, in his usual fashion, a silent and methodical perusal.

Tara's attention, meanwhile, was caught by Jason's bruised knuckles, which were already marked in various shades of blues and purples. "What the hell happened to your hand?" she asked.

"Don't worry about it," Jason muttered, flexing his fingers. Nothing was broken, that much he could tell, but he felt his face flush with embarrassment. *That*, at least, he should've known better than to try.

"All right," Tara sighed. After a moment's hesitation she strode across the room and sank down onto the couch, content to let the others examine the photo without her supervision. The room fell silent as Jason waited for Alex's judgment, though after a minute or so a faint snore drifted up from where Tara had curled herself up into a catlike position once again.

"You must be tired too," Alex said, a half smile crossing his face as he glanced over at Tara's sleeping form.

"Not too bad," Jason replied. "You? How's your leg?"

"I'm fine. I mean, considering the circumstances."

"So, uh, what do you think?" Jason asked. As he did, he suddenly felt like his excitement had been hopelessly optimistic and misguided. What did he expect, some sort of preternatural insight from Alex that he himself couldn't manage?

"This is going to sound crazy," Alex said slowly, "but okay, we agree the taller of the two was the victim"—he paused, and Jason nodded—"so we know him, and I *swear* I saw this other man at the party."

"Are you sure?" Jason's heart was racing again, even as he

scolded himself for leaping to yet another hopeful extreme with every fragment of information.

Alex nodded. "Ninety percent. We bumped into one another and made eye contact. I remember him looking surprised and kind of confused. I thought he was just drunk but now it makes more sense."

"Okay! This is good; we can work with that." Jason was on his feet again, and he began to pace the kitchen. "If he was at the party, there must be some way to figure out who he is, and where he lives, and where he could have taken Max, and—"

"Jase, hold on," Alex interrupted. "We can't take this to the police."

"I know—"

"No, really, they could prove you broke into that house."

"I know, I know," Jason repeated hurriedly, "we'll figure it out ourselves. We just have to think." He continued to pace, feeling the frenetic energy take over once again. Out of the swirling currents of his mind, an idea resolved itself and he immediately knew it was a good one. "What about a reverse image search?"

"Like, scan the photo and do a search?" Alex's tone betrayed his skepticism, but Jason decided to ignore it.

"Yeah, exactly." His mind was still racing. "We—we can crop it and run a search on the other guy's face and see what turns up."

"Okay," Alex replied slowly. He laid the photo back down on the table and removed the glove from his hand. "Actually, Jase, that's kind of brilliant."

"Yeah?"

"Yeah. But I don't think we should crop it. It's 2018. Anyone who's proud enough of a photo to physically hang it on their wall probably has it posted online somewhere."

Jason nodded. "You're right. Go for it."

Alex snapped a photo and seemed to have the search results instantly. The photo-matching wasn't perfect, and he set to scrolling through pages of similar images. Even so, it was only a minute or two before he alit on a match and followed a quick sequence of links to track down its original poster. "Found him," Alex reported. He clicked another link and began scrolling through a series of social media posts. "This is definitely him," he confirmed.

"Okay, well, now we just need to *find him*," Jason said, thinking aloud. "Like real-life find him. What does his page say? Does he give a town at least?"

Alex scrolled back up. "Virginia, USA. That's all."

"Shit," Jason cursed. "So that's it. We found the guy who has Max, and all we need is an address—"

"Which the cops could get for you if you hadn't gone on a crime spree in the meantime!"

The voice that cut him off was Tara's, causing Jason to do a double take. "When did you wake up?" he asked.

"Few minutes ago, whatever, I don't know." She rose from her spot on the couch and shuffled over to rejoin the group, arms crossed tightly for warmth. "When did you come around on taking a photo of your stupid stolen picture?"

"I mean, maybe the cops can help," Jason insisted, ignoring her latest jab. "If we put the picture back, we're in the clear, and we can say we got a threatening message from that guy or something."

Alex shot him a skeptical look. "Jase, the detectives still haven't called back about the ransom note, and in the meantime, you broke into that house."

"Well, I wasn't planning on sharing that part of it!"

Tara scoffed audibly. "No, they'll just figure it out from the cell phone GPS you managed to leave on."

Jason let out a groan of exasperation and set off on a lap of the room. "It's absolutely fucking ridiculous," he spat. "We have all this technology, all this information, and it isn't any fucking easier to find someone than it was . . ." he trailed off, struck by a new spark of inspiration. "Hang on a sec," he muttered, darting out of the room.

He returned a moment later, laboring to carry a large cardboard box overflowing with papers. Alex turned in his chair and instinctively started to rise as if to offer help, but stopped himself, wincing slightly, as the motion shifted his injured leg.

"Jase, what are you doing?" Tara asked, sweeping coffee mugs aside to clear a landing space for his unexpected burden.

"Hold on, hold on," he replied absently, digging through the papers. As his search took longer than expected, he continued, "We're pretty sure these guys are local, right? So, odds are pretty good they've been around a while. Maybe even in the same spot since . . ." he paused, withdrawing a well-worn tome from the box, and gestured to its cover, "2005?"

Alex gave him a look of disdain. "The *phonebook*?"

Tara stifled a giggle. "This is your phonebook? It's so little."

"Yeah, yeah," Jason muttered, already paging through the whisper-thin sheets, which clung together from a stubborn combination of age and persistent humidity. He licked his index finger to better separate sheets of the white pages, provoking another snicker from Tara. Finally, he had the page and began scanning through the names. "Well," he announced, shoving the book across the table, his finger poised above a familiar name.

"Sure, okay, you found where someone with the same name as this guy lived over a decade ago," Tara said. She shrugged. "How do you know it's even him? Or that he still lives there?"

Alex wrinkled his brow as he scrutinized the address. "We don't."

"Let's find out," Jason declared, reaching for a pen to scribble the address on a scrap of paper. He glanced from Alex to Tara and back, and was once again met with skeptical looks. "Jesus, enough with the doubt," he said. "We've had this same argument a hundred times today and it never leads anywhere."

"Jase, I'm not arguing," Alex replied. "You're going."

Jason nodded. He looked to Tara once again. "What do you say? Shall we head out?"

She managed a half smile. "Let me guess, you know where this place is, too."

"Approximately."

Shaking her head, she reached for her coat. "You're driving."

"All right," Jason replied with a flicker of a grin, the first genuine smile he'd managed in quite some time. "That's more like it." He snatched up his jacket and keys and was halfway to the door when Alex's voice arrested his progress.

"Hey Jase, do me a favor."

"Yeah?"

"Return that Goddamn picture first."

Chapter 10

MONDAY, 4:30 A.M.

With the photo safely returned to its rightful home, Jason and Tara wound their way back toward civilization—at least for the time being. Jason recognized the street name of their new destination and knew they wouldn't linger in Charlottesville longer than a one-exit jaunt down the interstate. Even close to town, the roads were deserted, and snowflakes were beginning to swirl in the cold night air. Somehow the snow made them feel more isolated, safely warm in the trusty old car on road after lonely road until it felt like they'd crisscrossed their way over half of Albemarle County.

"You ever been to Monticello?" Jason asked as they turned east onto Route 53.

"Nope, and not that tavern place either." Tara nodded to the road sign that had prompted his question, which directed drivers to an array of the area's historical sites.

"We can go sometime," Jason offered. "The views are pretty good."

Tara shrugged, shifting in her seat, and Jason could sense her discomfort.

"What? C'mon, Tara, don't get freaked out now. We're just going to stop by this place and see what's up. Drive by even, see if anyone's home."

"I'm not freaked out." She fell silent for a few moments, then continued, "I mean, that's not true, I'm totally freaked out, but that's not what I was thinking about."

"Okay . . ." Jason trailed off, not sure how to interpret her statement.

"Jase, it's just, I don't know, this place. Charlottesville."

"What about it?" He could feel a defensive edge sliding into his voice.

She sighed. "You and Max love it here and come running back every chance you get, like it's some magical place where everything's going to be okay. He *hides* here for months on end whenever the rest of the world starts 'getting to him' or whatever he calls it. But just . . . I don't know, fuck this town." She shivered involuntarily. "It's like every time I'm here something goes to shit."

"What do you—"

"August. That was a nice fun time for everybody, wasn't it?"

He wasn't prepared for the memories her statement conjured up, and it took Jason a moment to respond. "No," he said quietly, recalling the other perpetual elephant in the room, "it wasn't."

It had been hot that week. Nothing outrageous or oppressive, just August hot, at that point in the summer when you struggle to believe it will ever be fall again. He and Tara were in town with the hope of dragging Max away from his already months-long absence, having convinced themselves that physical proximity would make them more likely to bridge the chasm separating them from his inner world.

The day before had been perfect, all things considered.

"You know, it's not so bad here," Tara had remarked on a stroll of the nearly empty University Grounds, pausing to stretch and inhale deeply as a light breeze whispered past. "It's good for me to get out of the city sometimes."

"Growing up, this was 'the city,'" Jason remarked.

Alex nodded. "Still is."

For once, Tara hadn't felt the need to push back against their quaint Southern notion of civilization and just accepted it with a nod. "How about a coffee?" she suggested, even the normally quick cadence of her speech seeming to move in slow motion in the afternoon sun.

"Sure," Jason had replied. "Let's go downtown."

They set out on foot, neither hurrying nor delaying, just enjoying the rhythm of the motion and the dreamy aspect of the normally bustling college town half emptied for the summer. Tara had paused atop the bridge over the train tracks, momentarily transfixed by something in the distance. She fanned herself, then continued on through the soft, warm air in silence.

Finally, iced coffees in hand, they had settled on a bench on the sun-dappled bricks of the Downtown Mall, and Jason raised the question they'd all been awaiting and dreading. "So, how's Max?"

Alex had shrugged. "Don't see him much. He's got a new place now, way out in the county, but he won't say where."

"County?" Tara raised an eyebrow.

"As opposed to city," Alex explained. "I never thought about it, but I think it's just Virginia that does it this way. The city"—he gestured to their surroundings—"is its own thing, not part of the county. It goes back to Reconstruction."

"Of course it does," Tara muttered.

Jason had refused to let their conversation be derailed. "Let me guess," he'd said, pausing to sip his drink, "it's his Walden Pond."

"How?" Alex laughed. "The two of you don't even need to talk to know what the other is saying."

Tara's eye roll was apparent, even from behind her sunglasses. "If that means he's actually coming back with new material, I'm all for it."

"Do you think he'll be around this week?" Jason asked, turning back to Alex. "I texted him to say we were in town, but . . . you know how that goes these days."

"Months," Tara corrected. She had seemed poised to say more, but swallowed her comment and fell to fanning herself once again. The ambient discontent seemed to linger in the air for a few minutes, but even that soon dissipated into comfortable silence in the slanting afternoon sun.

"Walk some more?" Alex had suggested. They fell back into their previous dreamy rhythm, meandering through the time-forgotten corners of town that—save for the occasional cars parked along the street—could have transported them to any perfect August day of the past two hundred years. Jewel-toned crepe myrtles swayed lightly in the breeze, their airy blossoms forming a constellation of colors in striking contrast to the blue of the sky.

Jason could still see those flowers, still feel the cool of a red-brick shadow and the sweating coffee cup in his hand. That *con-*

tent feeling of a summer day, pure and unspoiled. That day wasn't so long ago, yet by every reasonable measure it was worlds ago, and now, thinking back on it, he was surprised to find it made him sad. It was like a snapshot of innocence: being home, knowing everything was all right, and that he would see Max again soon—at some hidden retreat in the Blue Ridge, no less.

Of course, none of that had been true.

The next day was dreamlike too, a stomach-churning nightmare. Those memories were just as vivid, but jagged, ripped apart into fragments Jason couldn't—or wouldn't—piece back together. He resented Tara for bringing it up again, just as it seemed like they might be able to move past one crisis to deal with another. But in the same moment, he realized it was an impossibly naïve hope. Once again, all that echoed in his head was Faulkner: *The past is never dead. . . .*

It wasn't past in August, and it wasn't past now either. The entrance to Monticello came into view of the headlights as snow continued to swirl, falling faster than before.

"Do we have to talk about this right now?" Jason asked.

"Why not," Tara said, a standoffish tone creeping into her voice. "You're worried Jefferson will weigh in?"

"I don't care about Mr. Jefferson. I just don't want to do this right now."

"God! Mr. Fucking Jefferson." She wanted to say more, was opening her mouth to speak, then all at once sank back in her seat with a heavy sigh. When she began again, her voice was quiet, subdued. "You're right, this isn't going anywhere. I just—" She paused, and drew in a deep breath. "I guess I just wish you . . . and he . . . would acknowledge that someone like me might have a different view of your perfect Southern town than someone like you."

The tone of her statement made him uneasy, and Jason leapt back on the defensive. "So what? Because I'm white I'm automatically wrong about Charlottesville?"

"That's not what I said."

"Well, what *did* you say then?"

"Nothing, Jase, I didn't say *anything*. I just think you have an easier time explaining away all of the Charlottesville-and-Jefferson nonsense than I do. We never really talk about it but since you mentioned it, yeah, you guys are white men, and I'm . . . not."

She sighed again. "I don't even know what I'm trying to say. It's just so easy for you to forgive this town that you forget it isn't like that for everyone."

"Jesus, Tara, what am I supposed to say to that?" Jason fired back. "You wish we'd made more of a fuss over you? You don't get enough of that 'girls can't drum' crap as it is?"

"I'm not asking you to be a jerk. You know what, forget it. If you wanted another perspective—on anything—you would have asked by now."

Jason forced himself to patiently exhale before taking the bait. "I would love to hear your perspective on where the hell Max might be, I really would." He could feel the sarcastic edge to his tone, even as he fought to suppress it. "But right now, I need you to help me look for house numbers. It's coming up and I can't see anything in the snow."

Tara's surprise overtook her snark as she asked, "The house is just like . . . here?"

"Uh, yeah." He waved a hand at the scrap of paper resting on the dashboard, "Thomas Jefferson Parkway."

Now there was a hint of laughter to her tone. "Fucking Virginians."

"What?"

Tara just shook her head as houses crept into view, clusters that might at one time have been neighborhoods but these days felt the sprawl of the city in rush hour streams of cars zipping through at—if you believed the conservative estimate of the signs—a decidedly un-neighborhood-like fifty-five miles per hour. "Our guy lives down the street from Jefferson and around here that's just normal. What a state." She leaned forward, focusing intently on the passing mailboxes. "Slow down, slow down. This one," she pointed.

Gravel crunched under the tires as Jason guided the car into the driveway. Immediately, a dog began to bark, and a moment later another joined the chorus with high, mournful whining.

"Shit," Tara muttered, visibly tensing in her seat. "He's got dogs."

The lights flew on at a neighboring house, and after the slam of a screen door, a woman's yelling voice rang out and the dogs quieted themselves.

"Not his dogs," Jason whispered, letting out a small sigh of relief. The neighbor's lights went off, leaving them with just the narrow beam of headlights once more. "Is he even here?" he asked, squinting at the empty driveway ahead of them. "I'm going to take a look."

"Are you serious?"

"Since we're here. I'll be quick." He cut the headlights and was already unbuckling his seatbelt and drawing a pair of gloves from his jacket pocket as he spoke. "Get ready to drive us out of here, okay?" He didn't wait for the protests he knew were coming, and set off at a jog up the empty gravel drive toward where he could feel, but not see, the house looming ahead of him in the early morning darkness. He hadn't grabbed his flashlight, but the thought only occurred to him as he drew near enough to the house to make out its outline—or reach out and touch it, for that matter.

Even before he reached the door, Jason knew he would find it unlocked, and with no trace of Max inside. Everything about the place was wrong. Neighbors, dogs, and passing cars, even at this hour—it all added up to just about the worst place to imagine bringing, much less holding, a hostage. You'd have to be the kind of professional who could write a convincing Russian ransom note before you could pull that off. But maybe there was *something* to be found. That was the hope that kept him fumbling, panting, blinking away snowflakes as he felt for a doorknob.

The door sprang open as his hand alit on the knob and Jason stepped hurriedly inside out of the cold. No warmth awaited him, however, and he shivered as he closed the door and held his breath, waiting anxiously for any sounds of life that would tell him he was wrong, that he needed to get out *now*.

He waited for what felt like a full breathless minute, but no sound was forthcoming. Emboldened, Jason felt for a light switch on the near wall, and a moment later the room jumped into too-bright view, leaving him blinking away shadows as he took in an unfamiliar home for the second time that morning.

This one was less sparsely furnished, but only just. There appeared to be more rooms, though not necessarily more space. He was standing in a small living room and could see through to a partially walled-off kitchen at the back of the house. To his right, a narrow hallway disappeared into shadow, toward bedrooms, he supposed.

Jason took his time as he crossed the living room, trying to absorb every detail of his surroundings. Nothing caught his attention, so he continued on to the kitchen, a narrow galley-style space drowning in shadows. A single dot of red light flashed ominously at the end of the counter. He felt a sudden flash of panic. *A bomb?* He rushed to find another light switch and sent buzzing fluorescent light tumbling into the kitchen. Not a bomb.

He felt both foolish and relieved as he approached the red dot, which indicated nothing more sinister than an unheard message on the answering machine. "Who still has a landline?" Jason mumbled to himself. He hesitated, then realized he had nothing to lose. "All right, let's hear who's calling you," he said aloud.

As the machine ran through one prescription refill reminder, then another, Jason allowed himself to wander once again, taking in the utilitarian space. But as he turned to the refrigerator, he stopped dead in his tracks. The photo. There it was, identical to the one he'd pored over, held up by a Confederate flag magnet.

The computerized pharmacy message cut off abruptly and Jason jumped at the human voice that leapt out of the machine next. It was a man's voice, low and raspy, with a heavy drawl that immediately placed him as a local.

"Hey," the voice said slowly, "it's me." After a pause it continued, "You reckon we still gon' take our lil friend up over the mountain? I figure I'll stop up at the cabin before, unless you was planning to." Another pause. "Anyway. We lookin' good so far. I'll keep you posted. Bye now."

The answering machine announced the end of its string of messages with a jarring beep. Jason remained fixed in place, his mind racing. Once again, *he was right*. The right partner, the right house, everything. And the message could easily have been the partner—he had nothing that supported that particular hunch other than a string of unbelievably lucky breaks, but it fit perfectly. Plans with the partner in crime. An unnamed "friend" he suspected was anything but. A secluded location out of town.

Wherever that cabin was, he was sure Max was there.

Jason rummaged in his pockets, hopeful he'd find a pen and something to transcribe the voicemail on, but all he had was his cell phone and Swiss army knife. "Sure, we'll do it that way," he muttered, swiping to his phone's camera and setting it to video mode. He restarted the answering machine and clicked ahead through the robocalls to the human message before tapping record on his phone. Tara would like this one better, he thought with some bemusement; at least there would be nothing to return later.

Recording completed, Jason pocketed his phone and set to retracing his steps through the house, turning off lights as he went, and slipped out the front door. He was careful to secure the latch before taking off at a bounding gait for the glowing taillights of the car, which Tara had turned around while he was in the house.

"All good?" Tara asked with some trepidation as he slipped into the passenger seat.

"Yeah," Jason replied, shaking away a shiver as he fumbled over the seatbelt. The car was warm, and he could feel the effects of a new surge of hope. "I got something—don't worry, I just took a video."

"Oh yeah?" Tara's interest was genuine.

"Listen to this." It took him a few moments to pull up the video, and the recording-of-a-recording made the audio fuzzy and distant, but the message came through. When the video ended, the silence in the car was almost unbearable as he awaited Tara's verdict.

She cast a glance in Jason's direction, a mixture of confusion and concern on her face. "You think Max is at that cabin."

"You don't?"

"I don't know. No, I do." She paused. "I'm just worried what's going to happen when you find it."

Chapter 11

MONDAY, 6:45 P.M.

"Jase. Jase, wake up."

"Hm?" Jason yawned widely and shoved his way up to a seated position. It took him a moment to remember where he was and what was going on. He was at home, having fallen asleep on the couch for who knew how many hours, given that it was dark outside once again.

"I think I might have something." It was Alex speaking, turning to face Jason from where he sat at the kitchen table, his leg elevated on another chair.

"Yeah, hold on," Jason mumbled, stifling another yawn. "Gimme a minute." He rose from the couch and shuffled toward the bathroom. "What time is it anyway?" He didn't hear Alex's answer from the other room but as he reentered the kitchen, he reached for his cell phone lying on the table and the glowing screen leapt into view. Later than he'd hoped, but at least the phone had charged.

"All right," Jason said, "tell me what you've got. Coffee?"

"Sure." Alex's voice sounded strained, and Jason realized he probably hadn't gotten any sleep since their midnight alarm. "I want to preface this by saying that voicemail is not a lot to go on, but bear with me."

"Yeah, yeah," Jason replied, already busying himself with the coffeepot. His head shot up with a sudden realization. "Wait, where'd Tara go?"

"She took your car to pick up food. We figured you wouldn't mind."

"No, thank God," Jason muttered. Eating, like sleep, had fallen by the wayside in the frantic hours—now going on days—since the party. "Okay, sorry, go ahead."

"That line about 'over the mountain' was pretty much all I had, and this may shock you," Alex paused, a sarcastic hint of a smile flickering across his pale face, "but a decent number of people head up over Afton Mountain on the weekends, most of them to places you might call a 'cabin.' So, the question becomes, where *exactly* is this cabin he mentions?"

Jason nodded absently as he set the coffee to brew. "I'm listening."

"Personally, no idea," Alex continued, "but on a map, it's not as bad as you might think. If we assume our kidnappers don't want to be within earshot of Skyline Drive or the Blue Ridge Parkway"—he referred to the scenic routes winding their way north and south respectively from the nearest mountain crossroads—"that narrows it down even further. We're left with three areas with any kind of road access if we take 'over the mountain' at face value and don't look too far north or south."

"Okay, three areas," Jason repeated, coming over to peer at the computer screen where Alex had been annotating a satellite view of the area.

"Those are circled in red," Alex explained. "Each one looks to have a couple of buildings that could be our cabin. But this one"—he pointed to the northernmost of the three—"is just off a road some of Jules' friends take to their hunting cabin, and she just texted me that they've never seen either of these guys before."

Jason squinted, trying to concentrate. "Jules . . . ?"

"Julie. My girlfriend." Alex spoke patiently enough, but Jason could feel the tinge of frustration he knew had every right to be there.

"Right, right," Jason said, trying to ignore the flush of shame that leapt to his face at not remembering Julie's name—or even that she existed, if he was honest with himself. He fell silent, watching Alex hunch over the screen as he traced unmarked routes leading up into the mountains. Alex had taken on the role of private investigator so eagerly and so expertly that it was easy to forget he'd been forced out of his element by the recent chaos as well. Jason searched his memory for what Alex would be doing these days, if not for this. Graduate school, he thought he remembered, but those words meant nothing to him, left him unable to picture what Alex should be *doing* instead of chasing improbable leads in the case of his own brother's disappearance.

"I think it's manageable," Alex said, jolting Jason's attention back to the map. "Though it looks like access isn't the best. There could be some hiking involved." He paused. "It's risky, but manageable."

"Risky is fine," Jason replied dismissively. "We could even go tonight." He was surprised by how quickly he'd become numb to the idea of putting himself in danger. Breaking into the first house had produced a tremendous rush of adrenaline; the second barely registered by comparison. The next one was sure to be even easier.

Jason refocused his attention on the map, hoping to gain a better sense of scale. The circled areas looked dauntingly large, even in miniature, and it would take at least half an hour just to drive up there, maybe more if—

He jerked his head up, as something in the corner of his eye caught his attention. He leaned across the table and peered through the windows into the darkened backyard. "Did we get snow?"

"Uh, yeah." Alex sounded confused. "It was snowing when you got back this morning."

"I know, but I mean . . ." Jason trailed off, glued to the window with curious fixation. After a moment's consideration, he headed for the back door and flung it open before reaching down to inspect the depth of the freshly fallen snow. "We've got like four inches." He straightened up and drew the door closed against the chill night air. "Shit, man, we might not even be able to get over the mountain tonight."

"Spoken like a true Virginian." Tara's voice carried through the house from the front hallway, where she had evidently just arrived. "The roads are fine. You guys don't know how to plow around here, but that's a separate issue." Already the aroma of Indian food was wafting over from the bags of takeout she carried, reminding Jason of just how long it had been since their last non-coffee-based meal.

"More important issue," Jason declared, pushing all thoughts of a drive up the mountain from his mind, "let's eat."

The kitchen became a swarm of activity as they gathered forks and distributed takeout containers, pushed Alex's workspace aside, and crowded around the table. All three ate greedily at first, but as their hunger faded, they fell back to talking, Jason and Alex taking turns as narrator to fill Tara in on their latest findings.

As Jason finished explaining the two sites they needed to check out, he could see that neither excitement nor relief was registering with Tara. Her expression was thoughtful, somewhere between a scowl and a frown, and she set her fork down across her empty plate with an air of finality.

"This whole thing stinks, you guys."

"No kidding," Alex muttered.

"That's not what I mean," Tara continued. "Like, stinks as in something's up, and honestly I'm sort of surprised I have to be the one to point it out."

Jason's thoughts leapt to their exchange in the car that morning. Part of him hated to think what Tara would say next, but he tried to ignore that feeling. "Okay . . ." he gestured for her to continue.

"I just keep asking myself: Who are these guys and why would they come after Max?" Tara frowned, giving the question a moment to sink in. "They're local, they're amateurs . . . and I know that probably doesn't mean anything, but then there's the ransom note. Things went sideways and they jumped right to xenophobic fear mongering when they needed a distraction."

"So . . . ?" Alex said slowly.

"So, what if this is some sort of hate crime?"

As she said it, the Confederate flag magnet holding up the photo of the two assailants flashed into Jason's mind. He hadn't given it much thought at the time; the Virginia he grew up in was filled with those flags, and only recently had anyone drawn any serious attention to what they *meant*. It could be nothing . . . or Tara could be right.

Alex, however, looked skeptical.

"C'mon, Alex," Tara pressed. "It's not that crazy, especially after last August. Now Max has this show all hyped up as a big Charlottesville love and unity thing . . ." she trailed off. "I'm just saying, not everyone around here is bought in on this peace-and-love 'real Charlottesville' vibe he's been pushing. And those

same people probably don't want to be associated with someone like him anyway."

"What do you mean, someone like him?" A defensive edge
had crept into Alex's voice.

"I said it at the police station. We've never kept our politics
a secret, Max least of all, and if you really want to go there, he's a
first-generation immigrant from the Soviet Union."

Alex shook his head. "I'm sorry, what does that have to do
with anything? We were practically babies when we moved here.
Dad had just been hired by the University—it was all by the
book."

"That's not my point," Tara interrupted.

"Hold on." Alex was insistent. "But you're saying, in the eyes
of his hometown, Max is still *different*. An outsider."

Tara bit her lip, clearly trying to suppress the frustration that
was starting to rise. "Not the *whole* town, obviously, but yeah, I
think there are people around here who aren't on board with his
whole deal. And the fake Russian note . . . it sounds kind of racist
to me."

"If this town were out to get us, we would know about it by
now."

"*Would* you?"

Alex scowled more seriously now, an expression that further
highlighted his resemblance of his brother. "Whatever you're
trying to say, just say it."

"Do I really have to spell it out for you?" Tara let out an exas-
perated sigh. "This town can be a nasty place for someone who's
even a little bit different. You and Max get a pass because you at
least look the part. You're white enough. Try looking like me in
this town for a day—for *one day*—and tell me exactly how welcoming and enlightened"—she traced a set of air quotes—"'y'all'
really are." With that, she shoved back her chair from the table
and stormed out of the room.

"Tara, wait." Jason was on his feet in an instant, trailing her
into the hallway. It was an eerie feeling, leaping in as mediator
like he'd done so many times before, but now with Alex—Alex, of
all people—as the offending party.

As he approached Tara, who stood with her arms folded
across her chest, staring out the front windows for a feigned look
of detachment, Jason heard the distinct buzz of a cell phone.

"Jase, your phone," Alex's voice floated in from the kitchen.

"In a minute," he called back, knowing Alex would say if the message were from Max.

The buzz repeated itself. "It's not a text. It's ringing."

"Then *answer* it!" Jason spat, and immediately regretted adding his own irritation to the already tense moment. He took a deep breath to steady himself before turning back to Tara. "Hey," he said quietly, "can we talk about some of . . . all that?"

"Jase, it's fine." Her reply was curt enough to tell him he'd made the right decision in following her. "I just needed to get it off my chest."

"So . . . what you were saying about those guys . . ." Jason trailed off, unsure of his question, but suddenly longing to understand.

"Forget it. I'm probably wrong anyway." She turned away and fell to pacing the half-darkened hallway, looking more shaken than Jason would have expected as she hugged her arms closer around her narrow frame. He was struck by a sudden urge to reach out and pull her into a hug, but something about the ghostliness of her pacing form gave him pause. It was a weightier repetition of his realization with Alex earlier that evening. *I don't know your world.*

All at once, he saw that he had never taken the time to understand her, not really. His thoughts drifted back to the day they met, at an open audition he and Max had held during their indoctrination to an unfamiliar urban music scene. The details of Tara's life—or history, or whatever it could best be called—had never mattered. She was the best drummer they heard that day. Period. They'd barely discussed the fact that she was a girl, much less the fact that she was Black, and it had rarely come up since.

Jason remembered the closed-door meeting Max had insisted upon to lend their audition an air of importance. It was just the two of them, and though they'd both adopted the pretense of carrying clipboards as the half-dozen or so drummers played, only Max had taken any sort of notes.

"The girl was pretty good," Jason remembered saying as he scanned the blank sheet of lined paper before him in a well-practiced show of studiousness that had failed to impress any of his high school teachers and wasn't about to fool Max.

"Tara," Max supplied the name without looking up from his

notes. "She wasn't just pretty good. She was too good to still be looking for a gig." The way he said it, Jason could tell he wasn't trying to invent an excuse not to offer her the spot in the band. It was a genuine observation, not an implied question about why she was still looking.

Jason had nodded. "Yeah, she was the best one." He hesitated, then couldn't stop himself from blurting out, "You don't think it'd be weird having a girl in the band?"

Max's head shot up and his eyes met Jason's in a look of stern reproval. "No. It'd be weird to have a shitty drummer when we could have her."

That was the end of the conversation; Max had spoken, and Jason's face stung with a flush of embarrassment at having voiced such a foolish concern. "You're right," he agreed, and just like that, the meeting was over. And, after they'd emerged with their offer and fell to chatting with Tara, the reservations that had prompted his comment evaporated. She seemed like a perfect fit for the band's evolving image: tough, cool, and with just enough of that signature pop-punk desperation for a voice.

"I'm not quitting my day job just yet though," Tara had been quick to warn them. "And sometimes it's more of a night job, so if that's an issue. . . ." She trailed off, and the look in her eye had sent Jason's mind spiraling, even as he told himself not to make assumptions. A moment later, Tara burst out laughing. "My God, the looks on your faces. I'm a *valet*. I just need advance notice so I can get off work if we have a gig."

And as he and Max began to laugh, too, Jason was sold. She was one of them. From that day on, he had—quite literally—never given her identity a second thought. She was Tara the drummer, the bandmate, the friend who could withstand even the most aggressive jokes and teasing he and Max could muster.

Sure, she had her policy of not drinking around fans and would make the occasional complaint about high heels or uncooperative bra straps, but Jason had never felt like any of that mattered. Now his mind swirled with all the possible times he'd said something wrong or glanced over a statement of Tara's without even realizing it, and how strange it was to have all of this thrown in his face when he felt least prepared to deal with any of it. But of course that was how she was feeling, and why it came up now.

"I don't think you're wrong," Jason heard himself say through the fog of memories. Tara stopped short and lifted her face toward him, her features marked by cascading light and shadow cast in from the kitchen. He sighed, struck by the feeling that he was only beginning to see the friend with whom he'd ridden out the storm of the past two nightmarish days. "What you said in the car about perspective . . . you're totally right."

"Thanks." Her voice was barely a whisper, but Jason could feel the emotion behind it.

"Tara, I'm sorry," Jason said, still feeling detached from the moment. "Alex and I love this town and we know how much Max loves this town . . . it's like, if we can't have him here, at least we have *here*, you know? It's our home, Max's home." His voice wavered with the sudden threat of tears. "And that's about all I have right now, okay?"

"I know," Tara whispered. "I'm sorry too." She drew in a breath, then continued in an only slightly shaky rendition of her usual tone, "Jase, it's just hard for me sometimes. The way you get when you love something . . . it's like all you can see is the good, and anyone who sees something bad is the enemy. I just . . . wasn't ready for Alex to add onto that, I guess."

"What do you mean?"

Now Tara managed a weak smile. "Really?" she asked gently. "C'mon, Jase, you do this with Charlottesville, you do this with Max; you act like they're perfect and if someone says otherwise you don't want to hear it."

"I don't—" he started to interrupt, but stopped himself as he realized she was right.

"You're not wrong to love the place you grew up, Jase." Tara's expression softened further. "I get it. I stuck around New York for a reason. Home is . . . something special. But I wish you could admit it isn't perfect."

"I never said Charlottesville was perfect," Jason mumbled guiltily. He could feel the weight of her words, the softly voiced indictment hitting him harder than if she'd shouted. Sighing, he continued, "I'm just tired of hearing how awful it is."

Tara's eyes narrowed at that. "I never said—"

"No," he cut her off, "I didn't mean you. Not just you, anyway. The past six months it's like . . . no one will even say what happened. No one talks about the rally or the Nazis, they talk about Charlottesville. Or what happened '*after* Charlottesville.'

Like we don't exist anymore, we were all just that one day."

Tara nodded slowly, processing. "You're right," she said. "That's not fair either."

"Do people here really treat you differently?" Jason asked. He tried to make it sound understanding, like he genuinely wanted to know—and he did. The question still felt clumsy leaving his lips, like maybe there was no good way to ask.

She shrugged, looking evasive. "Half the time I don't think people even realize. But I swear, the next time I introduce myself and someone goes, 'Oh, Tara, like the plantation.' . . ." She shook her head, then continued with renewed confidence. "Look, I know I'm not crazy. I also know it's not just here. Probably everyone who keeps throwing Charlottesville around as a euphemism for racism does too, but it's easier to say something about the rally than start looking at your own hometown and end up feeling . . . how you do right now."

Jason nodded. As he watched her, still closed off and cloaked in shadow, he didn't know what to say, but a blundering "I'm sorry," slipped out.

"You said that," Tara replied, offering a slight smile once again. "Jase, personal feelings about Charlottesville aside, I brought those points up to be productive."

"It's okay," he said, as much to Tara as to himself. He sensed there remained a lot to be said but could feel a new understanding beginning to take shape.

Tara wiped at her eyes, and Jason realized she had been holding back tears as they spoke. "Sorry," she blurted out, "this isn't what I was going for."

"Me either," Jason replied, sneaking in a weak smile of his own. "Look, Tara, I really am sorry." He paused, swallowed hard. "I don't want you to think Charlottesville and Max are the only things I care about. You're pretty high on that list, too, and I guess I kind of suck at letting you know it."

"Yeah, yeah," Tara said, but even through the tears there was a twinkle of a smile in her eye as a teasing note crept into her voice, "we only fight like this because we're like family."

He gave a sheepish shrug. "Hey, it's true."

Tara nodded, giving only a small eye roll.

"Are we . . . okay?" Jason knew he was rushing a resolution, but the weightiness of the moment seemed to have passed, and he felt his attention drifting back toward the kitchen and Alex's phone call.

"We were always *okay*," she shot back. "Just, thanks for hearing me out, I guess."

Jason nodded. "Sorry it took me so long to be ready to listen."

Tara responded with a nod of her own. "Now, are we gonna go see what that phone call is about, or what?"

"Sure." Jason flashed a grateful smile and fell into step beside her as she started back toward the kitchen.

They returned to find Alex absorbed in a conversation on Jason's cell phone, though he paused to mouth an "I'm sorry" of his own in Tara's direction as she and Jason slipped back into their chairs. He held up an index finger, indicating he still needed a moment with whomever was on the other end of the call.

Tara seemed prepared to wait in silence, but with every "Mm-hm" and "I understand" from Alex, Jason felt himself growing more and more desperate to know what was happening. Sitting there letting his mind race was unbearable. He turned to Tara, and, keeping his voice low, asked, "So what were you going to say?"

Tara took a moment to gather her thoughts. "Look, you've worked miracles figuring things out up to this point, but have you thought about what happens next?"

"We go find Max."

"No, like, what do our bad guys do next? We still don't know what they're after, not really. I just thought piecing together some of that might help."

Jason frowned. "We don't know," he agreed. From his perspective, it was easy to feel like Max himself was the target, the prize, but it was foolish to think the kidnappers saw things in the same light. He tried to think, running through all of the evidence again, desperate for something he'd missed that would answer the unbearable question of *why*. Why Max, why here, why now?

Tara bit her lip, deep in thought as well. "Hm," she said, "you said you saw a pay stub in the first house. That's how you knew the guy was working at the mansion."

Jason nodded. "He started there in January. It can't be a coincidence."

"It *could* be," Tara hedged her reply, "but it probably isn't. He got that job after we announced our tour dates—after Max booked the mansion for our party. Doesn't the timing sound like this is about the concert?"

Jason hesitated. He still hadn't bought in on Tara's urge to place the band's message about Charlottesville at the center of the kidnappers' motives, but he didn't want to push back and risk another argument. Fortunately, his thoughts were interrupted by the conclusion of Alex's phone call.

"Yes, thank you. Goodbye," Alex said to whomever was on the other end of the line. He ended the call and slid the phone across the table toward Jason. "Tara, I—"

"I'm sorry, too," she replied quickly yet with obvious sincerity as she cut Alex off. "What was the call about?"

With a guilty look and a brief nod, Alex acknowledged her apology. "That was the detectives calling back," he said, sounding slightly dazed. "They want us to meet with them again, eight o'clock tomorrow."

"Did you tell them about the note?" Jason asked.

"Their translators agree it's a misdirect," Alex replied. He exhaled slowly. "But the list of demands they just received might not be."

Jason's phone buzzed again, interrupting the otherwise serious moment as he and Tara tried to process. His thoughts were drifting—to Max, the demands, the police—as he cast a quick glance at the screen. Just a text from a high school friend. It could wait.

"Demands?" Tara repeated. "What do they want?"

Alex shook his head. "Also in Russian. The police say their translators will have it by morning."

"That sounds serious. Do they think *we're* safe?"

"Not sure." Alex continued to sound shaken. "Let's hit pause on looking into those cabins until we hear what the cops have to say."

"Wait, come on, this is ridiculous," Jason interjected, trying to shake the dark mood that had settled over the room. "It's just one guy, probably hiding out on the mountain and keeping an eye on Max himself. What's he going to do to any of us? Those demands are as phony as the ransom note, I guarantee it."

"Do we know it's one guy?" Tara asked. "We think it was just the two of them at the party, but now that you say it, how do we know?" She shuddered. "I don't like it."

"Well, the picture . . ." Jason trailed off, realizing Tara could be right. They happened to have a photograph linking the two men who seemed to be partners, but for all anyone knew there could be dozens more.

Alex shook his head. "I don't want to think about it right now. We'll talk to the police tomorrow and go from there." He glanced at his own phone, which was illuminated by the arrival of a text. "Guys, it's been fun, it really has, but I'm going to head home and try to get some sleep. Jules is on her way." He looked to Tara. "Where are you staying? She can give you a ride."

Tara was momentarily flustered, though Jason couldn't place why. "I, um, thought I might stay here actually," she said, sounding apologetic as she looked in his direction. "I stopped by my hotel on my way to get the food, so I'm good anywhere."

"Sure," Jason replied, sensing that Tara's fumbling words were meant as a request. She had always preferred having her own space when the band traveled, but given the circumstances, he was just as glad not to be alone in the house. "If you want a bed, I don't mind sleeping on the couch."

"Couch is fine," she said. "Let me go grab my things."

Tara headed out to the car, and Alex was drawn back into his phone. Still typing away, he gave a nod in Jason's direction. "What was that text you just got?"

"Oh." The message had slipped from Jason's mind, and his thoughts were still elsewhere as he swiped it open, but he gasped as an image materialized on his screen.

"What?" Alex sounded understandably concerned.

"Take a look." Jason slid the phone across the table, and a look of alarm registered on Alex's face before he even picked it up. On the screen was a social media post, a photo of Alex and Tara leaving the hospital. The poster, clearly a fangirl, had tagged the accounts of both Max and the band, and included a caption, "Don't worry baby, I'll carry you" and a series of broken heart emojis. The accompanying message from Jason's friend was a long string of question marks, and had been sent to both him and Max.

Alex exhaled slowly as he passed the phone back. "Oh boy."

"We knew it was coming," Jason said, not that it helped. An ill-informed story that drew attention to Max was the last thing they needed, and yet here it was, courtesy of an unsuspecting undergrad eager to advertise a celebrity sighting on her way home from class. He tapped out an evasive reply to his friend, "LOL it's all good. One drink too many."

"What are you telling him?" Alex demanded to know, craning his neck for a better look at the screen.

"Just brushing it off," Jason replied, hitting send on the message. He turned the phone toward Alex, who scanned it quickly and nodded his approval. "I thought Izzy was on top of this shit," he grumbled.

"You never told her I was hurt," Alex said, and as he spoke, a new message from Izzy appeared on Jason's screen.

"Right on cue." Jason held the phone up for Alex to see: "I see u found Max. Thx for the heads up about his leg? Oh wait. . . ."

Alex shrugged. "You wanted to keep her in the dark anyway. No reason not to let her think it's Max."

"That's true."

"And besides, playing a show on Thursday is starting to feel pretty unlikely. Here's an excuse to postpone."

"I guess," Jason muttered. He sighed. "I just don't like to think we might not have found Max by then."

Chapter 12

Stepping into the hot, steamy shower felt heavenly. Jason drew in a deep breath as the water rushed over his aching, under-slept body. He reached for soap and his hand closed on the flowery body wash Tara had left behind after her own long-over-due shower. After sniffing the pink concoction skeptically, he decided there was no harm in trying something a little stronger to eradicate the lingering odor of two days of sweat, still tinged with the acrid scent of Saturday night's liquor.

Jason closed his eyes as he worked up a sweet-smelling lather first in his hair, then across his entire body. As he reached down to wash his feet, his back offered a throbbing reminder that it had been days since he'd slept in a proper bed. Maybe at eighteen he could have afforded it, but those days were starting to feel like they were a long way behind him.

The stiffness of his left hand was another reminder of his lack of invincibility, and he paused to inspect the bruises left behind by his first reckless attempt at window breaking. On any other day, his primary worry would be how the fingers would hold up under the stress of rehearsals and the upcoming concert, but right now, picking up a guitar was the furthest thing from Jason's mind.

As the hot water continued to stream over him, he let himself slip down to a seated position in the bottom of the bathtub and fell to thinking once again. Surreal was the only way to describe the past two days. He was struck by the sudden, impossible urge to call Max and have a laugh about this whole mess, as if it were a bad dream, as if the feelings of helplessness and worry had just been conjured up by his overwrought psyche.

I fucking miss you, man. The words were so vivid it was like he'd spoken them aloud.

Jason's thoughts drifted back to childhood, to all the promises he and Max had made to themselves and one another never to lose touch. From their first secret club in kindergarten to setting off for New York together after high school, it had always been the two of them. And it always would be, if not for . . . this.

And what even was *this*? He could feel himself struggling not to conflate Max's withdrawal during the hiatus with his current disappearance, but the two seemed to open the same wounds. Max was gone, ripped away from him by some force he didn't understand.

A painful thought struck Jason. *He's my best friend in the world and I don't know what I'd even say to him if I found him.* Over the past year, he'd gotten so used to Max not wanting to be found that the question now entered his mind as to whether he was doing his friend a favor by going to the metaphorical ends of the earth to bring him back.

The thoughts were growing oppressive, and Jason rose and turned the water off. He stepped out into the bathroom, shivering as the cold air rushed to the water droplets clinging to his naked body. His teeth chattered as he toweled himself off and studied his reflection in the mirror. He looked like hell. Dark circles were prominent beneath his tired eyes and his face prickled with three days of stubble that would have to wait until morning. Most concerningly, he was losing weight; he probably had been since the chaos of tour preparations began, but the past few days of neither sleeping nor eating properly had taken a visible toll. *And it isn't over yet.*

Even in its current state, his body was that of an athlete, his muscles maintained by a workout regimen left over from his high school days. For a few years he'd toyed with the idea of sports as his escape, but it felt like every accomplishment came with a qualifier: his height. Coaches had invariably referred to him as undersize; it wasn't until senior year that he even reached his current height, just shy of five foot eight. The choice was easy. He could either be a too-short, too-small point guard, making apologies for his stature at every turn, or a guitarist, full stop. As much as he loved basketball, he knew he could never escape the condescension, and his decision was made. Max had laid out a path for him, and he was happy to follow.

Although, he remembered, it wasn't clear back then that Max was ready to commit to a life of music either. Both boys had been solid students, floating somewhere near average in a large high school class—with one notable exception. When the subject was literature, Max was a devoted straight-A student.

One English teacher in particular had taken an interest in Max, and even convinced him to take the literature AP test their junior year. Jason recalled the exchange vividly, the day he'd realized *their* dream might be more his own than that of the person whose talents made it viable in the first place.

He had inadvertently eavesdropped on the deciding conversation, waiting in the hall at the end of the school day for Max to emerge from last period English. Any other class, Max would reliably be the first one out the door, but when it came to English, more often than not, he would invite himself to linger and continue debating the topic of the day.

"But I'm not going to college," Max had insisted, the scholarly self-assurance of his earlier literary arguments draining from his voice. "It doesn't help me any."

"You won't regret taking the test," the teacher had patiently replied. "You're what—how old are you, Max?"

"Seventeen."

"All right, at seventeen you don't want to go to college." Her tone was genuine, more understanding than Jason had ever known a teacher to sound. "That's fine, but things can change. Maybe at, say, twenty-seven you'll feel differently, and you deserve an unquestionable piece of proof of your abilities."

Max was petulant. "If I decide I want to go later, I can take the test then." Even from around the corner, Jason could hear him shifting uncomfortably in place, or maybe even edging toward the door.

"An opportunity is presenting itself to you now. I think you're smart enough to know you should take it."

"I mean . . . I might not even do well."

It had sounded like the teacher was laughing to herself. "Do you remember the first essay you turned in to me, way back in September?" By then it was December, just over a week shy of winter break.

"Yes ma'am. *A Separate Peace.*"

"And do you remember what I wrote on it?"

"Yes ma'am." In the silence that followed, the teacher must have motioned for him to continue, which after a lengthy pause, he did, sounding uncharacteristically embarrassed. "You wrote that it was the best student analysis of the text you had read."

The teacher sighed. "You're extremely talented, Max. I don't know how else to tell you. I've had countless students with no-where near your level of ability walk away from that test with a perfect score and college credit in hand. There's no reason to think you won't do well."

"Okay. I guess."

Jason had dared to venture a peek around the corner of the door frame, and regretted it as he made eye contact with the teacher. He hurriedly ducked back out of sight.

"Go ahead, your better half is waiting," the teacher had in-structed, but Jason again sensed a hint of laughter in her voice. "I'll see you in class tomorrow."

"See you tomorrow." And Max strode out of the room, launching an elbow into Jason's side as soon as they were out of sight of the door. Jason could only laugh, pleased with himself for how effectively he'd embarrassed his friend. As they rounded the next corner, Max finally spoke. "You still know your mom's credit card number?"

"Yeah, why?"

"I gotta pay for that AP test somehow."

That was when the sinking feeling had first registered with Jason, the worry that he might lose his best friend to an academ-ic world where he had even less of a chance of keeping up. Then, at least, the combination of their bond and Max's contempt for authority had prevailed. In the years since, one of the two must have broken, and there was no point in pretending Max had come around on the issue of being told what to do.

Some good that test did him, Jason thought to himself with only a hint of bitterness. Twenty-seven had come and gone with-out so much as a mention of college, and Jason wasn't about to remind Max of his golden ticket to yet another means of placing distance between the two of them. He now eyed his reflection with cautious disdain, regretting the stab of resentment brought about by letting his memories take over. Reminiscing could wait; present-day Max could not.

Pushing the thoughts from his mind, Jason inhaled the scent of just-washed sweatpants and a clean T-shirt as he drew the clothes over his shivering body. He tousled his wet hair, sending droplets of water flying, and shoved a toothbrush in his mouth for a halfhearted effort at scrubbing away the latest round of coffee stains.

His bare feet were silent on the carpet as he retreated—finally—to his own bedroom and dove into the mess of sheets and blankets that awaited. After a few restless minutes of straightening the covers and pulling them close around his chilled body, Jason settled into a state of exhausted comfort so complete he felt as if he wouldn't move for anything.

The bedside lamp was still on, and from where he had nestled himself in the center of the queen-size bed—one of the only updates he'd made to his childhood bedroom—he didn't bother trying to reach it. The light was dim enough; he closed his eyes and immediately drifted off.

Jason's eyes sprang open and a shudder of energy tore through his body. He was startled to find the room still lit, and complete darkness intact outside. His heart was pounding as he fumbled for the cell phone resting on his bedside table and punched it to illuminate its clock. *Not even midnight.*

It was as if panic itself had jarred him awake, out of the long-awaited rest into which he'd slipped so effortlessly only an hour earlier. *What is happening?* He couldn't recall a bad dream but had been jolted awake as if out of a nightmare. His hands shook as he let the phone drop into his lap. Still sitting upright, he nervously eyed the darkened corners of the room.

And suddenly a dream did come flooding back to him—only it wasn't a dream. Scenes from the past had been replaying themselves over and over in his mind, an endless montage of Max in freefall.

He could hear the slight, sudden tremor in Max's voice, backstage after one of their final concerts before the hiatus. They were in State College, one of several college-town stops on the last leg of the tour as they circled back toward home. The crowd had been unbelievable, an endless source of the passionate, nearly violent energy the band loved to feed on. Jason remembered tearing off the stage, feeling on top of the world as he greeted Max with a hearty slap on the back. "Fuck, man, this *crowd!*" he'd half shouted, ears still ringing, "Have you ever felt so *alive*?"

And then the singular, unmistakable moment as Max's expression, previously ecstatic, clouded ever so slightly. He'd mirrored Jason's gesture, striking a return blow across the top of his shoulders, and as he did, he leaned in close, his whisper competing with the din in Jason's ears, "Every day. And it's killing me."

Jason knew better than to ask what he meant. Max's eyes were locked on his, fixed in an expression he could only describe as haunted. That moment later registered with Jason as his first glimpse of the demon, that invisible, destabilizing force that had set Max ranting about love songs and later brought about the collapse of life as the band knew it.

He could see the transformation beginning, as if in real time, stepping in out of the damp autumn drizzle into their New York rehearsal space to find Max holed up in a corner of the room, his back to the door. At first, all Jason had heard was the thunderous punch of the bass as Max's hands leapt and bashed across its heavy strings, but as Jason stood transfixed, a single pained cry had distinguished itself among the deep, rumbling notes.

Suddenly Jason's presence had been detected, and the wall of sound died away, leaving just Max, seated on a wooden stool, bass in hand. Max turned slowly, swallowing a grimace, and his expression was stoic as he met Jason's gaze. It was a look of absolute denial; the noise must have come from somewhere else, could not have been him.

"Hey," Jason had managed as a somewhat shaky greeting. He was willing to believe that look in Max's eyes, the now-impenetrable wall of ice, until his attention was drawn to a single, deep red drop of blood slowly tracing its way down the clean, white oval of Max's pickguard.

"Hey," Max repeated softly, "hand me a rag, will you?"

That was all he had to say, remaining quiet and uncomplaining through the three hours of rehearsal that followed. Every time they paused, he would reach for the rag and silently wipe away the latest damage.

"You're bleeding," Tara had remarked multiple times, but Max would only wave her off, and after the second or third mention, made a point of keeping his back turned to her drum set.

Jason's own fingers had tingled with sympathetic pain as he watched his friend press through, never shying away from a booming strike of the thick, coiled strings. Once, catching Max's eye, he held out a spare pick as a silent offering, and was met with the look of scorn he knew the gesture deserved. Max would never use a pick on his bass; "She deserves better," was the only explanation he had offered Jason at the age of fourteen, when they were beginning to talk seriously about forming their first band. The "she" in question had since been upgraded at nearly five times the cost, but his teenage logic stuck.

From there it was a spiral, spinning faster and faster out of control, Max lashing out at anyone who got too close, Alex thrust into the fray, Tara adding her frustrations to the madness and looking to Jason for answers. And then the wall of the hiatus came crashing down on them. On all of them, at first, except himself.

He had felt the partial relief in Max's exhalation of a sigh as they walked together, rid of the expectations of rehearsals and public appearances, bundled up in comfortable anonymity against the frigid winds of a brewing Nor'easter. Jason had sensed Max was still fighting, but now that it was just the two of them, the internal storm seemed to be letting up, or at least they'd found a momentary shelter from the tempest.

But days became weeks, weeks became months, and still the storm wore on. Any shelter he and Max had shared was coming apart at the seams. That night in May—catching fireflies in that roadside field—felt like a breakthrough, a sign of better days ahead. Jason wasn't fooling himself by assigning a particular significance to the look Max had given him as they stood atop his car in the rising summer sun. But any effects of that night unraveled as quickly and mysteriously as they had appeared.

He could still hear the buzz of the final message of that summer illuminating his cell phone as it lay in the midst of his usual early afternoon coffeeshop breakfast: "Jase . . . I need some time. Not forever . . . just some time."

It wasn't the reply he'd expected to his question of when Max was coming back to New York, but deep down, he'd known it was coming.

And then every time he looked at his phone, that message was all he saw. He couldn't stop himself from opening that conversation, wading through sent message after sent message to the last incoming one. He'd open it daily, reread those final words, often send another fumbling attempt of his own, then return the phone to his pocket, only to repeat the ritual the following day.

Jason could still feel his hands shaking as he typed out his final reply at the end of that long and horrible August 12. He had fought back tears as he wrote it; it was the first one he hadn't agonized over, the shortest, most to the point: "I fuckin miss you. Text me back."

He could see the reminder of that most-recent message lighting up his screen with the incoming call four months later, could feel the churn of anticipation in his stomach—mixed, he was surprised to find, with dread—as he answered the call. And he could feel it all rush away, the frustration, the loneliness, the months of worry, everything, as Max's voice broke through the static of the rural connection: "We're back."

It had all come flooding back to him at once, the events of the hiatus playing out over the course of a half hour's fitful sleep. Jason never wanted to be back in that state, facing a life without Max, and yet here he was, literally reliving his worst nightmare.

The vividness of the memories rattled Jason, seemed to be closing in on him, and he was struck by the sudden sense that he would only be safe with his back against a wall, able to survey the room in its entirety. It was a childish preoccupation, one that had entered his mind from time to time as bad dreams disrupted his sleep, but now Jason couldn't logically back himself out of it. His reminiscences were eerie enough, but the reality of Max's disappearance was even worse. Before, he'd known the raging storm was confined to Max. Now, nothing was certain.

Jason's heart was still racing as he forced himself to rise and make a cursory lap of the house. The stairs creaked underfoot as he made his way down to the living room, where he was relieved to find Tara asleep, curled up on the couch in a comfortable nest of blankets. Jason tiptoed past, checking the back door, then the front, before returning upstairs and collapsing onto his bed once more.

Any relief he felt at the partial return to normalcy—his own bed, his own space, some sense of routine—was gone. *I can't take any more of this*, he thought. The sleepless nights had been grueling, but a failed night of trying to sleep was even worse. He rubbed at his aching eyes and yawned widely. *Demands be damned. Seems like a perfect day for a trip to the mountains.*

Chapter 13

The blare of his alarm at seven o'clock wasn't enough to shake Jason from the fitful sleep he had finally fallen into sometime in the early hours of the morning. It was Tara's concerned knocks on his bedroom door that had awakened him and set off a frenzied set of preparations.

The thought may have come to him in a compromised state, but in the clear light of day, Jason was only more convinced. No matter what the police, or his friends, or anyone else had to say, he couldn't wait. He was going to go find Max himself. He dressed and shaved quickly before returning to his room to scavenge for whatever supplies he might need on a snowy mountain in pursuit of his kidnapped best friend. The task was somewhat beyond his grasp.

"Jase? We're late." Tara's voice had floated up the stairs. He reluctantly dropped the half packed backpack and joined her in grabbing coffee on the way out the door. Her warning had proven premature, but now, as they turned into the driveway of the mansion, they really were late.

"Alex could have mentioned they wanted to meet here," Jason grumbled, more to himself than anyone else. They had arrived at the police station fifteen minutes earlier, only to be redirected by an officer. Still, his frustration was misguided, and he knew it. Now that his mind was made up, every minute of delay was time he could be spending searching for Max.

"Well, we're here now," Tara replied, her voice carrying a forced cheeriness that Jason knew was masking a serious case of nerves. The car had barely rolled to a stop before she was out the door, hurrying toward the gathering that had formed near the front steps of the house.

In addition to the two detectives they now knew by sight, a few uniformed officers milled about. Alex and his girlfriend were already talking with the detective who had first interviewed Jason and Tara. The girlfriend—Julie—was the first to notice Jason and Tara's arrival, and she beamed and waved as they approached.

Now that he saw her in person, Jason realized he did know Julie, and felt even worse about how he'd brushed Alex's life aside. Julie was tall, blonde, and decidedly *cute*, with long legs that just skirted the boundary between elegant and awkward. She was younger even than Alex, by how much Jason couldn't recall, and smiling in the bright morning sunlight as Alex slumped against his crutches, she could have passed for a decade his junior.

"Tara, Jason, so good to see you again!" Julie gushed, motioning them over. "I'm sorry we didn't get to talk last night." Suddenly Jason recalled Julie's other defining trait, and the reason he'd avoided her in the past: her overwhelming friendliness. Even on a good day, her cheeriness grated on Jason, and he was in no mood for it today.

"Yeah, no worries," he mumbled.

Julie turned to Tara and placed a hand on her arm. "How are you holding up?"

Tara responded with a look and a nod that Jason could only place as a mode of girl-communication, with its secrets and signs that had never made sense to him.

"Aw, honey," was Julie's reply as she pulled Tara into a hug that was immediately returned. She nodded in Alex's direction and added, "Him, too. I'm so sorry."

Jason's patience for pleasantries was running out, and he turned to the detectives. "Did you translate the demands, or what?"

"Still in progress," the female detective replied, joining her partner in the circle that had formed. "In the meantime, we'll need the three of you"—she pointed to Jason, Tara, and Alex—"to show us what modifications to the house you did and did not approve for your event." She started toward the mansion, motioning for them to follow.

"Hold on, Alex can translate," Jason said, hoping to derail the detective's plan, which felt like nothing more than busy work. "We can go through the house later." And by *we*, he meant everyone except him. The second he knew those demands, he'd be on his way to Max, ideally with the required cash or whatever else in hand, but to bring him home regardless.

"We trust our translators," the female detective replied. She shot a glance at her watch. "They should have that for us . . . any minute."

Jason suspected that was code for the translators being late with their work, but decided against bringing it up. Begrudgingly, he fell into line for the tedious journey through the house. It hadn't sounded like much when Max described the setup—instrument storage, an informal stage, the coatroom, an additional bar—but now the changes felt endless. If a piece of furniture had been moved an inch, the police wanted to know about it.

As they crossed yet another room, looking for yet another modification Jason only half remembered, his eyes fell on the crumpled banner bearing the band's name and logo. Max had insisted on it, a triumphant announcement of their return, but now, messily stashed along the back wall of what looked to be a sitting room, it looked anything but triumphant. Out of place, certainly, and even a little bit sad.

All these years and we never got around to changing that stupid name, Jason thought as he stared at the folds of canvas, not processing whatever question the detective was asking now. He couldn't help but recall the day they chose the name, and how pointless calling themselves The Generation had seemed even at the time.

It was in the early days of his and Max's time in New York, and Jason had returned to their shared apartment earlier than expected and in a foul mood. The less-than-legitimate nature of his fake ID had been discovered, earning him a prompt dismissal from his bartending job and a long walk home in the gusty, bone-chilling winds of early spring in the Northeast. He wanted nothing more than to sprawl on his uncomfortable futon in peace and quiet and crack open a few beers—which, naturally, he hadn't been able to snag from work this time around. But he returned to find Max, bass in hand, sitting by the open window, listening to the sounds of the city and deep in the creative process.

"It's cold out," Jason had grumbled. "Close the fucking window."

Max didn't reply. He never did when a musical thought was working its way through his head. But even as disgruntled as he was, Jason's curiosity was piqued, and he shuffled over to the window to inspect the scene below. It was nothing out of the ordinary, just the usual throng of cars and pedestrians on the tail end of the evening rush hour. "What're you working on?" he asked.

"Listen," Max instructed, and after tapping out a tempo for himself, began to play, an uncharacteristically rumbling, muddy bass line.

"Sounds like a fucking 737," Jason muttered irritably when Max had finished. He'd been prepared to let his bad mood dissipate if the song were something compelling, but he heard nothing distinct in the low jumble of notes Max had just played.

But Max was beaming. "I've been listening to planes land all day, trying to get it just right."

"Great," Jason had mumbled, wandering over to the futon and executing his long-awaited flop onto its sagging cushions. He was itching to make some comment about how he'd been out earning rent money while Max sat in the apartment listening to airplanes and letting the heat out, but a brief reflection on his own day halted Jason's tongue. He'd awakened mid-afternoon in an unfamiliar apartment, painfully hungover and only half sure he'd even slept with the girl who'd left him there with an unsigned note reading "Get out by 3 p.m." And then, of course, he'd managed to lose his job—the first step above menial labor he'd been able to find in nearly eight months of city living. With only his legitimate driver's license remaining, he was at least *another* eight months away from another bartending job, far too long to go with only the occasional gig as a source of income.

"I still don't know if I have it," Max continued, unbothered by the silence that had fallen over the room. "I don't like the planes here, you know."

"Me either." Jason only half intended to keep the conversation going, but at least Max had found something they could agree on. His middle-school memories of watching the Twin Towers fall were too vivid for him to ever be comfortable with the number of takeoffs and landings that took place so close to the sea of skyscrapers.

"No, not that," Max replied, apparently reading Jason's mind. "They're so . . . lonely here. It's not like at home, where you hear a plane land and you know everyone on it is there because they mean to be, not just passing through. Half the people here would just as soon be in Philly or Dulles or—I don't know—fucking *Detroit*." He paused, looking over at Jason to see if he was still listening. "You know the sound I really want?"

"Hm?"

"The last flight of the night coming into Charlottesville at, like, eleven o'clock. I always loved that sound. You just know everyone on it is coming home."

He played the bass line again. This time, with the image in his mind of a lone propellor plane hanging low in the starry night sky, Jason could hear why Max had been so excited about the riff. It did almost sound like home, like drifting off to sleep with the windows open in his childhood bedroom or traversing a moonlit field with a group of high school friends as the woods came alive with the chirping of cicadas.

He hadn't wanted to surrender his frustration just yet, though, so Jason quickly changed the subject. "You find us a drummer, or what?"

It had taken Max a second or two to snap back to reality. "Oh," he said finally, reaching to close the window. "I couldn't make flyers. We don't have a name."

"We have a name."

"Max and Jason?" Even without looking up, Jason had known Max was rolling his eyes as he spoke. "That's not a band name; it's just *our* names."

"Fuck, man, I don't know. Name it whatever you want."

"That's the problem. I don't know what I want." Max had gotten to his feet and was beginning the process of coiling up his cables and wiping down his bass. From the self-assurance in his voice, it was clear that it had never occurred to him to wait on Jason's approval of a name, if only he could come up with one himself.

"No," Jason had said, shaking his head. "Words are your job. I just play guitar, man."

"It's not like naming a *song*," Max contradicted. "You name a song when it's finished. The band . . . I don't know what it's going to be. We're just getting started."

" . . . if we can ever find a drummer," Jason muttered.

Max pretended not to have heard, and continued to flip shut the latches of his case. "All we know about this band right now is a genre and an era," he said, talking more to himself than to Jason. "And even that combination is tenuous. We know what punk sounds like in the eighties, the nineties, even the two-thousands, but here we are on the brink of a new decade." Sensing Jason's urge to interrupt, he quickly hedged his statement, "Fine, *pop*-punk, if you will, but we both know it's not a new genre, it's how punk evolved to survive." He sighed. "It's like naming a child. You don't know who they'll turn out to be. All you know is what fucking generation they are and you're supposed to slap a name on them to last the next eighty years."

"Well, fine," Jason quipped. "Just call it 'The Generation' if that's the only thing you know about this band."

"That's a dumb name."

Jason had groaned and rolled over to face Max and prop himself on his elbows for the remainder of what was proving to be an inescapable conversation. "Fuck, man, I told you. Words are your job."

But Max was still thinking, and it was close to a minute before he responded. "Actually, I like it," he said finally. "The Generation. A dumb name for a dumb punk band no one will ever hear about anyway." He reached for a pencil, lying discarded on the windowsill. "Hand me some paper. I've got flyers to make."

Something in Jason suspected that even then, Max knew that they were onto something great. Which is part of why it bothered him now to see that name discarded in a heap on the floor. And the feeling was only heightened by Max's absence. Jason held his tongue, though, waiting for the detective's inspection of that particular room to finish before falling into line once again.

"Really, why are we doing this?" he finally asked. He and Tara were the only ones with the detective now, standing upstairs overlooking the ruined balcony.

"Well, for one thing, *sir*, we have a positive ID on the man who fled from the scene. Both he and the victim were employed here in recent months. The nature of—" she stopped short, cut off by the crackling of her radio. "Yes?"

The male detective's voice on the other end was staticky, but clear enough. "Just heard back from our translators. You'll want to get down here."

Just like that, the ambient boredom gave way to a rush of nerves. Jason and Tara exchanged a brief look of mutual worry and were instantly two steps ahead of the detective, heading back downstairs. One of the uniformed officers waved them over to where the others had gathered in a spacious dining room lined with tall, curtained windows that admitted both sunlight and chill air through their thin panes.

They were barely through the door when the words burst forth from Alex. "Jase, it's the concert."

"They want us to call it off?"

"No. They say you can't."

"Huh?" Confusion was all that registered with Jason. His mind raced with a million questions. The kidnappers *knew* the band couldn't perform. Not without Max. Sure, he'd been reluctant to postpone, but only because he was counting on getting Max back in time. But if playing the concert was a prerequisite to his release . . . it didn't make any sense.

The detective across the table from Alex and Julie motioned for Jason and Tara to sit. By this time, the female detective had caught up with them as well. "We have a lot to discuss," she said, exchanging a brief glance with her partner as she slipped into a seat beside him.

"What exactly are they demanding?" Tara asked.

The male detective cleared his throat and, as usual, took his time in answering. "The note we received asks that you maintain the façade of proceeding with Thursday night's concert as planned. However, your band is not to perform. The perps intend to provide a video message from Max to air for your fans and on your social media. If you obey, they claim he will be returned unharmed."

Alex's voice was soft and serious. "That message isn't really from Max, is it?"

"Most likely, no."

"And if we don't obey?" Tara asked.

"The note says there will be consequences."

The mood in the room was turning somber, for reasons Jason couldn't quite place. To him, the news could hardly have been better. One video. That's all they wanted. "Fine," he said, his mind made up. "We keep the show, air their stupid video, and get Max back. Easy."

The detectives exchanged another look, and this time it fell to the female detective to speak. "These demands may not tell the whole story. It's entirely possible our perps have no intention of releasing their hostage, whether or not their message airs."

"But they told us what they want—"

"And if you give it to them, you endanger the lives of thousands of civilians," the female detective replied firmly. "For whatever reason, this concert seems to be a flashpoint for these individuals. We have no way of knowing that their plans end with the airing of the message. An attack of some kind seems entirely possible at this point."

Now some of Alex and Tara's worry began to register with Jason, but he refused to let it take over. "So, what's the alternative?" he demanded. "Letting them kill Max?"

"Sir, I understand your concern. That said, the consequences are unspecified in the note. This leaves open the possibility that our perps have not committed to resorting to violence against your friend."

"Well, *I'm* committed to making sure they don't," Jason replied defiantly. He folded his arms across his chest. "Increase security, or whatever. We're not cancelling the concert."

He looked to Tara and Alex, sure that they, too, would see that it was the only option. But instead of nods of agreement, he was met with the same dejected expressions. "What?" he demanded. "I'm not letting them hurt Max."

"What about us, though?" Tara asked. "Our safety, our reputation. If we air that video, who knows how it makes us sound. Our careers could be over."

"Max's *life* could be over!"

"I know," Tara whispered miserably.

"And that could happen anyway." Alex's voice was barely audible, swallowed up with worry. "Jase, I get what you're saying, but I don't know. . . ."

"Well, at least don't call it off *now*!" Jason could hear the desperation in his own voice as he turned back to the cops. "We still have two days."

The female detective nodded. "That was going to be my next point. Even supposing you need a full day's notice to cancel, that leaves us roughly thirty-six hours to continue our investigation while appearing to comply with the perps' demands."

"Good. So keep investigating."

"I assure you we have every intention of doing so."

"That said," the male detective interjected, "our leads in this case are . . . limited, and thirty-six hours is not a lot of time. You need to be prepared to cancel."

"Yeah, sure," Jason muttered, already forcing that possibility from his mind. An entirely different set of preparations had taken over his attention. The cops might not have much to go on—and the break-in and GPS trail were too damning for him to fill them in—but his resolve to find Max himself was only growing stronger.

Tara gave Jason a disapproving look, silently urging a more convincing show of agreement. "Okay," he said. "If no one's found Max by tomorrow night, then sure, we'll cancel."

"Tomorrow night," Tara repeated, eyeing Jason all the while. "It's not a lot of time."

"No," he agreed, returning her stare. From her expression, he knew she understood. "But a lot can happen between now and then."

Chapter 14

The sun slanted low, growing redder and redder in the western sky as Jason sped along I-64 and began the long, slow climb up Afton Mountain for the second time that day. Patchy snow lingered on the ground, only partially melted by the afternoon sun. For what felt like the hundredth time, he ran through a mental list of his supplies, hoping nothing had been forgotten.

Even as he tried to focus, he couldn't shake the memory of that morning's confrontation with Tara. After the conversation with the police, tempers had flared, and though they'd reached a resolution before he departed, Jason found himself still trying to make sense of all that had been said.

"No way," Tara had declared, eyeing him with a disapproving look. They had been sitting on opposite sides of his kitchen table, sipping coffee over the remains of breakfast when he'd made the apparently unforgivable mistake of suggesting they drive up the mountain and each search one of the areas Alex had identified on the map. "That was not the plan."

"What are you talking about?" he'd replied. "It was always the plan. We found the cabins, now we go find Max."

"Nooo . . ." Tara drew the word out, "*we* were never planning to go up on that mountain. *You* were."

"Nooo . . ." Jason matched her tone, "we both were."

Tara shook her head. "I'm not going. This idea is beyond reckless and risking your life for it is bad enough."

Jason heard the finality in her statement, but stubbornness took over and he blurted out, "Of course I'd risk my life for Max.

And honestly, I'm pissed you don't feel the same way."

There was a brief silence in which only the rustling of a paper takeout bag could be heard as Alex and Julie busied themselves with staying out of the conversation.

"This isn't about how I *feel*, Jason." Now Tara's tone was icy, her eyes narrowed into a scowl. "Think about it for a moment. *You* going up there is one thing, but what's going to happen to someone who looks like me?"

"I think you're making too big a deal of—"

"Oh no." She cut him off. "Remember what we know about these guys. About why we think they went after Max. If they see me up there, I get shot."

"And you think I wouldn't?" His voice had risen as he spoke. "Of course I'd fucking get shot, but that's a risk I'm willing to take."

"I know. So, *you* take that risk. I'm sorry, I don't see how getting more of us killed helps anything!"

"Obviously it doesn't, but that's not the plan!"

"And what a well-thought-out plan it is!"

"Better than anything the cops have going!"

From there, the debate had devolved into a shouting match. Jason couldn't remember much of what had been said, just his sense that Tara was being selfish and refusing to play her part in the obvious next step toward finding Max. He knew what she was getting at, even knew she could be right about facing a different set of dangers, but past a certain point, what did it matter? Danger was danger, and they could at least face it together.

Finally they had reached a tipping point—what turned out to be the central point of the argument, in fact—as Jason's exasperation spilled over into the anger he'd been feeling all along, but had been scared to confront head-on.

"Do you even care about him, Tara?" he'd blurted out, "Really, I mean, why'd you put up with Max all these years if this is how much you care?"

An eerie silence came over the room, displacing the cacophony of their argument. He saw just the slightest quiver of her lower lip as she quietly, coldly replied, "Jase, don't do this."

"No, I want to know," he insisted. "Why? Why'd you even stick around?"

He could tell he'd struck a nerve. Tara's eyes narrowed into a glare. "Jason, that man means the world to me, and it makes me sick to think I might not ever see him again." Now she paused, drawing in a deep breath. "I can't believe you're asking me this right now. I have so much respect for Max and you're acting like . . . I don't even know. It's ridiculous."

"You . . . respect him?" Tara's statement had caught Jason off guard and the words slipped from his mouth before he knew what he was saying.

"Yes, I fucking respect him," Tara shot back, irritation coloring her tone once again. "That doesn't mean he doesn't frustrate the hell out of me from time to time." After a moment's consideration, she added, "You too, by the way."

"Yeah, well, you've got a funny way of showing it," Jason muttered, straightening out of a defensive posture he hadn't even realized he'd assumed. "You talk about Max like he's this obnoxious kid and you're about to bail on us the first chance you get."

Tara's response was immediate, and surprisingly firm. "This past year should have made it pretty clear. I'm not going to bail on you." As she eyed Jason, her expression shifted into a scowl, "Where would I go?"

Jason had stifled a laugh. He knew they were getting side-tracked, but he didn't care. "Like you haven't had other offers? Tara, you're a fucking incredible drummer. There must be a dozen bands out there trying to steal you from us *right now.*"

She shook her head ever so slightly. "No."

"What do you mean, 'no'?"

"I mean, no, I haven't had other offers." She leaned back, folding her arms across her chest as she continued. "Not serious ones, anyway, now or ever. And that says it all. It's why I respect Max and the opportunity he gave me. At this point, even if something did come up, I wouldn't take it."

"I don't get it," Jason said, still not seeing what any of this had to do with Max, but too baffled not to wonder. "No one's ever tried to get you to ditch us?" He'd been solicited by a number of other bands since news of the hiatus broke—not that he would ever leave Max—and even if he flattered himself, his talent wasn't anywhere near as impressive as hers.

"Jesus, Jase, a little awareness of your own genre? How many Black women have you seen in a punk band?"

"I—I mean, I don't know," he stammered, for some reason

flustered by her question. "I never thought about it."

Tara nodded knowingly. "Yeah, exactly." She paused. "I just get the sense Max *did* think about it."

Jason nodded. It was yet another item on an endless list of things he'd never thought about, chief among them Tara's feelings about Max and the band. Her statements of loyalty were reassuring, but it unsettled him to realize just how differently they felt about the man who had united them, both musically and on their current quest. Tara's respect for Max, as she called it, sounded professional, almost impersonal, and Jason struggled to imagine anything that could feel *more* personal than an attack on his best friend in the world.

"I . . . I don't know," Jason had fumbled for words once again as he attempted to bring their conversation full circle. "I'd do *anything* to get Max back—"

"I know." Tara cut him off firmly before he could muster another halfhearted accusation. They both knew what he was going to say next, and that it wasn't going to lead anywhere. Now, in retrospect, Jason was grateful to Tara for ending that discussion before it could take another unpleasant turn. "You do what you have to do. I'm here to help," she said, "but by that I mean *here*, not out on that Goddamn mountain."

Jason had nodded, accepting the uneasy truce. And Tara's offer to help had proven genuine. Once again, she took charge of the whiteboard, jotting notes and drawing Alex and Julie back into the conversation as they began to plan his search.

It *was* his search alone, a feeling that hadn't bothered Jason as he set out in the bright midday sun, his car skimming through slushy puddles on the way up the mountain. The beginning of the adventure had felt like a breath of fresh air; for the first time all week, he was setting out with even the slightest chance of finding Max.

Of course, the hopefulness of his expedition had drained away as quickly as it began. After half an hour's hike, he'd encountered the cabin Alex identified from the satellite images. But one cabin turned out to be several—a clustered campground, deserted for the winter, if not long since. He'd returned home riled up with a new rush of frantic energy that sent him scrambling to prepare for a second outing, even as Tara and Alex cautioned against a search that would stretch into the night.

"I can't waste any time," he'd insisted. The hours he'd once had for this search were quickly evaporating, and he couldn't stand the thought of losing an entire long winter night to sitting and waiting.

Now he could feel the car's engine straining as the incline grew steeper, and he watched the first of many vehicles zip past. He patiently downshifted into fourth and felt the car spring forward, engine roaring just to keep pace with the eighteen-wheeler up ahead.

Food, water, sleeping bag, cell phone, flashlight, knife. Jason silently repeated the list once more, casting a glance toward the passenger seat to see how many of his supplies he could account for while driving. It was a more robust set of preparations than his earlier search had necessitated, but even so, he couldn't shake the feeling he'd forgotten something.

He hadn't taken the decision to set out at night as lightly as Tara and Alex seemed to think; with the cancellation deadline looming, it was the only option. It felt like he was the only one who could find the cabin in time. He was going to find it. He had to.

Atop the mountain, the sign for Exit 99 swept into view, and Jason clicked on his turn signal before easing onto the ramp. He slowed the car to a sedate pace, mindful that up here at elevation, the snow lay in deeper drifts. The roads had been wet but easily passable in the bright afternoon sunlight, but as darkness approached, he knew they would turn icy within a matter of hours.

Turning south this time, he saw that the gate was down, blocking traffic from entering the Blue Ridge Parkway for the winter. He was unphased; the parallel state route was his preferred path anyway.

In among the densely clustered bare trees, the approach of night was even more palpable. He illuminated the car's headlights and slowed to a steady crawl along the mountain ridge, watching for icy patches along the road.

Jason had committed the route to memory, knowing better than to rely on a GPS signal this far out of town. Still, every few seconds, he found himself glancing down at the unchanged odometer, worried about missing the upcoming turn—quite literally—off the beaten path.

Finally, the correct mileage ticked into view and Jason surveyed the roadside for the opening in the woods that Alex's careful map reading told him would be here. They'd pored over the satellite images, trying to pin down an identifying feature that marked the turn onto the gravel road—the *private* road, Tara had been quick to point out—but the street view photos had been taken mid-summer, and the best Jason could do was slow down and look for a break in the wall of trees.

Sure enough, an opening presented itself. Jason felt a slight shakiness in his hands, and a flash of paranoia prevented him from clicking on his turn signal as he eased the car off the pavement. He downshifted all the way to first as his tires sank into the snow, but even in its old age, the Subaru was reliable on unplowed roads. As the engine surged, he felt the tires gripping the snowy ground.

"Okay," Jason whispered aloud, bringing the car to a stop. He reversed, testing out his traction, and stopped once again without a hint of a slip. The road was passable. Now it was just a question of how far he could go.

He could still hear Tara's voice clearly in his mind. "Do *not* go on private roads!" she'd protested, just as he and Alex were closing in on a plan of how to reach this particular cabin.

Jason had swallowed his comeback, trying to manage something more civil for the sake of the peace they'd only just restored. "Pretty sure I have to," he replied, looking to Alex for support.

Alex, as usual, had hesitated. "You don't *have* to," he began slowly, shifting his gaze from Jason to Tara, "but, if I'm reading this map correctly, the closest public road access is miles away. And on the other side of the ridge."

Tara frowned. "Seriously? That far?"

"I don't mind hiking, but I'm not going over the mountain," Jason declared, shaking his head. "Look, at least this one has a road."

Tara shifted uncomfortably in her seat. "A private road. I don't like it."

"You'll like it when I drive up to the cabin, grab Max, and make it home in time for dinner." The words felt over-confident leaving his lips, and Jason could tell Tara was itching to call him on it, but it was Alex who spoke next.

"I wouldn't do that, either."

Jason had shot a skeptical look in his direction. "Why not? I'm trespassing anyway."

"Yes . . ." Alex drew the word out, "but you don't want to announce it. What are you going to do if the kidnappers hear you coming?"

Jason could read the answer forming on Tara's lips, not that he needed to. "Get shot, probably," he muttered.

"Right," Alex agreed. "Don't do that." He paused, thinking. "Your car doesn't run too quietly these days, does it?"

Jason shook his head. "C'mon, man, you know the Subaru is old enough to drive itself."

Alex nodded, but his attention was already elsewhere, and he motioned for Tara to slide the whiteboard in his direction. A moment later he was hunched over it, jotting numbers and symbols and muttering both to himself and to Julie, who nodded answers to his unspoken questions and supplied numbers in a cryptic little back-and-forth.

Jason barely had time to wonder what they were working on before Alex's head shot back up. "Point-six-four kilometers."

"Point *what*?"

"Point-six-four kilometers," Alex repeated, pointing to the corner of the board where he'd boxed the final answer to several rows of neatly stacked equations: 0.64 km. "That's how far away you need to leave your car if you don't want them to hear you coming."

Jason and Tara each leaned over the board, adopting expressions of concentration as they tried to make sense of what Alex had written, but to Jason's eyes at least, the pile of numbers and letters was incomprehensible. It was like waking up halfway through a math lecture in high school and having no idea where to even begin his attempt at taking notes. Tara looked similarly lost. "You're gonna have to explain," she said.

"Right." Alex was unphased. "So, sounds get quieter the farther away from them you are. Six decibels quieter every time you double the distance, to be exact. I made some assumptions about Jase's car and the level of ambient noise, and there you go." He tapped his answer with the back of the whiteboard marker. "Point-six-four kilometers."

"That's how close I can get to the cabin?" Jason asked.

Alex nodded.

"And, uh, what is that in miles?"

"Less than half a mile," Alex replied, catching Julie's eye as a shared half smile flickered across their faces. "I knew you kept an engineer around for a reason."

"Yeah, uh, thanks, man," Jason replied hurriedly. The thought clicked in his head. Engineering. That was what Alex was studying. Julie, too, he could only assume from the way she'd leapt in to help.

Less than half a mile to hike had sounded comfortable, but a closer look at the topography provided a harsh reality check. According to the online maps, the private road meandered through the woods for about a mile before twisting into a series of increasingly steep switchback turns.

"You'll have to leave the car here," Alex had explained, indicating a point on the map just under two miles' drive short of the cabin.

Jason scowled. "What? You said half a mile."

"Half a mile as the crow flies. Sound travels in a straight line." Alex gave a small apologetic shrug. "Just physics, sorry."

Now physics seemed to be working against Jason's car, too. The traction he had found just off of the main road was giving way to deeper snowdrifts, and he found himself gripping the steering wheel tighter and tighter as the car alternately slipped and plunged ahead. Even worse, the light was fading quickly, and his eyes were already straining.

It had been years since Jason had navigated unplowed roads, and he could tell his winter driving skills were rusty. "Don't panic," he whispered aloud. "Nice and steady." Even as he said the words, the next slip sent his heart leaping into his throat. The car sank into a slushy patch and lurched violently into a skidding engine roar.

"Okay," Jason whispered, letting out a tense breath as he eased the car to a stop and weighed his options. He was sure the car could make it closer to the cabin, but with each slip he grew less and less certain of its ability to make it back out. No need to be reckless, he told himself, not when he was this close and well prepared with his stash of supplies. He'd turn the car around and hike from here.

The snow made it difficult to judge the width of the gravel road, and Jason's paranoia about getting his tires stuck in icy mud turned what should have been a three-point turn into nearly a dozen tentative, lurching segments. But at last the Subaru was facing the main road, ready to retrace its own tracks for what he could only hope would be a less dramatic return trip.

Jason tried to calm the shaking in his hands as he withdrew the key from the ignition, but his adrenaline was surging already, and for all the wrong reasons. He took his time stowing his spare key in the glove compartment; if he lost his key in the woods, at least he could break a window and still drive home. And now he knew better than to waste time punching the glass.

He gave his phone a last hopeful glance before setting off, and a new message from Alex sprang to his attention: "Hope you see this in time. Police can't find the victim's truck: black Ford. I'm wondering if his partner has it?"

The lead was a good one, and it grounded Jason immediately. His hands were steady as he began typing out a reply of thanks, only to find he had no reception. He hesitated before pocketing the device; if he was already beyond the range of cell service, there was no hope of sending or receiving messages from the cabin. But it felt like a waste to leave it in the car. He zipped the phone into one jacket pocket and his Swiss army knife and flashlight into the other.

Jason paused to take stock of his new plan as he stepped out of the car. He hadn't wanted to carry much on foot, and had only packed the sleeping bag, water, and granola bars in case he needed to spend the night in his car. But now, with the road impassable and a longer hike ahead, he wasn't sure what he might need.

It's still only a few miles, he told himself, taking a long gulp of the water before returning the bottle to the car. He was sure it would be fine, quick even. It had to be.

But even a short hike could prove challenging in the snow. Jason felt like he could barely move, layered up with two pairs of socks stiffening his ankles in his hiking boots and his winter coat zipped tight over a sweatshirt and flannel shirt. *We couldn't have done this in April?* he mused as he slammed and locked the car door before pocketing his key.

He set off along the road at first, promising himself he'd take any shortcut he could find once the switchbacks up the mountain began. He was barely out of view of his car when the darkness really settled in, its presence like a heavy blanket thrown over the land. Pausing only to pull out his flashlight, Jason pressed on, equally hopeful and fearful of what lay ahead.

Chapter 15

TUESDAY, 7:15 P.M.

Jason's muscles were burning as he strained against the snowdrifts and rocky terrain. He'd abandoned the road some time ago, convincing himself a straighter path up the mountain would be faster, though he was feeling less and less sure his gamble would pay off.

The exertion was enough to break through the chill of the frosty night air that stung his exposed face but was refreshing to breathe. He had long since worked up a sweat, and wished he'd brought his water, at least. But he had to be close by now.

Jason tried to focus on the climb, to not lose track of a single footfall and risk an icy tumble down the mountain, but his mind kept wandering. All he could think about was Max, what he would say when—not if, but *when*—he found him. He could see himself storming heroically into the cabin, taking down the remaining kidnapper with the swing of a fist or some improvised weapon, freeing Max from whatever dungeon they'd trapped him in, and—

And he didn't have an answer for what came next. That was where the fantasy always cut out, him appearing by Max's side and not knowing what to say.

It was a familiar feeling, one he'd experienced most acutely the December morning after Max called to announce the end of the hiatus. That call had left him with both nothing and everything to say, adding a layer of uneasiness to his anticipation of their reunion.

He'd awakened that morning to the buzz of an incoming text, having slept with his cell phone under his pillow on the off chance that Max would call back later. As it was, they had talked until well past midnight, but Jason had been determined not to miss any calls or texts once the line of communication had been reopened. And indeed, it was barely nine o'clock as a new message rolled in.

Yawning, Jason had swiped the message open, then done a double take at the words on the screen: "Buzz me in. It's freezing out here." His stomach fluttered with a rush of nerves, but he was out of bed in an instant, on his way over to the call box. *It's not true*, he told himself, trying to subdue a surge of hope. *Max wouldn't. He's not actually here.*

But there he was in the doorway a minute later, smiling shyly and carrying a white takeout bag Jason recognized immediately.

"You brought *bagels* to New York?"

In the moment, it was the only thing that had popped into his head, and that was how he had greeted his best friend, the person he'd spent the past six months dying to see. Making fun of him for bringing breakfast all the way from Charlottesville.

Max didn't seem to mind. "I got your usual," he replied, his smile broadening into a grin. His face was flushed with cold, and his hair, longer than he typically let it grow, had been teased in all directions by the gusty winds that Jason had heard howling through the night. But he looked like himself, dressed not for New York but for a Virginia winter in a flannel and jeans, and was just shaking off the morning chill as he stood in the doorway. He hesitated for a second, as if he, too, were searching for what to say. And then any pretense of talking fell away as he threw his arms around Jason, clapping him hard across the shoulder blades. "I missed you, man."

"I missed you, too."

There had been something desperate in the tight squeeze of Max's embrace, something that made Jason suspect he was trying to convey a message that words had failed.

As they parted, even through the lingering smile, Jason could see something more restrained, more subdued about Max. In manner, though, he was still himself, already headed for the couch with the bag of bagels, motioning for Jason to follow as if he—in his own home—were the one awaiting an invitation.

At first, they had eaten in silence, and Jason found himself darting glances in Max's direction every few seconds. "I'm not dreaming?" he asked finally. "You're really here? We're really coming back?"

Max had nodded, his expression serious. "Tara still needs some convincing, but I sent her sheet music this morning. And some tour dates I may or may not have started looking into."

"Tour dates?"

The somber expression had dissolved, and Max was smiling again, looking rather pleased with himself. "Hear me out: I wrote a love song for Charlottesville, so obviously, Valentine's Day weekend at home, and then . . . I don't know, we hit the road in March?"

"Insane," Jason had replied, shaking his head. "Absolutely insane." But he was grinning, too. And then the words had started spilling out, as he wanted to ask Max anything and everything, but most of all where the past six months had gone. And why he'd spent them alone.

"We should talk about that," Max said quietly. He suddenly seemed to be avoiding eye contact, and was at an uncharacteristic loss for words. The weighty silence tightened Jason's throat and had him on the verge of backpedaling, apologizing, doing whatever he could to chase away the darkness that had clouded Max's expression.

But after a moment's consideration, Max had continued, "I'll tell you everything." He looked up again. "I promise I will . . . but let's just enjoy this, okay?"

Jason had managed an uneasy nod, then a genuine, "Yeah," as the slightest flicker of a smile returned to Max's face. He didn't know whether Max was referring to the breakfast or the tour—not that it mattered. None of it mattered, as long as Max was really back.

A more approachable question came to Jason, and he blurted it out, eager to move on from the serious moment. "How'd you even get up here? You were in Virginia last night."

"I was. In the one corner of my house that gets a decent cell signal, to be exact."

"You're avoiding the question."

"Oh." One of Max's signature smirks was forming. He reached into his pocket, withdrew an all-too-familiar set of keys, and placed them on the table between them. "I kind of stole your car."

"You did *not* just put another five hundred miles on the Subaru!"

"Oh, definitely not. Four hundred at most."

From there, it had devolved into the sort of serious-but-not-serious fight that only happens between longtime best friends, Jason demanding to know why neither of the cars Max kept in Virginia would do, and why he couldn't have caught an early-morning flight instead. Max bore it all, shooting back increasingly snarky answers about his last-second planning.

Finally, a thought clicked in Jason's head that brought the whole web of excuses crashing down. "You drove all night—you bought the bagels yesterday! Before you even called me! You *knew* you were coming up here!"

Max had shrugged sheepishly. "Guilty." With a smile, he added, "You mad?"

"No." Jason's reply was immediate and sincere. *How could I be anything other than happy to see you?*

Now, Jason longed to recreate that feeling, that ease with which he and Max had reunited. But it seemed impossible. His rescue mission was guaranteed to hit snags, and even if he envisioned it going perfectly, there was no telling what their conversation would become. He hadn't lied to the police; Max really had been acting more like his usual self lately, but still holding back the way he had been in December, and Jason couldn't help but worry that Max would have retreated further by the time he arrived.

And if he hadn't been willing to open up about the hiatus before, Jason could only imagine the resistance any questions would be met with now. *It doesn't matter*, he reminded himself. *This isn't about the past. It's about getting Max home now.*

With that, he leapt into a quick scramble for what appeared to be a small plateau up ahead, but a lapse in concentration and loss of balance sent him slipping, and he fell to his hands and knees. His feet clawed at the snowy ground but found no traction, and he felt himself sliding backward. His foot struck a tree trunk, sent him spinning, coasting on top of the snow, and he was another twenty or thirty feet down the mountain by the time he regained control and shakily recovered his footing.

"Shit," Jason cursed, easing his way to his feet. He'd lost a lot of ground, and a new danger was suddenly more real in his mind: what if he slipped again as he neared the cabin? He was painfully aware of every sound he made, the crunching of snow and leaves underfoot, the rustling of his coat as he moved, the laboring of his breath. Any one of them could be a dead giveaway.

He adopted a more cautious approach, zigzagging his path as he climbed. He regretted giving up on the road so soon. If only he hadn't been so stubborn, so sure he could find a shortcut, he would have been at the cabin by now. Now, without the road to guide him, was he even sure he'd find it?

But with no other options, Jason could only keep climbing. He was barely past the site of his earlier fall when a noise made him jump. A distinctly human noise. A voice. He surged ahead in the direction of the sound, crested a small rocky outcrop, and had to pull up suddenly as the faintly illuminated sketch of a house came into view. He rushed to extinguish his flashlight and crouched behind a tree, waiting breathlessly for a look of suspicion or flashlight beam to be cast in his direction. Nothing.

He could just make out the figure of a man, moving purposefully in the vicinity of the cabin. As he watched, the man paused by what appeared to be a back door, stomped the snow from his boots, and went inside.

Jason's heart was racing, his mind filled once more with images of his heroic entrance and reunion with Max.

Is it even the right cabin, though? The thought weighed on Jason as he crept toward the house, pausing behind every tree wide enough to shield him from view. He suspected he was still cloaked in darkness from the perspective of anyone inside, but didn't want to risk it, especially if a loud footfall drew unwelcome attention. *Who else would be out here in February?* It felt too coincidental to find another occupied cabin this far up the mountain on a snowy night, but he had to be sure.

Alex's text about the truck entered his thoughts with renewed importance. It wasn't a sure thing, but if that truck happened to be up here. . . .

He scanned the scene, searching for signs of a vehicle, only to realize he'd arrived on the opposite side of the cabin from the road.

Careful not to draw too close, he began to trace a semi-circle toward the drive. He felt like he was moving blindly with only the glow from the cabin's windows and the moon overhead, its silvery light fragmented by the treetops all around. His heart raced as his hopes surged; he had to restrain himself from breaking into a sprint for the door. But he couldn't afford to leave tracks so close to the cabin—not yet. He had come too far to make such a reckless mistake.

Finally, Jason's feet crunched on snowy gravel, partially cleared by a series of boot tracks. He could just make out a dark mass interrupting his view of the illuminated windows. He'd have to get closer. Now he did run, a light, eager jog with cautious footfalls, and stowed himself behind the vehicle—definitely a truck, he could tell that much—before drawing out his flashlight once more. Glossy black paint sent the beam scattering in all directions, and he hurriedly guided the light to the center of the tailgate . . . and the familiar blue Ford logo.

He had found them.

Oh my God. The words caught in Jason's throat as he turned the flashlight off and returned it to his pocket. Instinctively, he grabbed his knife, held it cradled in his gloved palm as he tried to process what it all meant. *Max is inside.*

I need a plan I need a plan I need a plan. The thought pounded in Jason's head as he rose to his feet and retreated to the cover of the woods. He drew out his phone to check the time, only to find its screen dark and unresponsive in the cold. At least one occupant of the cabin was clearly awake, but without knowing the time, it was impossible to even guess for how much longer.

Moving more quickly, Jason continued his wide arc around the cabin, now on the uphill side. The higher ground afforded him a slightly better view, but he still wished he could see more. He'd spied the front door on his loop of the property, but that was no use; with a hostage inside, there was no way the man would leave it unguarded through the night. The back door could be more promising, but if the man had other partners, what was to say it wouldn't be guarded as well?

There must be another way, Jason thought. His path was leveling off, beginning to slope back down toward where he began his circle, and so far he'd come up empty. Small cabin, two stories, front and back doors. That was all he knew.

He was almost back to where he'd first spied the cabin when he saw it—a distinct interruption in the roofline. He squinted, trying to convince himself he could just make out the faint glow of a window—no, larger than a window—a sliding glass door. It had to be a second-story deck, facing down the mountain and no doubt offering stunning views of the valley opening up to the west.

He knew immediately. That would be his entry point; he just had to figure out how.

Chapter 16

Spotting the deck was one thing; figuring out how to get up there was quite another. Jason hurried toward the cabin, ducking from tree to tree in case his movements could be seen from inside. He wished he still had the benefit of his flashlight, but it was far too risky this close to the house. Now he lurked among the closest few trees, only about twenty feet away. He hardly dared breathe as he pressed up against a broad tree trunk.

As he peered around the side of the tree, Jason's hand met something metal protruding from the trunk. He hesitated, fumbling blindly until both hands closed on a horizontal bar. He felt above it, found another. *A ladder?* Sure enough, higher up, he found a third rung, and, pausing only to pocket his knife, he felt for a foothold, heaved himself up, and began to climb.

The ladder had been mounted on the side of the tree farthest from the house, and Jason felt confident he couldn't be seen as he made his ascent. He was moving by feel, unable to see where the ladder was leading him. The treads of his hiking boots were packed with snow and provided almost no traction on the slick metal rungs, forcing him to cling tightly with both hands. By the time he reached the top and realized where he was, his forearms were burning and he was breathing heavily once again.

The ladder ended at a high fork in the tree, and as Jason stepped onto a wooden platform barely wide enough for his boots, the thought finally clicked in his mind. *It's a tree stand.* Of course a cabin like this one would have a nearby hunting perch; it was just unexpected to find one so close by. Maybe the house was so rarely occupied that animals were no longer wary of approaching.

Now he was nearly level with the roofline of the cabin. By facing the tree and peering through the space enclosed by the forking branches he could see the deck clearly. His plan was looking even better from his new vantage point. The room into which the doors opened was lit only dimly by the light that floated up from the story below. If he timed it right, he could have the second floor to himself and wait in silence for the lights to go out.

Jason's first thought was the ladder. Maybe there was a way to free it from the tree and climb up onto the deck. He quickly ruled that out, though, realizing he had neither the tools nor the time to disconnect the ladder, assuming it would even release its years-old grip on the trunk. *I'm already up here*, he thought, eyeing the plane of the deck some twenty feet away but only five or six feet below where he stood. *If only there were a way to get . . . over.*

His eyes shot up to the branches. One continued nearly straight up, but the other . . . the other curved and leveled out invitingly in the direction of the house. If he followed it, that would cut the distance in half at least, and from there. . . .

The idea was still incomplete in Jason's mind as he started to climb, pulling himself up hand-over-hand until he crouched on all fours atop the sloping branch. He inhaled deeply, willing himself not to look down, though in the darkness he wouldn't have been able to judge the distance to the snowy ground below.

Inch by inch, he eased his way along the branch. As it leveled out, he realized it extended closer to the house than he had initially judged. But it was growing thinner, too, down to a width of about six inches where he found himself perched.

The deck was enticingly close now; just a few more feet and he would be practically on top of it. Or so he told himself. But he could feel the branch beginning to sag under his weight, and he knew he had no choice but to make his move. Slowly, carefully, he drew his feet up underneath him, readying for a leap.

What am I thinking? A wave of fear washed over Jason. If he aimed to land inside the railing, he would have to cover eight feet or so of horizontal distance, and a slightly greater vertical drop. It was doable. Not ideal, but doable. He checked the stability of his footing, hoping to give himself the best push-off, and—

Crack.

The sound was unmistakable. Jason felt it more than heard it, whirling in panic just as the branch lurched beneath him. There was no time for thought, only motion. He scrambled to heave himself from the collapsing limb, pushing off of what felt like equal parts tree and air as he hurtled toward the deck.

The deck grew closer, closer, closer, as if in slow motion, and Jason willed himself to reach farther, to somehow cover that last critical distance.

Impact was dizzying, a blow to the gut that knocked the wind out of him. He grabbed blindly, anxiously, for anything to hold onto as he felt himself slipping. He'd landed on the railing of the deck but was on the verge of sliding straight off. In his breathless desperation, he managed to hook his hands over the top of the railing, and hung for a moment, panting and wheezing, before kicking out, searching for a foothold to ease the burden on his burning forearms.

Just breathe, Jason told himself. The shock of impact was fading, and he focused on drawing deeper breaths, the chill night air filling his lungs with the force of a sucker punch. Finally, the toe of his boot caught on the protruding edge of the deck, and he swung upward to stand, still outside the railing, but anchored by both feet.

Jason stood there for a few moments, still gasping for air as he tried to take stock of the situation. He would know soon enough whether or not his arrival on the deck had been detected. In either case, he needed a plan. He couldn't afford to be spotted from the ground if someone inside decided to investigate the fallen branch. His breathing was becoming steadier but not quite controlled, and he felt vaguely bruised; he was relieved not to feel the stab of pain that would have meant a broken rib, or worse.

Holding tight to the railing with his right hand, Jason reached into his pocket and withdrew the Swiss army knife once more. He wasn't sure how he'd defend himself, but it felt better to be armed in some small respect. The heft of the knife in his hand was reassuring, yet small enough to not slow his motion as he raised himself up on both hands and swung his left leg over the railing and—

Blinding light filled his field of vision, and he could hear the swish of a door sliding open and the pounding of heavy footsteps running toward him. Caught off-balance, Jason heaved himself into the frenzy of light and sound, fighting to land among the feet on the deck and make his first strike—only to collide abruptly with some unseen force that shoved him back and sent him free-falling, frantically grasping for the railing once again.

This time, he didn't catch it.

He didn't remember landing, just a flash of burning red pain that overwhelmed his vision and the coppery taste of blood stinging his tongue. He cried out as the agony resolved itself to his right shoulder, and flailed desperately to roll over and unpin it from the icy ground. A wave of nausea struck as he righted himself. Cradling his injured arm, he crouched on his knees, his head lowered to the ground to hold the spinning world in place.

Through the haze of pain, Jason heard a man's voice shout, "I'll keep watch. You go get him."

And the reply, "Think he's armed?"

"Make sure he ain't."

Run. Go. Get out of here. The words pounded urgently in Jason's mind, but motion wouldn't come to his dazed limbs. He tried to shift his feet, to at least scramble into the darkness beyond the trees, but every movement sent a bolt of pain coursing through his body. A new realization cemented itself in his mind. He was about to be captured.

Jason felt himself shaking with the furious cocktail of adrenaline and pain, but tried to focus. They'd take his phone, his knife, and then what? A frantic idea popped into his head and he released his hold on his injured arm, letting out an involuntary wail even as he tried to ignore the shockwave of agony. He'd held onto to his knife through the fall, and now made a desperate reach to shove it into his boot. It took all of his remaining strength to wedge it along the inside of his ankle, hopefully out of sight and beyond the imagination of anyone who would empty his pockets.

The effort came just in time, for a moment later, a man's boots appeared at his side. "Hey! You!" He felt a prod in the back and nearly cried out again. "Get up, asshole!" the man shouted. "I'm talking to you." Jason heard the click of a gun being cocked and his stomach churned as he realized it was a barrel pressed against his back.

"Okay," he choked out, "I'm getting up, I promise."

"You hurt or something?" The question was accompanied by a harsher jab in the back that sent Jason sprawling, writhing in pain as he clutched at his shoulder. "Well, fuck, I'll get you up myself then," the man decided, and the next thing Jason knew, he was being lifted roughly, pulled to his feet by the back of his coat. He swayed unsteadily, still woozy, and stumbled as he was shoved ahead into the unknown.

Chapter 17

"Who the fuck is this?" The man's voice was incredulous as he looked Jason over. His partner had flung Jason down on a wooden bench just inside the door of the cabin, and continued to aim a shotgun in his general direction.

"I'm—I'm just—" Jason gasped for words, still dizzy and half blinded by pain.

The man with the gun cut him off. "I reckon he's our little friend's boyfriend, don't you?"

"Oh yeah?" The first man now squatted close, peering into Jason's face. He was tall, heavyset, and at close range, his breath reeked of alcohol and cigarettes, but that was all Jason could make out in his compromised state. "Sounds about right, don't it?" The man straightened up and turned to his partner. "You check his pockets?"

"Ain't got much. Flashlight, car key, and a dead cell phone."

"There a car outside?"

"Nah. Woulda heard."

"Wonder he made it up here at all."

Jason willed his vision to focus, trying to take in his surroundings, but the brightness of the cabin's interior compounded the effects of his fall, and he could barely distinguish the two forms standing over him. A faint whimper of pain escaped his lips.

"What are we gonna do with you, boy?" the man with the gun asked, giving Jason's feet a hard nudge with his boot. The pocketknife shifted, precariously close to sliding out of Jason's boot.

"We got room," the other man interjected. "Watch him," he instructed. "I'll be right back."

Jason let his head drop back against the wall behind him, wondering if he was going to pass out from the pain. It was unlike anything he had ever experienced in his years of sports and misadventures. *Broken, ruptured, shattered.* The pain was all he could think about, even forcing thoughts of Max from his mind. *I'm useless like this,* he thought. *Maybe they'll see that and let me go.* But even that was only so reassuring; left alone in the woods, he doubted he could make it out.

The second man's return announced itself with the jangling of metal, followed by a hard tug on Jason's uninjured arm and the closing of a handcuff. Jason felt himself being dragged to his feet once again and stumbled hopelessly along, pulled by the left wrist as his right arm dangled limply, searing with pain at every step.

A door creaked open, and Jason was shoved ahead into a musty, stale-smelling space, a small room cloaked in near darkness. He heard the other side of the handcuffs click shut and the slam of the door behind him. Now crouched on the floor, he found himself bolted to a horizontal section of metal pipe protruding from the wall just above his head, unable to move more than a few feet in either direction even if his body had allowed. This was it. He had failed.

Quietly, desperately, he began to sob.

"*Jason?*"

His head shot up, and he immediately had to steady himself. The voice had come from across the small room, and in the dim light he could just discern another human form, seated against the opposite wall, chained up by his right wrist in an identical manner. The young man's face, ghostly pale in the dark, was gaunt, haggard, and streaked with either dirt or blood—but even looking like he'd been through hell, Jason would have known him anywhere. *Max.*

"Oh, thank God!" Jason burst out. "Max, Jesus, I'm so sorry." The tears flowed freely now, and he found he had no more words.

"Man, are you okay?" Max sounded shaken. He stretched out a hand in Jason's direction but came up short, shackled as he was. As Jason sobbed, Max drew in a deep breath and continued.

"You're not okay. What the hell happened out there?"

"I—I came to find you," Jason choked out. "I'm so sorry."

"Whoa, hey, why are you sorry?" Just hearing Max's voice was a reassurance, an unexpected calm in the middle of a nightmare. "I know you came to find me; it sounds crazy, but I knew you would. You're hurt. What happened?"

Jason slowly worked his way to a seated position, resting his injured arm across his lap. "Fuck, man, I almost did it. That stupid fucking tree."

A grin flickered across Max's face. "You went for the deck, didn't you? That's why they ran up there." His expression suddenly darkened. "Oh my God—and you fell."

"Landed on my fucking shoulder," Jason spat.

"Jesus, Jase, it doesn't look good." Max strained against his handcuffs once again, but could only reach to within a foot or so of Jason's outstretched legs. "We've got to get you to a hospital."

"We've got to get *you* home."

Max smiled weakly. "Hey, we're gonna. Don't worry about that." He paused, worry clouding his expression as his attention shifted back to Jason's injury. "Shit," he cursed softly.

Jason's instincts told him to offer a reassurance that he was fine, but through the pain and dizziness he couldn't manage it. There was no point, anyway. Max could read him like a book, and clearly saw how serious it was.

"Try to support it, okay?" Max offered. "We'll get you out of here. I promise."

"Yeah, sure," Jason muttered. He pulled his knees in close and tried to brace his arm against them. He wished he still had the use of his other hand; he strained at his cuffs but found them unyielding.

Max was silent for a few minutes, apparently listening to the sounds of movement beyond the door. Finally, in barely more than a whisper, he said, "God, it's good to see you. They'll be asleep before too long. Then we can talk."

"Please tell me you have a plan."

"Jase, how long have you known me? Of course I have a plan."

"Okay, two things to know about these guys," Max began.

The house had fallen silent at least twenty minutes earlier, and without the benefit of light seeping under the door, he and Jason were immersed in complete darkness. "One, they're heavy sleepers, but two, they wake up early and then it's high alert. I can hear them in and around the house most of the day, so if we're going to get out of here, it has to be at night."

"Sure," Jason agreed. His shoulder continued to throb, but he'd been careful not to move since repositioning himself. As long as he stayed perfectly still, the pain was at a more manageable level.

"Actually," Max said, considering, "I'm not even sure where we are; you might know more about these guys than I do."

"More than the cops, anyway."

Jason could practically feel the smirk on Max's face. "Atta boy."

"We're just on Afton Mountain," Jason said. "I don't know," he continued, "they've been trying to fake us out with notes in Russian, but it's all a mess. One of them accidentally killed their other partner."

"Ah! Okay, that's what they were arguing about the first day."

Jason was astounded by the conversational ease in Max's tone as they rehashed the events surrounding his kidnapping. It was strange; a situation that would have brought out the worst in most people seemed to have energized him. There was a brightness in his voice, an eagerness to talk that had been missing for quite some time.

"These two are no geniuses," Max continued, "and they're in deep on some nasty ideology. We're talking Fox News all day long, and that's not even where they get the worst of it." He froze suddenly. "Oh God. Jase, you didn't air the video, did you?"

"The 'message from you' or whatever? We haven't even seen it."

"Good." Max's voice was firm.

"What—what was it about?"

"Fucking racist bullshit," Max muttered. He was obviously uncomfortable, and Jason would have been willing to let the topic drop. But after a moment's consideration, Max continued. "Look, I get that these are guys whose families have been here forever, and they feel like all of a sudden they're being villainized for being proud of their so-called heritage. But, fuck, man, the things that come out of their mouths . . . the words they put in my mouth . . . it's just ugly."

"We . . ." Jason trailed off guiltily before correcting himself. "Actually, Tara thought that might be what this was about."

"Now they're trying to make *me* the voice of their message. Fuck. We have to get out of here."

"We're gonna."

"I mean it, Jase. No one can ever see that video."

There was a finality in Max's statement that registered with Jason, not that he needed further incentives to make sure their escape was successful. "Okay, then what's the plan?" he asked.

"Right, the plan." Already the solemnity was fading from Max's tone. "When they're asleep it's not exactly high security around here. All we need is a way to get these fucking cuffs off"—Jason heard him pulling against his restraints as he spoke—"and it should be a clear shot to the front door as long as we're quiet. I've been trying to get a sliver of wood from the floor, but getting one solid enough to release the latch—"

"Hold on," Jason interrupted, suddenly feeling stupid. "I think I still have my Swiss on me."

"They didn't search you?"

"They did. It's in my boot. Let me try to get it out." He made a move to reach for his foot with his injured arm, but just raising his hand sent a renewed shock of pain through his body. "Fuck," he muttered. Gingerly, he extended his legs toward Max. "Can you reach? Left boot."

He heard Max straining, invisible in the darkness. After some time, he felt a tug at his shoelace, and he was able to kick his foot free. "Wait," Jason instructed, "let me slide it to you." With his socked foot, he felt for the knife, then sent it skittering across the rough wooden floor.

"Got it."

"Can you still pick a lock with one of those?"

"Of course."

"All right then, get us out of here."

It sounded like Max must have shaken his head. "We can't make that much noise yet. They could still be awake."

"Okay. What's the rest of the plan?"

"Once we get the cuffs off, this door is no problem. Then, ladies and gentlemen, we're free to move about the cabin"—Jason could sense the self-satisfied smirk that accompanied this line—"and as long as we don't wake anyone up, the rest is easy. If we're lucky, they left the keys in the truck. Worst case, it's a footrace, but with darkness on our side." He paused, the optimism draining from his voice. "Oh shit. You can't run like that, can you?"

"Well, I'm fucking gonna try."

Jason heard a faint scrape of metal as Max started searching for the tool he'd use to pick the lock of his handcuffs. "Fuck it, man," Max whispered, "we have to get you taken care of."

It took several minutes, but sure enough, Max worked his way free. "Oh, finally," he whispered. "That thing has been grating the skin off my wrist for three days now." He seemed momentarily distracted by his own success, but a second later appeared by Jason's side, kneeling to inspect the handcuff's connection to the wall. "Let's get you out of there and see how bad this thing is."

Jason could hear the steady rhythm of Max's breathing as he crouched close, working at the small lock until the latch gave way. It took only a fraction of the time he'd needed to free himself. "See, I'm not so bad at this now that I have my right hand back," Max whispered. He hesitated. "Shit. Sorry."

Max rose to his feet as Jason shook his left hand loose from the cuff and cradled his injury once again. "One sec," Max said, stepping across the room. With a soft rasp of metal, the room was abruptly illuminated by a single bare bulb, its pull chain swinging overhead. "I almost forgot there was a light in here. Haven't been able to reach."

Max hurriedly fell to jamming the door crack with the debris available around the small room, mainly scraps of newspaper that had been pressed into service to fill a crack that had opened along the bottom of the single, boarded-up window.

The brightness was startling, but Jason's eyes adjusted, he was relieved to see his friend in greater detail. The past few days had not been kind, but in the light Max looked no worse than Jason suspected he himself did—better, in fact, given his own hasty removal from the deck. The smudges on Max's pale face seemed to just be dirt, and he was moving with most of his usual grace and purpose, despite having been chained in place for the past few days. Evidently satisfied with his work at the door, he stretched, his hands nearly brushing the low ceiling as he extended them, then knelt by Jason's side once again.

"Oh, Jesus," Max whispered, seeing Jason's face contort in

pain. His look of concern sent a knot of worry to Jason's stomach; he didn't dare try to inspect the shoulder himself, dreading what he might find.

Max considered for a moment, looking Jason over. "I hate to do this, but let's try to get your jacket off," he decided. Jason nodded, instinctively trusting him. "You have to promise not to yell."

Max tugged his gloves off and together, they eased Jason's left arm free of the coat, then carefully, inch by inch, managed to work it down his right arm. Jason could taste blood once more, though it might have been from the tight clench of his teeth that prevented him from crying out.

"All right, let's see the patient," Max said softly with a half smile as he knelt by Jason's right side. "I'll be as careful as I can, but shit, man, I think it's bad."

"You think?" Jason shot back, twisting a grimace into a forced smile of his own.

"Give me your hand," Max instructed. Just raising his arm those few inches proved impossible, and Jason resorted to using his left hand to lift his right to meet Max's. "That bad?" Max breathed, sending the knot in Jason's stomach flip-flopping.

Slowly, gently, Max ran his fingers along Jason's arm, starting from his wrist and working his way up toward the shoulder. Through the layers of his shirt and sweatshirt, Jason could barely feel his touch, but it was somehow instantly soothing. All at once he knew he was going to be okay; Max would make sure of that.

As he neared the site of the injury, Max locked eyes with Jason. His look was one of absolute calm. With the lightest touch, he traced over the shoulder, pausing with a look of concern at a point that left Jason feeling like he might actually vomit. Doubling over, Jason let out a soft whimper, and Max quickly withdrew.

"You landed right on it?"

"Pretty much."

"Fuck, Jase, it feels like someone wedged a crowbar in there and pried up the end of your collarbone."

Despite the nausea, a genuine smile flickered across Jason's face. "Sounds about right."

"Okay," Max sighed. "We've got to make you a sling, at least." A moment later, he had freed himself of his own coat and was tugging his shirt over his head.

"Whoa, where's this going?" Jason asked teasingly.

Max's shaggy dark head popped back into view a moment later. "Well, I wasn't about to suggest we try to get yours off. I don't exactly have a first aid kit on hand."

"Okay, okay," Jason replied. He watched as Max set the shirt aside and felt his arm once more, working with the deliberate purpose of an expert. Max's bare chest prickled with goose-bumps, but he didn't let the cold unsteady him. "You seem like you know what you're doing," Jason remarked, impressed and somewhat surprised at Max's command of the situation.

"Yeah," Max replied. "Think so." He had returned his attention to the discarded shirt and was preparing a series of careful folds.

Jason's curiosity was unsatisfied. "You learn all this when you got your place out in the county, or what?"

Max shook his head, not looking up from his handiwork. "Nah. You remember that summer at camp that I got that awful poison ivy?"

"Yeah. You were in the infirmary for like three days."

Max looked up and flashed a quick grin in Jason's direction before resuming his methodical preparations. "That may have been by choice. One of the counselors stuck in there was prepping for this wilderness first aid certification, and he let me help him out for a few days."

Jason's eyes widened. "Really? I thought you were dying in there, man."

"Nah. I never told you because I figured you'd be mad at me for having so much fun without you."

"Fun?"

"Oh yeah."

As Max talked, Jason could see that summer in his mind. They had been twelve—maybe thirteen—just the right age to eat up every minute of a long, hot Virginia summer. At first Max had worn a look of pride as he gloried in the red, blistering welts that appeared on his legs after a hike, but the unbearable itchiness on a sticky July night sent him banging down the door of the camp infirmary.

Back in their cabin, Jason had laid awake at night with concern, and each day of Max's absence he'd crept over to peer in the shuttered windows of the infirmary, feeling badly for him and his derailed summer. But now he could imagine it from Max's perspective.

The counselor, Jerome, had been seventeen, effortlessly charismatic, and a three-sport high school athlete; in short, automatically cool in the eyes of a twelve-year-old. His mention of an extra first aid course had landed him in the unenviable position of overseeing the barrage of bee stings and sunburns that a hundred-odd campers would accrue over the course of two weeks. He, too, must have been thrilled by the goriness of a severe case of poison ivy, and eager to strike up a conversation with the boy who immediately showed an interested in his studies. And indeed, Max would have shown an interest in anything Jerome wanted to talk about, as long as he was allowed to take part in the conversation.

"Yeah? You'll be my guinea pig?" Jerome had asked, and young Max had replied with a vigorous nod that sent his unruly dark hair cascading into his eyes. Max was right; if Jason had known what had really gone on during those days, he would have been jealous, and let that jealousy ruin the remainder of that perfect childhood summer.

"He showed me how to act out every sort of injury, what would hurt, what wouldn't, and then what to do about each one." It was present-day Max speaking now, his folded shirt draped across one shoulder. He motioned for Jason to move toward him. "With a shoulder, the best thing to do is immobilize it until we get an actual doctor to take a look. Lean forward, if you can."

Jason eased his back off of the wall, and as he did, Max leaned in close, carefully sliding the makeshift bandage under his arm. "Hold it here." Max gestured for Jason to support his arm. He shifted ever so slightly nearer, practically in Jason's lap as he deftly knotted the sleeves of the shirt behind Jason's neck.

Jason could feel the warmth of Max's breath against his cheek as the knot worked its way into place. He inhaled the slightly sweaty, but mostly just familiar scent of his friend's body, typically only this close in the midst of a scuffle, rolling on the ground and striking at one another as only childhood friends can do without fear of repercussion. Now, that closeness was reassuring. Their eyes met as Max slid back, sharing another moment of complete trust.

"How's that?" Max asked, sitting back on his heels and looking Jason over.

"Yeah, better." Jason wasn't just saying it to soothe Max's ego; the relief was immediate. His shoulder still ached, but it no longer felt the constant tug of the weight of his arm. Even better, he had his dominant left hand free again. He extended it toward Max, offering a high-five. "You're good, man."

Max returned the gesture silently, tapping Jason's outstretched fingers with his own. He reached for his coat, throwing it on over his bare torso. "Now you're glad I ditched you that summer, huh?" he replied with a teasing smirk. "We'd better find a way to get your coat on, too. At oh dark thirty, we ride."

Chapter 18

With his jacket zipped tight around him, injured arm held close inside, Jason could convince himself the pain was subsiding further. An unknown—unknowable—number of hours had passed since he and Max had fallen silent, awaiting the moment when they would finally make their move. "I think I might be able to run," Jason whispered, testing out his mobility with a few jogged steps in place.

"Good," was Max's curt reply. He was deep in a state of concentration, apparently involved in a series of mental calculations he wasn't ready to divulge just yet. Finally, he said, "There's one thing we forgot."

"What's that?"

"Our good friends out there." He gestured to the door.

Jason shook his head, not understanding. "They're asleep, right? That's all we need."

"Wrong," Max insisted. "That's all we need to get out of here. Fuck these guys, man. If we just run, they could get away with this whole thing. Their message is one thing, but those sons of bitches hurt you."

"And Alex."

Max's eyes widened in alarm. "Alex? What happened?"

Only then did Jason realize he'd failed to fill Max in on the events of the past few days. Everything had been forgotten in the wake of his injury, their reunion, and the plan to escape. "Shit, I should've started with that. The first guy—the one who's dead—threw him down some stairs at the party. He's got a broken leg but he's gonna be fine." He recalled how stoic Alex had been as they talked and planned; Jason couldn't imagine the useless mess he would have been in Alex's place, knowing how well he'd muddled through the past several hours.

"Fuck!" Max spat the curse out angrily, almost too loud for their cautious hushed tones. He ran a hand through his hair, roughing up the tumbling mess of curls. "Okay, we have to think. What can we do?"

They'd been talking quietly for quite some time, but still, Jason held his breath as Max set about picking the lock of the door. He held the cord of the overhead bulb in his free hand, ready to pull it and run as soon as the door yielded. The last thing they needed was for light spilling out of the room to give them away.

"Got it." Max's whisper was terse, matter of fact, betraying the incredible nerves they both felt as the lock gave way. He extended the knife for Jason to take—since he was already at a deficit in the arms department, as Max had joked earlier. Jason accepted the knife and restored his hold on the pull-chain.

"Ready?" Jason asked softly. At Max's nod, he sent the room plunging into darkness. They waited, as planned, for their eyes to adjust, then a tap on his arm let Jason know Max was about to open the door. Silence was the code until they were out of the cabin.

Every sound was deafening. The click of the latch, the faint brush of the door sweeping the forgotten newspaper aside, a swishing noise so close behind him it made Jason jump. He reached out, felt the trailing jacket sleeve that must have slipped from his pocket, and immediately felt foolish. *Leave a wide berth*, he thought to himself, not that the reminder was necessary. He felt a deep, dull stab of pain with every step but tried to block it from his mind.

Max led the way, patiently choosing his footfalls so as not to disturb a loose board. Jason could just make out his dark outline up ahead, but distances were impossible to judge with so little light. He could be keeping up or falling behind and wouldn't know which.

The main room of the cabin felt endless. Jason could only vaguely remember its layout and more than once had to steady himself against an unseen piece of furniture. With each stumble he felt his heart rate jump. Surely this would be the bump that got them caught. Suddenly he sensed that Max had stopped moving, and he halted his own motion just in time to avoid a collision. There wasn't supposed to be a stop here.

Slowly, silently, Max turned to face Jason and leaned in close, his head nearly touching Jason's—fortunately uninjured—shoulder. "Locked," he mouthed, his voice too quiet to even be considered a whisper.

Jason felt for Max's hand and pressed the knife into his palm. He felt useless standing there while Max fiddled with the lock, unable to help or even effectively stand guard. Suddenly a thought struck him. "Wait!" he whispered urgently, stooping low over Max's crouched form to be heard. "How is it locked from the outside?"

Max didn't move. "Oh fuck."

It was too late to turn back; they had left the relative safety of the locked room behind, and once their ability to remove handcuffs became known, any hope of escape would be dashed. But this was something new, not accounted for in Max's plan. They had assumed both men were asleep inside the house, but now it seemed that one—possibly both—was anticipating their escape attempt and had stationed himself outside to keep watch.

"Just go," Jason hissed. He'd come this far for Max; he was willing to do whatever it took to bring him home. "Leave me the knife, and go!"

"Are you sure?"

"Absolutely." He paused, hesitating for a moment. "Whatever happens, Max, I just—"

"I know." Max cut him off. "Me too."

Neither had to say it; they huddled there in the darkened cabin, scared to death of what awaited them beyond the door, in perfect mutual understanding.

"Here goes," Max whispered, giving the lock a final nudge. He extended the blade of the knife and handed it back to Jason. Silently, slowly, the doorknob turned, and a gust of cold night air swept into the room. "Run!"

The door flung wide, and as it did, an alarm blared overhead, causing both Max and Jason to jump. Not part of the plan either. Regathering their composure, each broke into a sprint, or as close to one as they could manage on stiff, cold legs.

"Hey!" a man's voice shouted, much too close behind them. In the moonlight, Jason could see Max more clearly, the gap between them widening as Max raced ahead down the gravel drive. Jason was panting already, willing his lungs to accept the icy blasts of air and his legs to shake free of the exhaustion of the climb up the mountain. The lights in the cabin clicked on behind him, casting another round of eerie shadows on the snowy ground.

The man was gaining on him—would reach him in a second or two. In a moment of clarity amidst the panic, Jason realized he had a decision to make. He'd committed to protecting Max at all costs; he just had to time it right. Still straining, trying for one last burst of speed, he thrust the knife into his jacket pocket and willed it to stay there. A fair fight he was sure to lose. Surprise was critical.

He felt the man grab at his back, his hand just missing the bottom of his coat. Another reach and he'd be caught. Jason braced for impact, and a moment later felt the sharp tug pulling him backward. *Shit.* The man had gotten a hold of the loose sleeve, giving him more leverage than Jason had counted on. But Jason had to stick to his plan; he allowed himself to be stopped and spun around to face his assailant.

"Where the hell you think you're going?" the man demanded, breathing hard from the sprint. For the first time, Jason could see just how much of a size disadvantage he was at. His captor—the unknown third accomplice—was easily six inches taller and outweighed him by a good seventy-five pounds.

"No—nowhere," Jason stammered. He needed to stall for time. With his right hand, he could feel the knife through the lining of his coat. If he could just get a hold of it. . . .

It took everything in Jason's power to maintain a look of calm as he fumbled furiously for the hilt of the knife. He could feel himself shaking as the man stepped closer, eyeing him with a look of suspicion. "*You*," he drawled. "You wasn't even supposed to be up here. And now you ain't gonna be."

Jason's trembling fingers closed on the knife. He only had one chance. His eyes drifted to his target: the narrow strip of torso protected by only a thin T-shirt between the open sides of the man's unzipped coat. "You—you got me," he said. He raised his left hand in surrender.

"Damn right." Over the man's shoulder, Jason saw the silhouette of his partner coming through the door of the cabin, beginning his approach—and almost certainly armed.

Now.

With all of his strength, Jason gripped the hilt of the knife. He heaved his body into the man and sent him stumbling backward. As he turned to run, Jason caught a glimpse of the knife blade protruding from the ripped front of his own jacket. The tip glistened with blood.

His shoulder had been jarred by the impact, but there was no pain, only speed. Jason tore down the driveway, barely aware of his body as the distance fell away behind him. He just hoped he'd bought enough time; the wound wouldn't keep the man down for more than a few seconds, but those seconds could make all the difference.

The sound of a shotgun being cocked echoed through the cold night air, followed by the roar of the truck's engine. Jason dove for the woods, hoping, praying that he could get out of sight before the headlights swept over him. Scrambling over rocks, he lost his balance, slipped, felt the prick of his knife as it tumbled from his pocket. *Shit.* Jason dropped to his knees, searching blindly for the knife. Shadows shifted around him; he could feel the approach of the headlights and knew he wasn't safe yet. Finally, his fingers closed on the blade. He ignored the sting of pain as the knife dug into his hand, and surged ahead into the underbrush.

A moment later, the truck roared past. It didn't stop, didn't even slow down. He was safe.

It only took a second for relief to be replaced by panic. *Max.* Jason had seen him take off down the driveway. There was no way to warn him the truck was in pursuit. . . .

He rushed back to the edge of the drive, looking hurriedly in both directions. As he glanced back toward the house, his heart caught in his throat.

Someone's still there. He could just make out a human form lying on the ground.

"Holy shit." The words slipped from Jason's lips before he could stop them. He was sure Max had run ahead . . . he'd been ahead of him this whole time . . . hadn't he? That couldn't—he couldn't—

Heart pounding, Jason broke into a run back toward the cabin. As he drew closer, he saw the body lay in the exposed gravel where the truck had been parked. Suddenly the form sat upright, sending Jason skittering to a halt. "Hey!" he shouted.

"Hey, yourself!"

Max. It was him. He was okay.

Jason surged ahead once more. "What the fuck, man? I thought you were—I thought that was—" He dropped to his knees, roughly pulled Max into a one-armed hug. "What the fuck?"

As they separated, Jason saw a broad grin spanning Max's face. "Those guys won't be coming back anytime soon." He wiped his hands on his pants. "Smell that?"

"Brake fluid." The odor was unmistakable. Jason engulfed him in another hug. "Jesus, Max, you can't scare me like that. I thought—" He stopped himself. It didn't matter. Here Max was. Here they both were. Together. Safe.

Max scrambled to his feet and extended a greasy hand to help Jason up. Standing, they embraced again. "Thanks, man," Max whispered.

"Of course." Jason couldn't help but smile, too. "Let's get the hell out of here."

"No shit," Max agreed with a laugh. "We've got to get you to a fucking doctor."

The words were barely out of his mouth when a booming crash seemed to shake the whole mountain. Jason's stomach churned, and his hand jumped to Max's shoulder to steady himself, but Max was unphased. "And call the rescue squad, I suppose," he added, flashing a smirk in Jason's direction. "Told you those guys wouldn't be going anywhere." He motioned for Jason to choose a direction, and they began to walk.

"And what about you?" Jason asked, struck by a sudden worry as he hurried after Max's retreating form.

"What *about* me?"

"Are you . . . sticking around this time?"

Max stopped, turned to face Jason, his expression deadly serious and bathed in moonlight. "Are you kidding? I'm never letting you out of my sight again."

Chapter 19

"Oh my God. Oh, thank God!"

The nose of the Subaru had barely cleared the end of Jason's driveway, and already Tara was upon them, racing up in socked feet, her coat unbuttoned and hair flying in all directions. Max, in the driver's seat, stopped the car and rolled down the window, flashing one of his signature smirks. "Miss me?"

"Maybe a little," she shot back, leaning into the car and throwing her arms around him in a tight hug. She planted a kiss on his cheek, immediately blushed, and stepped back to wave them along the driveway.

Max made a show of wiping his cheek with the back of his hand. "Thanks for the cooties!" he shouted out the window. Tara stuck her tongue out at him and raced lightly along after the car.

Only as they stepped out of the car did she seem to notice Jason's presence. Her eyes widened as she looked him over. "Jase, what the hell? Are you okay?"

"Of course," he replied with a clumsy smile, feeling self-conscious. They had finally finished navigating the emergency department of the hospital, and he had emerged with a proper sling and a robust cocktail of painkillers. The only major loss was the sweatshirt that had to be cut off of him. Even his car's windows had been spared, thanks to Max's lock-picking abilities. He turned to Max. "You didn't tell her?"

He grinned sheepishly. "It may have been implied."

"Oh no, not even implied," Tara insisted, playfully shoving

Max away before wrapping him up in another hug. "You just said he was getting checked out while you talked to the police."

"Hey, it's true," Max insisted, returning her embrace. "All right, all right, let's get inside before you freeze like that."

But Tara didn't seem to hear, now turning her attention to Jason. Her voice swelled with emotion as she said, "Jase, thank you. Really. I—" She stopped short, then blurted out, "How am I supposed to hug you like that?"

"You don't need to hug me," he muttered.

"No." Tara's voice was firm. "I do." She drew up close on his left and gave him a half squeeze of a sideways hug. "I can't believe you found him," she whispered. "Thank you."

All Jason could do was nod, but there was something meaningful in the look they shared. Then Tara peeled away, reattaching herself to Max's side as they made their way into the house.

Alex greeted them at the door, only to be nearly bowled over by his brother, who grabbed him by the shoulders and pulled him into a hug as well. "Welcome back, man," Alex said softly. His voice sounded like he might have been crying, but his head was downturned, and when the two separated, his eyes were clear.

"*What* is this injury ward we have going here?" Max demanded as he slipped out of his coat. "I can't leave any of you alone, can I?"

"No," Jason replied, tossing his torn and bloody jacket on the growing pile as well. *Please don't*, he was tempted to add, but didn't want to risk spoiling the reunion with an overdose of sentimentality.

Within a matter of minutes, they were all settled in the living room with Max eagerly at the center of attention. "I'd say you wouldn't believe the week I've had, but I'm starting to think you would," he joked, flashing a grin in Jason's direction.

Jason's sense that something had changed in Max was only growing stronger. As Max narrated the events of the past few days, there was no hesitation, no evasiveness, no moodiness, just the friend they were all unconditionally glad to have back in their lives.

Finally, Max gave the emphatic report they'd all been waiting for: the police had, in fact, caught up with the kidnappers around the time the EMTs picked them up from their crashed truck.

"So, it's all over?" Alex asked cautiously.

"All over," Max replied. "And that's all Jase," he added with a grin, nodding in Jason's direction. "I'm serious, he saved my fucking life."

"No problem." Jason brushed off the praise. "You would've done the same."

"For real, man." Max was suddenly serious as he extended his right hand, then quickly withdrew it, offering his left instead. "Thank you."

Jason reached out, completing the off-handed shake. This time, there was no mystery to the emotion he could feel in Max's firm grip. As they locked eyes, he gave a small nod, which Max returned, the soft glow of a smile lighting up his face.

"So, Jase," Tara's teasing voice cut in, "you about ready to cancel the concert now?"

It was the first time she'd directed a question his way, it seemed, but still it was Max who responded. "Hold up," he interjected, releasing Jason's hand as his eyes darted first to Tara, then back to Jason, "you didn't cancel?"

"The demands said not to," Jason replied with exaggerated sincerity. "I wasn't about to risk your life like that."

A spark ignited in Max's eye, barely perceptible but unmistakable. "You're telling me we still have a show tomorrow?"

Tara shot him a skeptical look. "Does he *look* like we still have a show tomorrow?"

"Definitely," Max decided. "Jase?"

Jason could feel a particular mode of Max-driven antic coming on, and in an instant he was unquestionably on board. In the end, the nightmare of the past week had been about the concert, about an attempt to drown out not only the band's message, but this particular call for unity. It would feel like a defeat not to play the long-awaited hometown show. Jason paused to test out the mobility of his right hand. "Maybe it's the painkillers talking, but yeah, why not?"

"Someone get the man a guitar!" Max exclaimed, leaping to his feet to obey his own instructions. He raced out of the room and reappeared a moment later, guitar case in hand.

Tara shook her head in mock disbelief. "The two of you. I forgot what it's like when you get going." She turned to Jason. "You really want to try to play?"

"Listen, it can't be any harder than stabbing a man," Jason retorted, rising to accept the instrument from Max's outstretched hand. He hesitated, realizing that even getting the strap over his head posed a challenge. Before he could start to ask for help, Max was beside him, undoing the bottom strap lock and standing ready to help him position the guitar. Jason felt in his pockets for a pick and came up empty. Max was still a step ahead of him, though, already holding one out for him to take.

"Looking *good*," Max declared, stepping back to admire the scene he had instigated. He wore a self-satisfied smirk, pleased with his role, as usual, in orchestrating such an ill-advised scheme.

"I feel like an idiot," Jason confessed, realizing as he palmed the pick that he might not even be able to reach the strings. "This stupid sling. . . ." The thick black fabric was hot and itchy, not to mention restrictive, which he realized was the point, but with his system full of morphine, it felt like more of an annoyance than anything else.

"We can take it off." Max was upon him again, reaching for the guitar when Tara cut him off.

"Absolutely not!" She sounded incredulous. "What the hell are you thinking right now? Either of you! Jase, you're hurt." Turning to Max, she continued, "He's got . . . what did you say it was, separated something? Don't encourage this. We'll postpone the tour."

"I don't know about *tour*," Jason replied, backpedaling. It had been almost two years since their last stint on the road, but he could still remember vividly the physical toll wrought by weeks of concerts and travel. Now, with the prospect of surgery looming, an extended trip of any kind was out of the question.

"Oh, the tour's not happening," Max agreed. "Not now. But we need to play this show. For Charlottesville. For us."

"And for that love song you finally managed to write?" Tara asked.

"Exactly."

Tara shook her head, by now ineffectively feigning disbelief. She turned back to Jason. "All right, rock star, at least play us a chord before we sign on to any sort of nonsense."

The first stroke of the pick was awkward, clumsy, but surprisingly not painful. Shifting his guitar to better reach the strings, Jason strummed at a power chord for a few seconds, feeling like a complete beginner. He continued, biting his lip in concentration as he started to find a rhythm. He picked a few single notes, then another chord. His left hand glided comfortably through a series of changes, the opening of a song they had slated to open the upcoming show.

"He can play!" Max was ecstatic. He didn't wait to hear any more before rushing back to Jason's side and freeing him of the guitar. "Do we still—? Of course we do. What time was rehearsal today?" He didn't wait for an answer, instead turning back to Jason and Tara in a dramatic performance of seriousness. "You two haven't been skipping rehearsal without me, have you?"

Jason laughed. "God, it's good to have you back, man." The infectiousness of Max's energy was overwhelming. Already, he found it hard to believe he'd made it through so much time without him.

Only then did Jason notice how Alex had faded into the background. He made a fumbling attempt to draw him into the conversation. "Alex, you want to come with, or what?" he asked.

Alex shrugged. "I'm good. Drop me off at home on your way?"

"Of course." Max's reply floated up from where he knelt, settling Jason's guitar in its case. He took every care with the instrument, gently wiping it down as if it were his own. "But before I touch my bass, I need one hell of a shower. Jase, you mind?"

"Oh, but touching my guitar was fine?"

"Key word," Max smirked, "*your* guitar."

"Thanks, man. But yeah. Use mine; my parents' is still leaking."

"Noted!" And with that, Max was gone in a flash.

The room felt quieter, emptier without him, but nothing compared to the loneliness that Jason, Tara, and Alex had shared over the past several days.

"He's back," Alex said quietly, a faint smile flickering across his face.

"And better than ever, apparently," Tara added with an eye roll. But she smiled, too.

Jason stayed silent as he sank back down on the couch, absently turning the guitar pick over and over in his hand. Somehow, he was at a loss for what to say to the friends who had been there with him through the whole ordeal. Everything he wanted to say was for Max alone, and he felt guilty about not knowing how to keep the conversation going with Tara and Alex.

Alex seemed to sense his unease, and asked, "Jase, are you really going to try to play this concert?"

"Yeah, sure." He tried to shrug it off.

Alex hesitated. "He won't be disappointed if you can't."

"I know . . ." Jason trailed off, feeling something deep within him gripped by that very fear. He couldn't disappoint Max, not after everything that had happened.

But as Jason thought back to their reunion in the cabin, to the worry and care with which Max had tended to him at his most vulnerable, he realized it wasn't Max himself he was worried about disappointing. *That* Max would never be disappointed. It was the performance of Max that would, the façade he had been constructing for their collective benefit from the moment the car pulled in the driveway. Alex could see through it; now he could, too, and Jason couldn't quite say why he needed to let himself be drawn in by Max's act, only that he didn't dare risk upsetting the happiness of any version of his best friend.

Finally collecting his thoughts, Jason continued, "We fought hard for this show."

Tara nodded, with a look of understanding. "It means a lot." A moment later, her serious expression faded, and a devilish smirk flickered across her lips. "Of course, there's no male ego at play here."

"Absolutely none."

"And all the fangirls who'll be eating up the injured bad boy vibe?"

"Hadn't even considered them." He grinned.

The room fell silent once again, this time comfortably, and Jason's thoughts drifted back to the events of the previous night. It seemed like a lifetime ago that he had set off up that mountain, and yet his reunion with Max had been effortless, as if they'd never been apart.

He lingered on the moments they shared huddled in the dark on the floor of their prison. The way Max had taken charge of the situation, taken care of him like that . . . Max would claim Jason had saved his life, but somehow it felt like the reverse was just as true.

"Hey Jase, you still have your phone?" Tara's voice drew him back to reality, but Jason didn't mind. The memory was reassuring, but the present was finally looking better, too.

"Oh. No. Max either, probably."

"Not even your work cell?"

"Oh God." He was on his feet in an instant. "What's Izzy onto now?"

He retrieved the phone from where it lay in the kitchen; it took only a few seconds to power back up . . . and for the notifications to pour in. This time, it wasn't just Izzy. One after another, missed calls and messages from agents, assistants, even his parents—with whom he rarely exchanged more than a "Happy birthday" or "Merry Christmas"—flooded the screen. "Shit," he mumbled. "Word got out after I left?"

"I know, I know," Tara said, "but I had to give Izzy something. Just that there was a threat about the concert, I swear. You know how she gets when she thinks we're lying to her."

"And then she went and told my *parents*?"

"To be fair, we all assumed you'd called them by now. Texting my mom was, like, the first thing I did."

"Look what you've done," Jason replied, brandishing the phone with mock indignation. Already it was buzzing again. He set it back on the counter and rejoined Tara and Alex.

Tara was laughing again, shaking her head. "That's fair."

"Well, shit, I'm in no state to deal with all of that *now*," he protested jokingly.

"Of course not." This time it was Alex who flashed a smirk before continuing, "I mean, you *are* injured."

"Ha," Jason muttered, knowing he deserved the jab—and that Alex deserved a proper thank you for everything he'd done to help find Max. Jason searched for the right words, but somehow the shared moment of levity seemed to serve the purpose better than anything he could have said.

The next thing they heard was running footsteps on the stairs. A moment later, Max came flying into view, shaking water from his hair like a wet dog. "Let's go!" he declared with a grin.

"Jesus, dude, are you wearing my boxers too?" Jason asked, laughing. Max did seem to be dressed entirely in borrowed clothes—a Western Albemarle boys' basketball T-shirt emblazoned with Jason's last name and high school number, and a pair of jeans that fit his waist but were a good three inches too short at the ankles. The effect was ridiculous, but somehow suited the occasion.

"I can take them off if you want," Max offered, reaching for his zipper.

The protest came from three places at once. "We're good!" Jason insisted.

"God, I feel like I need to remind you two to put on coats and not fight in the car," Tara remarked, looking from Max to Jason and back. "All right, I'll drive. Let's see if we can do something normal for a change."

Chapter 20

Jason was beginning to dread the band's reception at rehearsal. He had stashed his work phone in the sling, and its nagging buzzes had driven him to finally read the flurry of messages in its entirety. His parents' concerns were easy to brush aside, and from the way the agents' texts trailed off, he could tell they'd been satisfied by whatever details Tara and Izzy had provided. That just left Izzy herself, who was not about to take the news of his injury particularly well.

Max led the way into the unassuming brick building, a centuries-old structure no passing observer would guess had been converted into a state-of-the-art music studio. It was their musical home in town now that the days of rehearsing in Jason's garage were behind them, but Jason knew this particular homecoming would not be met with the warmest of welcomes.

"The prodigal band returns!" He could hear Izzy's voice, tinged with annoyance, as Max pushed open the door to their practice room. "And you're . . . walking?" she added.

Max stopped short in the doorway, blocking his bandmates in the hall. "Why wouldn't I be?" he asked, his tone effortlessly casual.

Jason heard Izzy tapping away on one of her many phones and tablets, then the tread of her boots as she crossed the room to hand Max the device. Right away Jason knew what it was. "Oh shit, is that Alex?" Max asked, suppressing a chuckle as he perused the same photo Jason had been sent earlier in the week.

Izzy's tone was icy. "He told me it was *you*. I confirmed it for the media."

"Well, you know, good news," Max replied with a shrug, passing the tablet back to her. He continued into the room, leaving Jason to brace for the moment when Izzy's gaze descended on him.

It only took a second. "Oh, for crying out loud!" Izzy stopped his progress just inside the door, and lifted away the hanging front of his jacket, which he'd hoped would hide the sling from view. "What the hell is this?"

"Just my shoulder," Jason mumbled, already feeling that he was about to be dragged back from his idealistic notion of playing a show by the furious woman looking him over. Her short, spiked hair was dyed bright pink, which they all knew was the Izzy equivalent of a red alert: do not cross. Izzy didn't scare him per se, but Jason respected her enough to know he was better off on her good side—especially on a pink hair day.

"What am I supposed to do with all this?" she demanded. "*Him*"—she gestured to Max—"hobbling around, I can deal with. Threats against the concert, sure. *You* and that thing, not so much."

"Jase can play," Max said calmly from across the room. "We're gonna get through tomorrow's show and take a break from there."

Now Izzy spun on her heel and turned on him. "You're cancelling tour dates *today*?"

"Postponing a little." Max was perfectly calm, unruffled by Izzy's interrogation. Even here, for an audience of one, he was ever the showman. "C'mon, look at Jason. He's got a grade four separated something or other. He can't play a whole tour like that."

"Can he even play a note?"

"Yeah . . . hold on. We'll get set up." Max paused, glanced around the room. "And if we get a camera in here, we can shoot some social media blurb for the masses. I'll handle it, I promise."

Izzy threw up her hands in disbelief. "And say what? Everything they've heard all week is a lie, but someone *else* is hurt, and the tour is cancelled except for one very special show?"

"Iz, we owe you one hell of an explanation for all this. But don't worry about the fans." Max was patiently insistent. "Please, I've got it. I'll take full responsibility for everything. Can you get a camera in here or not?"

"Camera is easy, but I want that explanation." Even in defeat, Izzy's tone was sharp, ready to hold him accountable for any misstep or poor decision. "What else do you need?"

Max hesitated. "You do tend to work miracles for us. Jase, you need anything?"

"I'm good," Jason replied automatically.

"C'mon man, seriously."

Jason shrugged. "I don't know. I mean, how bad is it going to be when the morphine wears off?"

The answer, evidently, was bad.

Forty-five minutes into rehearsal, Jason was doubled over in pain. He could feel tears coming, tried to swallow them down as he stumbled to a seated position on top of one of the smaller amplifiers, his guitar still slung over his shoulder. "Fuck!" he spat, frustrated by his inability to push through the pain. He had discarded the sling for rehearsal, a decision he now deeply regretted as his shoulder felt like it was being ripped apart by the weight of his arm.

An instant later, Max was kneeling in front of him, gently lifting the guitar away. "It's okay," he said. "It's okay. We don't have to do this."

Now Tara appeared by Jason's side too, placing a hand on his knee. "Seriously, don't hurt yourself on our account."

Jason tried to shake them off. "Just give me a minute," he insisted. "I'll be all right."

"That's a big fucking lie," Max replied with a laugh. "I hate to see you like this, man." He was silent for a moment, eyeing Jason with the same look of worried sympathy he'd worn as he examined his shoulder in the cabin. When he did speak, it was clear that his thoughts had drifted, but Jason knew they were inevitably circling back toward a relevant point. "Do you remember that game sophomore year when you broke your finger?" Max asked, as if it were the most natural question in the world.

Jason narrowed his eyes in a display of confusion. "Sure. Why?"

"What'd you tell me about playing injured?"

"I don't know," Jason replied evasively. "I mean, it was years ago. . . ." But he did know. And he was secretly, begrudgingly impressed by Max's ability to conjure up a memory that would make his point for him.

Max had made a rare appearance at one of Jason's basketball games, and tracked him down afterward, a childlike look of concern on his face as he approached where Jason stood outside the boys' locker room with a dripping bag of ice balanced on his hand.

"Why didn't he put you back in?" Max had asked, apparently oblivious to Jason's injury.

"Trainer says it's broken," Jason explained, lifting away the ice for his friend to inspect the finger, which was bent at a slightly unnatural angle but otherwise looked fine, not even swollen or bruised.

"It doesn't hurt, though," Max said. Oddly, it was a statement, not a question.

"No," Jason had agreed, wondering how Max could tell. It *didn't* hurt, and hadn't, aside from the moment it had happened, when he swatted for a loose ball and immediately pulled up, shaking the sting away. Max must have been watching as he sat on the bench, inconvenienced by the bag of ice, but cheering on his teammates and jumping in the middle of every huddle like he was about to go back in the game—which he'd been counting on until his conversation with the trainer at halftime.

Max eyed Jason curiously. "That tall boy, the one with the blond hair—"

"Christian." Already Max had adopted a policy of refusing to learn the names of any athletes beyond those he knew in another context. Jason had been annoyed on his teammates' behalf at first, but he had grown used to indulging Max's stubborn disdain.

"Sure," Max conceded. "He was hurt way worse than you and he kept playing."

As usual, Jason had found himself amazed by Max's perceptiveness. He was right; Christian had been pushing through practice with a sore knee all week, but Jason had barely seen him flinch during the game.

"Well, it's different," Jason explained. "He's just hurt. I'm injured."

"What's the difference?" It was a genuine question, coming from a boy who wanted nothing more than perfect command of the English language. If he didn't understand the meaning of a word—especially such a simple word—he had to find out.

Jason had tried to hide the smile creeping up as he realized he was, for once, the one who knew something Max didn't. "If something just hurts, you're hurt. But if there's something actually wrong with it, you're injured."

"Okay."

"Coach always says you owe it to your team to play hurt, and to yourself not to play injured."

Max had nodded understandingly then, as he did now, waiting for Jason's reply.

"All right, I'm trying to play injured, I guess," Jason mumbled, letting his head drop down to hide his embarrassed expression. "Now you're going to tell me not to?"

The room fell silent as they awaited Max's verdict. "I didn't say that," he said finally. It seemed to be dawning on him that his latest scheme might have gone one step too far, but he was never one to surrender so easily. "Maybe we just have to be a little creative."

Jason dragged his head up to make eye contact with Max. "I'm listening."

Whatever idea had come to Max, it was clearly a good one. He jumped to his feet, heading for the whiteboard on which they had written out the set list for the show. "First of all," he said, marking a handful of songs as he moved down the list, "we scrap your solos. I'll take some, Tara can fill in the rest."

Jason nodded, even as he felt a pang of disappointment. He hated the feeling of holding his bandmates back and being helpless to do anything about it. But a modified concert was better than no concert, and he was relieved that despite Max's moralizing, he wasn't going to be benched this time around.

"We can swap in acoustic versions here and here"—Max indicated two more songs on the list—"and give you a break for those." He was poised to say more, but a knock on the door stopped him short. "Yeah?"

Izzy let herself into the room, camera and tripod in tow, followed closely by a man Jason didn't recognize. "It's going well, I see," she said, casting a pointed look at Jason, who still sat holding his injured arm in his lap. She nodded to the man behind her. "You let this guy take a look at you, or what? He's from sports medicine."

"Izzy, you're a lifesaver," Jason replied gratefully.

She nodded. "Don't you forget it."

Chapter 21

THURSDAY, 8:15 P.M.

It had been years since Jason felt pre-show jitters like this. The opening act was on stage, and he found himself pacing his dressing room, hair and makeup done, but only half dressed for the show. His shoulder was engulfed in a web of electric blue sports medicine tape, and at the doctor's recommendation he held an unwieldy bag of ice to the area as he paced.

A knock at the door startled him. "Come in," he blurted out, only afterward realizing he didn't have a shirt on and wasn't in a state to be seen.

Much to his relief, it was Max who slipped through the door, swiftly closing it behind him. He, on the other hand, looked stage-worthy, dressed in slim black jeans and a black V-neck, with a healthy dose of eyeliner and hair gel to complete the look. It was good to see him like this. A wave of nostalgia washed over Jason as he remembered all of those earlier concerts when he'd taken for granted that he'd see his best friend on top of the world again.

Max smiled broadly. "How's it going?"

"Good," Jason replied. He could hear the nerves in his own voice. "Just didn't want everyone making a fuss." He nodded to his shoulder; the combined effect of brightly colored tape, ice, and a sling was more than he felt the need to take out in public.

"It's almost time. Let me give you a hand with that."

"Sure." Jason handed over the ice, then ran his fingers over the half numb muscles of his shoulder. The thick tape felt bulky and alien on his skin, but it did seem to be holding things in place. He didn't feel the aching tug of the weight of his arm pulling against his shoulder as Max stepped behind him and detached the closures of the sling.

"You're good?" Max asked as Jason slipped free and tossed the sling onto the pile of clothing that was spilling off of the dressing room table. Jason could feel Max watching him as he began the process of getting into his shirt. He hated the restrictiveness of long sleeves for a sweaty night on stage, but it was the only option that would cover the tape, and he wasn't about to distract from the night's true purpose by drawing attention to his injury.

Max continued to watch as Jason struggled with the mass of fabric. "You're going to be boiling out there, man."

"It's a better look than this."

Max's expression was thoughtful, half smiling. "I don't know. I think you look good. You know, badass."

"Fuck that, man, I'm not sweating into my guitar all night without a shirt." Jason gave the shirt another tug and finally managed to pop his head through. He was still struggling to steady his nerves and knew he wasn't hiding it well.

Max didn't respond and appeared to be sinking into thought, his eyes downcast. When he did finally speak, his tone was more serious than before. "I really have to thank you, Jase. For everything."

"Yeah, of course," Jason replied automatically, not sure how to read the shift in mood. He didn't know quite what Max meant by *everything*, but he had more than a reasonable guess. His mind scrolled back to the previous evening of conversation and laughter, culminating in Tara's declaration that she was never going to get any sleep around the two of them. She had ceded her claim to the couch to Max, who eagerly accepted. It was like old times, waking up at noon to find his best friend downstairs brewing coffee, getting ready for a show together like they had since they were teenagers. Somehow that felt just as significant as the escape they'd engineered together less than two days—but what felt like months—earlier.

Max leaned up against the wall opposite Jason, still not lifting his gaze and looking uncomfortable, like maybe he was fighting a case of nerves before the show as well. "So, listen," he began slowly, "there's something I have to tell you."

"Uh, sure." For lack of anything better to do in the uneasy moment opening up between them, Jason reached for the bag of ice and spent several seconds adjusting its position on his shoulder.

He could just see Max's expression, could sense something guarded in the faint sadness of his smile. "It's . . . you know what, never mind. It can wait."

"Okay. . . ." Jason's reply was uncertain as his thoughts leapt to the worst-case scenario. Max had said he wasn't going away again. He must have meant it. Right? But the look on Max's face provided no answers, no reassurances.

Max gave a small nod. "So really, just, thank you. I mean it." He drew in a deep breath that seemed to steady him, and a moment later the spark was back in his eye. A grin flashed across his face. "I wouldn't be here right now if it weren't for you. And this is too good to miss."

Jason forced himself to offer an uneasy smile in return. "Best job in the world."

From the hallway, a call of "Fifteen minutes!" floated into the room, spurring them both into action. Max nodded a goodbye and was quickly on his way, leaving Jason to contemplate the ice before tossing it back onto the pile of clothes and attempting to tame the mess his hair had become in the process of getting dressed.

Max's sudden moodiness weighed on Jason. It was fleeting, had come on in a flash and dissipated just as quickly, but it reminded him too much of the worst days of the hiatus. He tried to push those thoughts from his mind and refocus on a safer worry, the pre-show jitters that only minutes before had felt ready to swallow him whole. All that mattered was here and now, the show they were about to play together.

The blinding spotlights, the roar of the crowd, it was all close enough that Jason could practically feel the energy ready to wash over them the moment they stepped onto that stage. They stood in the wings now, he and Tara on one side, Max on the other, no doubt making faces he hoped they'd see despite the sea of lights and equipment separating them.

Jason's hand closed on the neck of his guitar, preparing to hold it steady as he crossed the stage. The nerves were gone; by this point it was all a routine, and he couldn't imagine a better one. He heard the cue in his headset and gave Tara one final nod of assurance before they raced out into the glowing void.

A rush of energy tore through Jason's body as he ran to his first mark, where he paused, eyes closed, breathing in the atmosphere of the stage, the crowd, the moment. He felt the waves of sound as much as he heard them—that is, until the unmistakable call to order of the opening riff echoed out from Max's bass and the yells reached a fever pitch. He didn't have to think, just let his hands fly and let the satisfying scream of distortion wash over him.

Fuck, I missed this.

Max's voice floated over the scene like the voice of the punk gods themselves, and Jason caught his eye just in time to see a signature wink and smirk before he launched into the first thundering bass solo, prompting a new swell of noise from the crowd.

The notes poured from Max's bass, a tumbling, rushing river of sound, as bright and clean as Jason had ever heard him play. For a moment, his bass was everything; the world dropped away. Then the thump of Tara's bass drum pulled them back to earth and the song surged ahead. Guitar and bass interwove themselves in an ebb and flow of harmony, dissonance, resolution—then a pause that seemed to freeze time, a moment of emptiness so complete it sent a shiver down Jason's spine, and they dove right back in, Max's vocals leading the way.

One song became two, then three, then four . . . Jason hoped it would never end. The exhilaration, the weightlessness, was indescribable. He drank it all in, for the first time in his life deliberately trying to commit every second to memory.

The acoustic interludes were the best. Jason perched on the edge of the stage, a spectator himself as Max crooned over the airy melody of an acoustic guitar and Tara's drumming was filtered down to a clean, simple rhythm. As the opening notes rang out, the noise of the crowd surged again. The fans' eager disbelief was clear. It was Max's first-ever public performance on guitar, saved just for them.

Jason found himself grinning with secret satisfaction; only he knew that it wasn't for the hometown crowd that Max broke his long-held policy, it was for him.

As he continued to watch, Jason was struck once again by his bandmates' talent. It was easy to be amazed by Max the performer, but with everything stripped away, neither he nor Tara missed a single beat. A fleeting worry crossed Jason's mind as he wondered whether they even needed *him*, but the renewed roar of the crowd as he leapt back into the spotlight and scratched out his next wailing, reverberating riff chased those thoughts away for good.

Finally, heartbreakingly, the concert neared its end, and Jason felt a rush of anticipation as Max stepped up to the microphone, poised for one of his signature speeches. Over the years, his topics had ranged from witty anecdotes to reflections on history or politics, but Jason suspected he knew where tonight's monologue would go. Especially given the surprise grand finale: the premiere of his long-awaited love song.

"Hey, Cville," Max said, his voice conversational and intimate even as it echoed through the arena's sound system. The crowd cheered, appreciating his colloquial charm. On the road, Max never missed a nickname, always casting himself effortlessly as a local. But here, it was personal, the name he'd used for this town for as long as he could remember.

"This is amazing," Max continued. "Y'all are such a great crowd. What a way to be welcomed back." He was interrupted again by shouts and applause, and stood grinning in the spotlight for several seconds before again calling the crowd to order with a booming riff. The fans knew the drill and quieted themselves with remarkable restraint.

"We are so honored to be here tonight. Here, home, in Charlottesville." Max drew in a deep breath. "This town has been through hell in the past year, and your resilience is inspiring. I have never been so proud to call this community my home." He paused to let the remark sink in. "But I feel like I've let you down this past year. I haven't been acting like I'm part of a community—this one, or any other." A series of hushed murmurs swept through the crowd, and Max waited for them to run their course before he continued.

"I want to thank you, and I want to apologize." His voice was even, measured, yet undeniably sincere. "When we went on hiatus, I left you all in the dark, and it's time I took responsibility for that. I was being selfish, and worst of all, holding back these incredible people up here, who shouldn't have had to waste the past year waiting around for me." Spotlights swung over Jason and Tara as he spoke, and Max gestured to each of them in turn, welcoming a roar from the crowd.

"I have to tell you," Max went on as the lights focused back on him alone, "this show tonight almost didn't happen. I was in some trouble this week, and I want to take a minute to thank the greatest friends in the world who made this concert possible."

So dramatic, Jason thought to himself with a smile, secretly relishing the attention he knew was coming.

"First, I need to introduce you to someone," Max declared. He turned toward the side of the stage and beckoned to a figure waiting in the wings. "Alex, come on out here." Uncertain applause slowly filled the arena as Alex, looking completely out of his element and on the verge of falling, made a slow and rhythmic approach to center stage. "This is my little brother," Max continued. "You may recognize him from earlier this week when y'all thought he was me. It's understandable"—he drew Alex in close beside him, maneuvering his bass to avoid its almost inevitable collision with Alex's crutches—"I mean, what a good-looking guy, huh?"

The crowd cut him off again, and this time Max waited for the noise to subside. Alex blushed noticeably, embarrassed by the attention.

"Believe me when I say you have no idea how much this guy has done for me over the years." At this latest remark, Jason cast a glance in Tara's direction, and they exchanged a knowing look. Alex's contributions really were beyond anyone's imagination.

Max gave his brother a hearty pat on the back before letting go of him. "He's a little shy so I'm going to let him get out of here, but only once you let him know just how appreciated he really is," he declared, freeing Alex to escape the spotlight amidst more robust cheers. As he started to cross the stage, Max continued, "And now I want to talk about the *other* person in that photo y'all got so excited about." He turned and gestured for Tara to stand, which she did, beaming as she waved to the crowd and accepted their applause.

"This girl," Max went on, "is the glue that holds everything together. You saw her in action looking after my brother, but that is just the tip of the iceberg. She is always there behind the scenes, making it all happen, keeping the rest of us in line. And *that*, let me tell you, is one hell of a job." He grinned, egging the audience on in their latest round of cheers. "Not to mention the fact that she's the best fucking drummer I've ever heard." From the roar of the crowd, it was clear they agreed with Max's assessment.

"And finally, my partner in crime." Now Max turned to Jason, and a spotlight swung over Jason as he did, catching him off guard as he stood cradling his injured arm. He made the mistake of releasing it too quickly and winced as all eyes were on him. A chorus of concerned whispers swept through the crowd.

"Jase, can I fill them in?" Max asked. Jason nodded, gripping his shoulder once again. The façade was gone; he might as well try to lessen the pain.

"Would you believe it if I told you this guy just played a show for you with a separated shoulder?" The murmurs turned to cheers, but Max continued over them, "Because he did. And do you know how he got hurt in the first place? Me again. He was bailing me out of a tight spot." Max paused, seemed to be laughing to himself as he looked in Jason's direction once more. "I don't have to wonder. I now literally know my best friend would give his right hand for me. And it's not just him. These three are so much better than I deserve, and it's about time they heard it!"

The roar was back to full volume as Jason and Tara exchanged a nod and leapt into an opening riff, knowing full well they were about to be cut off by Max. "Stop, stop, stop!" he called out in mock alarm, immediately silencing the drums and guitar. His eyes darted to Tara, then Jason, then back to the crowd. "Didn't anyone tell you? We've got a new song."

Now the crowd truly erupted. "I have to warn you, though," Max continued into the microphone. "We're trying something a little different this time. This one's called 'Charlottesville.'" He gave a nod, Tara counted off the rhythm, and over Max's melodic bass line away they went, exorcising the demons of the hiatus once and for all.

From the first cascading arpeggio of the bass line, the crowd clearly felt what Max meant by something a little different. The riff was dreamy-sweet and steeped in nostalgia, but there was an urgency to the song too, a power that began with Tara's drum kit but was evident on Max's lips as he started in on the opening verse:

"*I fell in love with Virginia summer nights*
"*Red clay to ground me, starry skies to fill my dreams*
"*Fireflies . . . could be fireworks for the way they make me feel*
"*Blue Ridge sunsets o'er the world that I call home.*"

Jason's guitar entered, its distortion thrusting the song into a punchy chorus, then a heavier, driving repetition of the opening arpeggio over which the nature of Max's love for his home crystallized:

"*My heart goes out to those who've never met her*

"*Seen Charlottesville up close and known her like I do*
"*My heart breaks for those of us who know her*
"*Who love 'despite the faults,' as we've been warned to do.*"

It was a love song, as demanded, and every note of it for Charlottesville. It was impossible to say who needed it more—Max or the town—but Jason could feel something restorative, healing, almost magical in the way both Max and the crowd threw themselves into it.

Jason's shoulder was straining, threatening to slow his pick, and it was sheer force of will that kept him on the tempo up to the final lines, the one concession of a hint at love not *just* for home that Max had allowed in his masterpiece:

"*Better by the day*
"*And better shared*
"*With you.*"

Max had admitted the line was a throwaway—a gift to the love-song-starved fans—but all the same, Jason felt a swell of emotion as the final chord rang out and Max's eyes darted in his direction.

That look sent Jason's thoughts back to Max's speech. His tribute rang over and over again in Jason's head as they exited the stage, devolved into a round of sweaty hugs, then lined up to go right back out for an encore. *Partner in crime . . . better than I deserve.* It was high praise coming from anyone, and Jason knew how Max must have agonized over his words to make them ring true, yet sound so effortlessly conversational. There had been no improvisation there, but rather a deliberately crafted message—one made all the more powerful by the song that followed. No wonder he'd been on edge before the show.

One encore became two, and finally, the concert came to a close. The next backstage reunion was messier, more exhausted, than the first, and this time they didn't let go. Jason found himself bundled between Max and Tara, all three breathing hard and dripping sweat but unwilling to move an inch. "I love you guys," Max said quietly, in between deep gulps of air.

"I love you idiots more," Tara replied.

Jason was surprised to feel tears spring to his eyes. "No way," he choked out. "Not more than I love the two of you."

Chapter 22

The concert was still ringing in his ears as Jason eased his key into the stubborn front door and jiggled it, waiting for the lock to give way. Max stood close behind him, jacket unzipped, radiating sweaty heat despite the cool night air around them.

They didn't say much as they stumbled, sleepy yet adrenaline-fueled, into the house and fell to their nightly routines. Jason took the first shower and returned downstairs to find Max stuffing his face with anything and everything that happened to be in the fridge. "You hungry?" Jason asked with a laugh, and Max vehemently shook his head as he continued to spoon peanut butter into his mouth.

Then Max disappeared up the stairs for his own well-earned shower and Jason wandered the kitchen, feeling like he should prepare something to commemorate the occasion. He knew this time should have been for the three of them, but was privately glad Tara had retreated to the peace and quiet of her hotel room. He couldn't explain that feeling, and it made him uncomfortable to think how selfishly he was hogging Max's time when she, too, might have been eager to share in an impromptu celebration.

Jason fell to pacing, too exhausted to still be on his feet but rejuvenated by the hot shower and easy hominess of a comfortable pair of sweatpants. The rough fabric of the sling itched against his bare chest, the only interruption of an otherwise complete state of drowsy comfort. A new round of painkillers had fought off the throbbing of his shoulder, but he knew, even so, that pulling on another shirt was out of the question. Another reason to be glad it was just him and Max.

Finally, his attention fell on the row of shot glasses lining the top of the refrigerator and he selected a pair. His personal stash of alcohol was nothing compared to what it had been in previous years, but he managed to produce a half-full bottle of whiskey, reasonable enough in quality for old friends to share. He was just pouring shots as Max reappeared, steamy and sweet-smelling from the shower.

"Cheers, man," Jason said, offering him one of the drinks.

"Cheers." They clinked glasses, then downed the shots, each making a face and trying to hide it as the alcohol struck its first blow.

"Well then, shall we get roaring drunk from sheer embarrassment?" Max asked, reaching for the bottle. He flashed a grin that told Jason it was a literary reference he was expected to know, then poured another pair of shots.

Max raised his glass again immediately, but Jason hesitated as he reached for his, racking his brain for where he'd heard the quote before. "Gatsby?" he asked hopefully.

"And a toast to the excesses of life even the Jazz Age couldn't imagine," Max replied with a nod. Another clink of glasses, another gulp of the bitter liquid, and a less restrained round of grimaces ensued.

Jason's head was already starting to swim. He suspected the painkillers and lack of sleep were compounding the alcohol's effect, but didn't want to dissuade Max from continuing the evening's revelry. Max seemed to be reading his mind, however, as he poured a third shot for himself only, then replaced the cap on the whiskey bottle.

They fell into their familiar mode of post-show conversation, reliving the highs and lows, scrutinizing every little thing that could have gone better. Max was always his own worst critic, but tonight even he seemed content with the performance. "It felt good to be back," he said, flashing a grin. "And how about that love song?"

By this point, they were draped over opposite ends of the sofa. The buzz, the company, the comfort of home—it was all just right. Jason nodded his agreement. "I can't even tell you how good it is to have you back, man." He yawned widely and craned his neck in an effort to see the clock on the wall.

"Time to crash?"

"Yeah, just about." Jason slowly disentangled himself from the couch. "Need anything before I head upstairs?"

"I'm good, I'm good," Max replied. He let his head drop back over the arm of the sofa and closed his eyes. "I think I'm already asleep."

Jason was nearly to the stairs when Max's voice stopped him. "Hey, Jase?"

"Yeah?" he replied, surprised.

There was a pause, then Max began slowly. "Actually, do you, uh, mind if I come up? Sleep on your floor like back in the day?"

"Uh . . . sure." It felt like a strange request, but if Max wanted to give up the cushy sofa to crash on his floor, Jason wasn't going to try to stop him. It had been a lifetime since that was their usual mode, middle-school sleepovers that their parents may or may not have known about. He supposed he wasn't the only one feeling nostalgic, and didn't mind an excuse to prolong their conversation from the comfort of his bed.

He heard Max stumble to his feet, then a moment later watched him jog into view, arms loaded with blankets. Max stuck out his tongue as he ran ahead, passing Jason on the stairs with a quick and childish declaration, "Race ya there!"

Soon enough, they were settled in the dark, Max sprawled in a collection of blankets and pillows that half filled the space between Jason's bed and the window through which a thin but persistent beam of moonlight streamed. Jason lay rigidly on his back, staring up at the ceiling, wishing he could find a more comfortable position. He was sure Max must be asleep already, but, struck by a suddenly urgent thought, he whispered, "Hey, you awake?"

"Hm?"

"Yeah, you're awake," Jason answered his own question, keeping his voice low.

"What's up?"

"I was just thinking about earlier . . ." Jason trailed off. "I mean, backstage, before the show, you said you had something to tell me."

Max was silent long enough for Jason to wonder if he actually had fallen asleep in the interim. Finally, he heard a sigh, and Max said quietly, "Yeah, I do."

Jason backpedaled, hearing the reluctance in his friend's voice. "It can wait, I just thought—"

"It's okay." Max cut him off. "It's waited long enough."

Jason rolled onto his side, propping himself up on his left elbow. He wished he could see Max's expression. What had started as curiosity was already reshaping itself into concern. *Don't say you're going away again*, he pleaded silently.

Max sighed again, then in a soft voice that sounded far away, he asked, "Mind if I join you?"

"Sure." Jason eased himself over to the far side of the bed, sitting upright against the headboard with his knees drawn in close.

Max sat stiffly at the opposite corner, half turned away as if refusing to make eye contact. "It's about last summer," he said quietly. Jason nodded, and after a brief but heavy silence, Max continued. "I never told you why I went away."

Jason's mind flashed back to that magical night of chasing fireflies and watching the sun rise from the roof of his car. "You said something about not having the right words," he recalled.

Max let out a small sound somewhere between a laugh and a sob. "Yeah, well, I kind of lied," he said, running a hand through his hair. "Not entirely," he corrected himself, "but when I said that, I'd found the words. I just wasn't ready to say them yet."

"So, what are the words?"

Silence.

Finally, Max stood up and slowly walked a lap of the room. For a moment, Jason was worried he was headed for the door, but he soon returned to his perch on the end of the bed. "You have to promise you won't hate me."

"Promise." Jason felt a throb of anticipation and drew closer to Max's side. The soft glow of the moon cascaded over them both now, but Jason still couldn't work out what he was reading on Max's troubled face.

"Jase, I'm gay." He could sense Jason's rush to respond, but quickly cut him off. "No, let me finish. And not the harmless, don't-worry-you're-not-my-type kind either . . . because you are." The statement hung weightily, tangibly in the air between them. Max sighed again, then continued, "You always have been."

A slow wave of confused, conflicted, overwhelming emotion

washed over Jason. He reached out his hand for Max to accept, and after a hesitant moment in which they locked eyes, he did. Question after question raced into Jason's mind, and one found its way to his lips. "How—how did you know?"

Max's eyes drifted downward, studying their interlocked hands. He sighed again. "The short answer is, how could I not?" Suddenly he looked up, examining Jason's face with a look of desperate admiration that made him look at once years younger and a world closer. "I guess it happened gradually," he said. "You know, as we grew up, spent so much time together, it was always the two of us. Somewhere along the way I realized I wanted it to *always* be the two of us." He paused, drawing in a deep breath, his head sinking down once again. "Jase, I don't expect you—"

"To understand," Jason finished. The rush of emotion was resolving itself into a shifting, elusive clarity. Max looked up in hesitant surprise, and their eyes met once more. Jason saw tears welling up in his eyes, darker than dark in the moonlight, and just the slightest tremble of his lower lip.

"I'm so sorry, man," Max whispered, fighting back the tears. "You don't need this. It's why I didn't tell you. I just need to know you won't hate me. Please."

"I could never hate you," Jason whispered back, giving Max's hand a soft squeeze.

"Thanks." His voice was barely audible, even at the close distance at which they sat. After another long pause, Max continued, his voice wavering, "I just needed you to know." He sighed. "And the hiatus . . ." he trailed off, drawing in a deep breath. "I can write love songs, Jase. I have notebooks full of them. I just could never write one that wasn't about *you*."

"Me?" The word fell from Jason's lips unbidden.

"I'm so sorry," Max repeated. "It's okay that you don't get it—"

Jason's heart was racing, but his mind was clear and untroubled. "I think maybe I do."

He leaned in close, and could just see Max start to do the same before he closed his eyes. Their lips met, softly, ever so lightly, just for a moment. Jason wasn't sure who had initiated it, just felt the surge of weightlessness, of butterflies, of inexplicable peace. He thought he felt something *else*, too, that he wasn't sure how to explain.

But suddenly everything made sense. He shyly met Max's gaze again.

The first kiss was just that, a first kiss, shy with the embarrassment of teenagers. The second was longer, closer, more passionate, and sent them tumbling backward on the bed, Max rolling underneath him to support his injured body, whispering "Watch your shoulder," as their lips parted and met again.

Now Jason knew he felt something. With his good arm, he drew Max close, felt the taut muscles of his bare back, the narrow line of his waist. . . .

I've wanted this for so long . . . I just didn't know it. The words formed in Jason's mind with astonishing clarity, but he didn't dare interrupt the moment. Now they rolled over onto his back, breathing heavily between longer, deeper, more urgent kisses. There was an unbelievable satisfaction to the strength of it all, the tension, the power, the desperation finally realized.

Time seemed to have frozen, the world waiting for their secret outpouring of passion to run itself dry. It must have been hours; the moon slipped low in the sky, then disappeared, leaving them shrouded in darkness. They didn't need to see, only to feel the closeness of their bodies and drink in the sweet softness of innocent lips.

That was all they did. It was all they needed. And as the sun was rising, they fell asleep, bodies intertwined, resting peacefully for what felt like the first time in a lifetime.

Epilogue

FOUR MONTHS LATER

It was June. The evening air hung thick and steamy, over-sweet with the aroma of honeysuckle. In the distance, the last rays of the setting sun glowed orange above the rich, deep blue of the mountains.

Jason reclined on a bench seat built into the side of the porch, absently picking away at a melody on his guitar. It had taken months, but he finally felt like he was getting his strength back, and his hands flew over the strings. In another three weeks, they would be restarting their tour, and as eager as he was for the rush of playing a live show again, for once Jason was content to soak in every moment of the present.

In the half darkness, he could just make out the figure approaching the house, coming up from the damp cool of the creek bed below. Without realizing it, he smiled, just watching Max draw near. Max traversed the steep, grassy incline in long, bounding steps, his hands cupped around some yet-unknown treasure.

His Walden Pond, as Max called it, had been their home as often as not over the past several weeks. The transition had happened gradually, seamlessly. At first, it was like everything was back to normal, then ever so slowly they started to allow themselves to reflect on that night together, to repeat it even, to reach a point where it made more sense to stop lying—if not yet to the rest of the world, at least to themselves.

Tara was the first person Jason had told. He hadn't been ready to divulge the details all at once, but it felt like as soon as he started talking, she could read the whole story on his face. He managed to get it out, haltingly, hesitantly, and then waited with a pit in his stomach for her reply.

Much to his surprise, her first reaction was to laugh.

"What?" he demanded.

"Jesus, Jase," she managed between giggles. "I thought you knew."

"Knew what? He told you?"

"Oh!" Her eyes grew wide, and her laughter resumed in earnest. "No, Max never said anything. I meant about *you*."

"What about me?"

"Yeah, okay," she replied with cheerful sarcasm, "we're going to pretend we didn't all see that you've been in love with Max for years."

At that, Jason had reddened with embarrassment. It had been hard enough to sort through his own thoughts and feelings, and it felt like a cruel punchline to learn he was effectively the last to know. But in the end, none of it mattered. Tara knew, and she didn't think less of either of them for it. If anything, she seemed gratified by the news. "At least now I know why neither one of you ever tried to hit on me," she quipped, forcing a sheepish smile from Jason.

As he thought about it, a lot of things made more sense. His parents' evolving aversion to the time they spent together. The photos from senior prom where they'd pantomimed sword fights, leaving their disgruntled dates scowling in the background. Even the way he'd felt when Max was gone, like he'd just *die* unless he saw him again. Any number of moments they'd shared that had felt so significant without ever being able to say why.

Of course, that was only one of the uncomfortable topics of conversation that became a necessity in the weeks after the concert. Relief dominated the band's emotions, but the nagging presence of the police investigation still tying up the loose ends of the kidnapping forced them to finally confront what had happened.

"So really—it *was* a hate crime?" Jason had said aloud to no one in particular, though Max and Tara sat beside him in the rehearsal studio. They had fumbled their way through most of a bitterly cold March marked by frequent visits to the police station, but among themselves had avoided the subject for as long as possible.

Max shrugged evasively. "It feels weird to call it that," he admitted.

"Call it what it is." Tara's tone was defiant and serious. "They felt so threatened by a message of unity and inclusion, they were ready to *kill* you for it."

"And turn you into their white-supremacist puppet," Jason recalled. Max had remained protective of the contents of the video staged by his kidnappers, but he had shared the general themes once the recording was safely in the possession of the police.

"That might have even been worse," Max said, giving a sad little half smile. His eyes drifted in Tara's direction. "I never want either of you to have to hear me say . . . those things."

"The real question, though, is what we call it for the public," Tara said. By that time, rumors of a threat against their concert had swirled for weeks, but they'd avoided making a statement beyond assuring the public of the safety of the band, their families, and the fans.

"Nothing," Max decided. Jason could see Tara preparing a rebuttal, but Max continued, "What does that do, other than make those guys famous? They're so afraid of becoming nothing, but it's exactly what their actions make them. They're zeroes."

"People should know," Tara insisted. "It's a blatant attack on the idea that this town can stand for anything other than its racist past." She gave Jason a knowing look. "There's a lot of good happening here, and we should be a part of it."

"Of course." But Max didn't sound convinced and seemed to be shrinking away from her accusing stare. "But maybe not like this."

"Okay, you're being weird," Tara said. "Since when do *you* not want to make a fuss about something like this?"

In the tense silence that followed, Jason could read the answer on Max's face, even before he exhaled slowly and began to choose his words. "They know," Max said. "Or they guessed. Or something."

"Know what?"

"About . . . me. One of them called Jason my boyfriend."

"Okay?" Tara eyed him, her expression torn between skepticism and confusion. "So what? I probably made that joke a hundred times before I knew. It doesn't mean anything."

Max shrugged, clearly still uncomfortable. "Maybe it doesn't."

"Even if it does, so what?"

"It just, I don't know, invites more of that to the surface."

"Again, so what? Weren't you going to come out to the fans anyway?"

Max froze. The look in his eye was one Jason hadn't seen since the hiatus, and he had to fight the urge to step in, to protect the friend suddenly walled off behind that shaken, panicked look. "I don't know," Max said finally, his tone clipped and terse.

"C'mon, Max, you know our fans," Tara said, her voice softening with obvious sympathy. "If anything, they'll only love you more."

"Sure. Maybe. I don't know." Suddenly Max was unfrozen, and the words came out all at once. "They're fine. They won't care. I'm not worried about that. It's just. . . ."

And as he trailed off, his hands shaking ever so slightly, Jason could see that it wasn't *just* anything. It was everything. The secret Max had carried with him for practically his whole life, the fear, the shame, the anxiety surrounding that secret—which might not be warranted in Tara's world, in present-day New York, but always had been in Max's.

It was a deep-seated panic constructed of small moments. The shrug to dismiss a parent's comment, the laugh forced at a classmate's joke, the suppressed cringe at every offhanded that's-so-gay. Over the years, their effect built up inside, planting just enough of a seed of doubt as to whether there really *was* something wrong with loving who you loved. And in the days when coming out was rarely an option, much less a celebration, that seed had taken root, had grown into a pernicious, invasive vine of terrified self-loathing that wound itself through the insecure corners of Max's heart. It wasn't the sort of weed that could be tamed overnight, not by a "We love you" from fans, nor even a "We accept you" from parents. It was the demon that had forced Max into hiding, and the one that almost hadn't let him escape.

"It's okay," Tara tried again, softly. Whether she could read the emotion in Max's face that was now so clear to Jason, he wasn't sure.

"It's not," Max cut her off. His hands were still shaking, but his voice was firm. "If it were okay, why the fuck would I have been so scared of the world finding out that I spent an entire year in hiding? Or did you really believe I just didn't want to be told what to write?"

Now Jason gave into the impulse that had struck him so often over the years—more often that he admitted, he realized—and slipped his hand into Max's. They exchanged a long look, a look of truly seeing one another. It was a look that gave more reassurances and did more to beat back that cursed vine than words ever could.

It took several seconds, but through that look, Max steadied himself. He turned back to Tara. "I know I should be ready to come out. But I'm not. And I need to do it on my terms, not any-one else's. So we don't bring this up."

That time, she didn't disagree.

A public coming out may have still been a ways off, but day by day, when it was just him and Jason, Max started to open up. Even so, it took weeks before they were ready to broach the next uneasy topic: girls.

"So you knew, like, a while ago?" Jason had asked, looking up expectantly from where he lay on the couch, his head resting in a reclining Max's lap.

"As soon as I had a word for it, I think I knew," Max replied, gently tracing the then-still-fresh scar that surgery had left be-hind on Jason's shoulder. The touch was cool, soothing, and after nearly six weeks Jason felt no pain. Max, too, seemed to have reached a respite from pain and fear, and he was almost laughing to himself as he added, "I sure remember the first time I thought *you* knew."

"Oh yeah?"

Max's face was flushed as he grinned down at Jason. "What was that girl's name, the one I played like I had a crush on in ninth grade?"

"Laurie Ann." Jason supplied the name immediately. And suddenly he knew what Max was going to say, recalling the in-cident himself and understanding for the first time why that day had gone the way that it had.

They had snuck the girl into Max's house—no longer the small apartment that Jason had fought so hard to gain access to—and settled in the basement with a rented movie and bowl of popcorn that Jason had eaten half of before she even arrived. He'd been there at Max's insistence, the excuse being he needed someone to keep the conversation going in case they ran out of things to say.

The movie was an old favorite, one they'd watched dozens of times, and now, Jason realized, Max had known exactly what he was doing when he piped up in the middle of one of Jason's favorite scenes. "This part is so *dumb*."

Jason had shoved him, paying no mind to the nervously smiling girl on Max's other side. "*You're* dumb."

And Max had shoved back, and within a matter of seconds they were rolling on the floor, wrestling and punching, enjoying the fight as much as the movie itself. The girl was completely forgotten.

By everyone except Max's mother, it turned out. Hearing the commotion, she appeared on the basement stairs, absently muttering Russian curses. The two boys froze mid-fight, still tangled on the floor, staring up at her as she eyed them with a look of disapproval. And then she saw Laurie Ann. "Maxim," his mother had said tersely. "Explain to me why there is a girl in the house."

"Oh, she can go," Max said quickly, and at the time, Jason had no explanation for the fleeting look of ashamed horror that crossed Max's face as he glanced down at Jason, still pinned beneath him on the floor.

Recalling it now as he eyed Max from a similar vantage point, Jason suppressed a laugh. "You never thought about girls?" he asked.

Max smirked. "I mean, I *thought* about them. It just never did anything for me, you know?"

"Not really, no."

"It wasn't like that for you?"

Jason laughed out loud. "No. It definitely wasn't. C'mon, man, you know I've dated." He paused, considered. "Wait, what about you? There were definitely girls, even after that."

"Hey, I wasn't the first seventeen-year-old to sleep with someone and wish I hadn't."

"Okay, fair." Jason fell silent, thinking, feeling the rhythmic rise and fall of Max's chest against his side. "Can I say something crazy?"

"Shoot."

"What if I still . . . like girls?"

Now Max laughed. "So what if you do?"

"No, I mean, I don't think I'm like you." Jason immediately regretted his choice of words, and tried to correct himself. "I mean, I like *this*," he could feel himself blushing as he spoke, "but if it were anyone else, I'd want it to be a girl, if that makes any sense."

Max nodded, still half smiling. "There's even a word for that." He paused and drew in a deep breath, his expression growing more serious. "But labels are . . . a burden sometimes. I don't care if we never put words to what *this* is. And even if it never goes anywhere, we'll both know that it meant something."

Jason let his eyes drift closed, trying to take it all in. As usual, an offhand commentary from Max seemed more profound than anything he could have generated by agonizing over his words. "I think I know what you mean," he said finally.

Now, watching Max bound up the stairs onto the deck, still clutching his mysterious treasure, he was sure he understood. "I caught something for you," Max announced, sliding into the seat beside Jason. "Hold out your hands."

"Yeah?" Jason set his guitar aside and eagerly complied. Max uncupped his hands, releasing the flickering green glow of a firefly onto Jason's palm. Jason smiled as he studied the insect as it crawled over his fingers, alternately illuminating and extinguishing its light.

After a few seconds, the firefly took flight, tracing a meandering course above their heads before disappearing with a final flash into the darkening sky.

"You let him get away," Max said, feigning disappointment.

"No," Jason corrected, pulling him into a long, slow kiss. "This one, I'm keeping."

Acknowledgements

Writing this novel has truly been a passion project and the fulfillment of a lifelong dream, and I am so grateful to everyone who helped me reach this point in my writing career. I want to begin by acknowledging the many authors and musicians whose own works have provided inspiration throughout this journey. William Faulkner, F. Scott Fitzgerald, John Knowles, Green Day, Blink-182, My Chemical Romance, and Fall Out Boy—I am indebted to you all.

Now for my personal acknowledgements.

First, I want to thank the State College Area School District (PA) for fostering my love of literature and providing a rock-solid platform from which to chase my dreams. In particular, thanks to Sandra Wyngaard, Kate Hoffman, Matthew Patton, Greg Somers, and Jim Robinson for helping to mold me, my writing, and my bass playing. And thank you to the University of Virginia for allowing me to make both college and graduate school my own—and never making me choose among physics, writing, and music.

Second, I want to thank the many friends and colleagues who have refused to be scared away by the time and effort I invest in fictional people. Special thanks to:
- Jo Jiang for reading messy drafts so early neither one of us imagined them becoming this book. I hope I've made the Gene and Finny pool proud.
- Eleanor Tsai for dutifully un-purpling my prose, and for the prologue suggestion that brought everything together.
- Rose Yankoski for being the ultimate hype-woman. You

were the first person to convince me that this is, in fact, a book—and you were right!

- Audrey Kreiser for enduring literal months of incoherent writing-related jabber, and for understanding the importance of a good old Subaru.
- Michael Sheaffer for pop-punk expertise, and for the tremendous compliment of thinking of my book alongside Fall Out Boy.
- Morgan Jensen for all things disaster boy and New Adult. I can't wait until the day I'm holding copies of both of our books.

Additionally, thanks to David Adewumi, Pete Spaar, Anika Kempe, and Kieryn Zeigler for your advice and encouragement.

Third, I want to thank my wonderful editor Jenny DeBell and everyone at Brandylane Publishers, Inc. for believing in my book and putting in the countless hours of work it took to make it a reality. Jenny, it is unreal to me how much your comments and suggestions have improved this book—yes, even the ones I argued with!

Finally, I want to thank my family. My parents have always supported me, but they deserve an extra shout-out for barely flinching at the idea that I'd put a graduate degree in physics to good use as a novelist. That said, my largest debt of gratitude is owed to my partner—who maintains I don't need to thank him at all—and to my horse—who requested his thanks in apples. You two have been my sounding boards, my inspirations, and my tethers to reality through an entire pandemic of writing, querying, and editing. We did it! I love you both.

About the Author

Liz Larson has spent half of her life in Charlottesville, Virginia, and the other half in State College, Pennsylvania. She loves both of her hometowns, faults and all. Despite her "real" job as a physics graduate student, her inner emo kid is still going strong. You can usually find her writing, playing bass, or out exploring the countryside—in all cases, surrounded by her animals and far, far too many Green Day albums.